The Fence Between Us

S.E. Fisher

BLUE DANDELION PRESS, LLC

eBook edition ISBN: 978-1-967734-00-9

Paperback ISBN: 978-1-967734-01-6

Cover by KiWi Cover Designs with The Author Buddy

Editing by: Revision Division

To my loving husband, who believes in me even when I can't see my own worth.

To my littles, I hope you always have the bravery to dream beyond tomorrow.

To my amazing parents and supportive friends, we did it!

To myself—see, I told you so.

Contents

Chapter 1

Rabble

Rabble rubbed at his eyes, the pads of his fingers digging into the corners and making sparks dance behind his lids. The drag of exhaustion pulled at him and his bones ached with long days and longer nights. One year had turned into eight in the blink of an eye. Some days he went to bed a young pup, fresh from the doghouse and others he felt like an ancient hound. Those ancient days were coming more and more often with each passing turn around the Sun.

He tugged at the stiff line of his collar, loosening the tie around his neck. Hopefully, adding space between his throat and the corporate noose would ease the feeling of being caged in. Frowning at the closed door of his office, he longed for the cooling breeze from the exposed HVAC system, knowing it would provide a welcome relief from the oppressive end-of-June heat. Enclosed spaces were not his friend.

Despite his disdain for the black painted panel wood door, he needed privacy for the phone conversation he just finished, which meant vacating the space he shared with his two closest friends and business partners. Even though he considered both men his brothers in every way that mattered, he wasn't quite ready to share the details of his new purchase, nor was Rabble willing to examine his motives too closely, at least not aloud.

He flicked the little yellow sticky note stuck to his index finger and reread the phone number of the real estate agent and a reasonable price tag for ten acres of land on the outskirts of his hometown. The requisite paperwork outlining his offer and the current owners' acceptance letter sat front and center on his desk, but he wasn't ready to look at them.

Staring at the note, the numbers blurred into smudges of graphite. When Rabble contacted the realtor, he hadn't planned what he'd say when she answered the phone. After he stumbled through an awkward and stunted conversation, the poor woman managed to determine which piece of property interested him. From there, it was just a matter of making an official offer and moving money from one of his investment accounts. Within a few days, he had a closing date.

Did he have plans for that property? No. The purchase had been impulsive and unlike him at all. Maybe that's why he couldn't seem to process the meaning of the numbers on the small square of paper. Returning to the place where his entire life had imploded hadn't been the plan, but now he found himself the owner of the very land he'd always despised. Rabble rolled his shoulders, trying to relieve some of the tension that worked to knot the muscles there.

Rabble glanced around his office, the pristine light gray walls, the bland cookie-cutter décor their decorator insisted on. He browsed his desk, taking in the stack of file folders on the corner that he still needed to sort and file. He frowned, noting the alarming number of coffee mugs he'd managed to collect just since arriving that morning. The only other personal touches on the entire L-shaped surface were the two worn photos in neat black frames nearest his computer. One contained the last unit picture taken of him and his brothers, along with the few other men he would always consider family. The other, a crinkled and creased wallet sized image of dreams he'd given up on long ago.

His eyes landing on the latest case file he'd compiled and he grabbed the manilla file folder, grasping it like a lifeline. Keeping his breathing as steady as possible, Rabble opened his door, nearly sighed at the cool blast of air that greeted him. He lumbered into the bright and open communal area where they all preferred to work even though they each had their own offices on the third floor of the renovated factory. Large windows lined two of the four walls, letting in plenty of natural light and an impressive view of the outer edges of Grand Rock.

Dash and Declan MacAlister, twins and Rabble's best friends, sat side-by-side, their backs to Rabble. Their considerable frames swallowed the chairs beneath them, courtesy of good genes and an intense workout routine. Identical in almost every way, Dash let his long, wavy hair grow to his shoulders, whereas Declan visited the barber religiously to keep his hair neatly styled within two inches. Aside from their hair, the biggest difference between the brothers was their attitude. While Dash hardly ever wore anything more than a frown, Declan remained all charm and smiles.

As Rabble walked toward them, he caught Declan's shit-eating grin just before he slid a five-dollar bill across the tabletop to Dash. Rabble raised a dark eyebrow in question.

Declan flashed his signature smile, the disarming one that kept anyone from looking deeper than surface level, "We bet how long it would take before the claustrophobia hit. Dash won."

Rabble couldn't quite bring himself to be aggravated with either of them, in part because he wasn't in the mood and because he was guilty of making the same bet on both of them. He slapped the manilla folder on the table in front of them, then turned to make another cup of coffee from the extensive and well-stocked bar. If all three of them agreed on one thing, it was that caffeine must be available at all times.

As he poured his third cup of the morning, the sound of rustling paper reached him. One of his friends had grabbed the file and thumbed through the documents. Rabble could practically feel their scowl behind his back.

Keeping his back to them, Rabble sipped his scalding coffee, burning his tongue in the process. He schooled his tone into mock casualness as he asked, "What are you doing for the Fourth?"

"Getting as far away from the city fireworks as possible," Dash said, his deep voice a mere rumble.

Rabble silently agreed. He didn't have many triggers, but enclosed spaces and loud booming noises... Yeah, those weren't his favorite. The city they'd settled in had been more of a necessity at the time and less of an ideal choice. Admittedly, they'd had many late-night conversations about moving the business somewhere else, somewhere less suffocating.

"Oh man, did I forget to tell you?" Declan winced. He leaned back in his chair and ran a hand through his short mahogany hair.

He adopted a wide-eyed innocent look that almost had Rabble snorting. He'd known the man a long time, and innocent was one of the last words he'd use to describe Declan.

Rabble and Dash stared at him, Dash managing a bit more patience than Rabble as his leg burned with the need to bounce his knee.

"Elyza called. She wants us to visit and help with the local town parade. Not only does the route go right by her bridal shop, but she also wants to make a big ass float. She went on about the benefits to small businesses and needing support." He shrugged. "Anyway, she said she'd supply beer and pizza."

With a sigh, Dash rubbed his temples but nodded. The twins' little sister was the apple of their eye; they'd do anything for her. While Rabble had met Elyza in person only a few times, always when she came to visit her brothers here in Grand Rock, he'd liked her. She had a spunky attitude and was as fiercely protective as her brothers as they were of her. At the end of her first visit to the city, she even adopted Rabble, claiming him as another brother. He'd been okay with that. As an only child, he figured maybe having a couple of siblings wouldn't be too awful.

"Looks like we're going to see Elyza," Rabble shrugged. He didn't have plans for Independence Day either, but Dash's idea of getting out of the city sounded good.

"Sweet, I'll let her know," Declan said, as if there had been any doubt they'd end up going to help her. He pulled out his cell phone to message his sister. "If we leave tomorrow, we can spend a long weekend in Shiloh Hills."

Rabble froze, his muscles seizing, his mug of coffee paused a scant inch from his mouth. The steaming liquid did nothing to warm his now chilled skin. *Shiloh Hills. Ah, hell.*

Located deep in the Ozarks of Missouri, Shiloh Hills was beautiful beyond compare. The hills wore huge old trees like a cozy blanket, covering every nook and cranny. In the autumn, the leaves turned varying shades of red, orange, and yellow, casting a fiery glow across the Ozarks that were visible for what seemed like miles. But Rabble's history with Shiloh Hills was long and loaded. His hometown held his best and worst memories. No matter that he loved the area, no matter that it contained an intrinsic part of his soul, staying as far away from that town remained at the top of his list of things to do.

If either twin noticed his voice going all funny, they gave him the courtesy of keeping their mouths shut. "When," he choked, struggling to form words around the lump stuck in his throat, "did she relocate to Shiloh Hills?"

Declan returned to reading through the file. "As soon as we settled here. She wanted to be near us, but city life isn't for her. She found the closest small town with an economy, or semblance of one, and set up shop. She's had the bridal shop for—what, Dash, about a year now?"

Dash nodded, taking a moment to scratch at the underside of his dark beard.

Rabble did the math in his head. When they'd finished their last military assignments about two years ago, they had wandered some, floating from town to city and back again. The three of them sought similar things, something light, something hopeful to combat the darkness that had become their world.

About eighteen months? Elyza had been settled in Shiloh Hills for eighteen months, and this was the first he'd heard of it. For as long as Rabble had known the twins, Elyza dreamed of opening a bridal boutique, frequently sending them long letters while they were away with her budding plans for a shop. Covered in mud and sweat from head to toe, they'd open the mail to find some soft scrap of lace or satin that all three scowling men would analyze closely. They knew, if they failed to give Elyza their honest opinion, she'd make them pay like all hell. She also expected them to ask the other members of their unit for opinions as well, something the other men never failed to hold over their heads. It was enough to give any man a complex.

Rabble didn't have that problem though. Any prospect of marriage had flown out the door when he was eighteen. He wasn't celibate by any means, finding momentary pleasure with women when he felt like it. But the thought of spending his entire life with one person? Yeah, not anymore. At one time, he'd seen a path for himself that looked more like that white picket fence lifestyle, but Rabble left those dreams, the potential for that life in the dust of a Greyhound bus. He'd boarded that bus with a hollowed-out heart and empty pockets. He left the final tether, along with those wishes and plans behind with a friend he trusted to dispose of the small felt covered box he'd saved so diligently to buy.

Without thought, Rabble took a long drag from his coffee, the hot liquid barely registering on his already burned tongue.

He savored the scorch as he worked to clear his head. What had he been thinking about? Oh, right. Elyza and her bridal boutique.

Rabble counted himself fortunate that Elyza had yet to turn her matchmaking interests to him as she had with her brothers. The number of blind dates Declan and Dash had gone to at the behest of their sister neared the double digits. Each.

"Rab, what's the deal with this case?" Dash asked, accepting the file his brother passed him and began skimming the details. "Do we need to wrap it up before we leave Grand Rock?"

Rabble gave himself a mental shake and finally felt his bones thaw enough so he could move. *Get your head back in the game!*

For the next half hour, Declan, Dash, and Rabble demonstrated exactly why they were good at what they did. The security company they'd built together specialized in providing safety solutions for women and children in shitty situations. They secured some government contracts and worked as freelancers at other times. None of them were interested in protecting pop stars from crazed fans or paparazzi, and they didn't guard the guilty. They prioritized women, children, and innocents who had been dealt a rough hand in life.

They worked together seamlessly. While they each knew all aspects of the company inside and out, the three of them had decided early on to lean on their individual strengths. Declan enjoyed handling the surveillance and protection details, while Dash had a way with technology that baffled Rabble. For his part, Rabble excelled in organization and deployment. He handled the majority of the government contracts and lined up resources for those who needed a fresh start. Alone, they were each skilled. Together, their team was formidable.

The file before them detailed a request for relocation from a young woman in southern California. According to the file, she had married a man straight out of high school, and he was not only abusive, but law enforcement also suspected him to have strong connections to dangerous people. The kind of people who shot first and didn't bother asking questions.

Declan read the file aloud. "Catherine Elnor, twenty-five, married to Edward Elnor, accountant. Requesting a new identity and relocation. Doesn't look like she's looking for an extensive protection detail."

Dash wearily rubbed his hand down his face. They'd seen this same act play out time and time again, and it usually ended with someone innocent going six feet under.

Rabble frowned. "I'll see if I can convince her to have at least a limited protection detail. She's probably going to need it before this is all said and done. I'm working with a lawyer in the area to get her divorce taken care of." In truth, he was hoping to get that finalized sooner rather than later.

Declan asked the question they all hated, his hazel-green eyes darkening. "So what threat level are we thinking here?"

None of them liked to speculate what type of danger may arise in individual situations. It wouldn't be the first time a low-threat level had surprised them. Those unique instances never ended well.

"Let's just err on the side of caution." Rabble slid them each another folder, this one containing the same information as the original but with additional documentation on the soon-to-be ex-husband and his associates. He waited and said nothing while they reviewed the forms he'd provided, Dash absently tugging on his long hair at the nape of his neck.

"Dec, if you could pick her up from the airport and bring her up to speed on the new identity? Dash, can you get accommodations set up for her and prep for the works on security? We haven't spoken specifically what kind of security she'd like at her new place, so we need to nail that down. Thanks, guys. I pretty much bet she'll turn down full-time protection, so let's just make sure we cover all the corners."

Rabble had a feeling Catherine Elnor just wanted to get away from the life she'd found herself trapped in. She wanted a fresh start, and he understood that, but the past had a way of sneaking back in when you least wanted it to. Refusing to fail her, Rabble would do his best to make sure she was prepared when that time came.

"I've got an idea, Rab, but you may not like it." Declan tapped his pen against the table, finalizing the plan in his head before speaking again. "What about Shiloh Hills?"

Dash looked curiously at his brother, not noticing Rabble choking on his fourth cup of coffee.

"Think about it." Declan held up his hand and ticked points off his fingers as he counted. "One, we're leaving for Shiloh Hills sooner rather than later. We'll be there during the first week or so, and it wouldn't hurt for us to stay a little longer. Two, Elyza could use the help at her shop, and, three, Dash can check with Elyza about a rental in her neighborhood."

Declan was right. Rabble didn't like the idea, but he couldn't see a fault in his friend's logic. Knowing the twins, they must have researched the neighborhood where their sister planned to buy a house, ensuring its safety. Hell, they probably knew more about Shiloh Hills now than Rabble did. That Shiloh Hills was barely a blip on the map also helped their case. The town was hardly a well-known destination. Damn. He searched for a bright side, and found the only one he could think of. Even if he returned to Shiloh Hills, for the brief duration of the Independence Day holiday, Skye was long gone, having left for bigger and better things long ago.

Rabble sighed and ran a hand through his dark, tousled hair, an errant curl scratching his ear. "Let's do it. We'll move her out in the next few days and connect in Shiloh Hills."

Damn. Damn. Damn.

Chapter 2

Skye

Skye and her fellow teachers stood in front of the school building on sweltering asphalt and waved as the final long yellow bus pulled out of the parking lot, taking with it the last of the summer students. She never minded working a few extra weeks after the official school year ended, enjoying the chance to explore fun activities that doubled as learning opportunities.

Though she loved her job and the kids, Skye couldn't deny that she looked forward to spending long hours lounging in the striped canvas hammock in her small backyard. She had spent several months creating a mini oasis behind the tall wooden fence that enclosed the space, placing sparkling pavers and short solar lights along the path from her back door to the two shady trees where she hung her hammock, and the tiki torches and potted citronella plants helped ward off blood-sucking mosquitos. The yard exuded relaxation, and she couldn't wait to spend more than a few minutes wrapped in the cocoon of the hammock, swaying in the gentle breeze.

Along with a slew of other instructors, Skye watched until the final bus disappeared over the hill, then retreated into the sweet relief of the air-conditioned building. She headed toward her assigned classroom, needing to grab the impressive collection of canvas bags and fancy stainless-steel thermoses she'd amassed during the month-long summer program. Now, she regretted waiting until the last minute to pack them all back home. As more teachers dispersed to their classrooms or left the building altogether, the lack of busy noise made her melancholy.

Halls that typically rang with all manner of sound, from the peeling of bells and papers shuffling to the happy laughter and chatting of children and faculty alike. Some teachers were less than thrilled to be around children all day and counted down the minutes until they could leave, but Skye had never felt that way. She craved the happy cacophony and chaotic nature of the elementary school. Sure, she was exhausted and didn't know where the children got their energy, but being at school, surrounded by noisy kids, was better than sitting in her soundless house, alone.

The short drive back to her tiny two-bedroom cottage did nothing to shake the gloomy feeling that snuck into her chest and stuck like a stone, and the silence that greeted her did nothing to lift her spirits. Still, Skye loved her little home, and she thanked her Mamaw every day for helping her buy it. Even though Mamaw had been gone for years, the moment Skye graduated college and her inheritance became accessible, she purchased the small cottage and had slowly restored it in the years since. The vertical wooden siding, painted a soft sage green, called to Skye's soul. Under the white-trimmed windows, the flower boxes stained with a light walnut color brought out the natural wood grain, and the color of the shingles matched the rich soil in the little garden she maintained in the backyard. Skye chose the color scheme with intention, invoking warmth and peace. Following a long day on her feet, mustering an upbeat attitude for her students, she wanted somewhere that calmed and soothed her. Best of all, it was one-hundred-percent hers.

Stepping over the threshold, Skye dumped her bag by the door and flopped onto the overstuffed reading chair, the only seating in the room besides the chambray gray loveseat pushed against the front window. Dishes waited in the sink, and several loads of laundry needed washing. Compared to her desire to lay on the chair and let herself sink into the stuffing, the need to clean did not even come close.

She tipped her head back against the rolled edge of the chair and stared at the popcorn ceiling, the stack of smutty romance books she'd been meaning to read catching at the edge of her vision. The tower threatened to topple over if it grew any taller. Maybe they'd find her buried under a stack of happily-ever-afters. That would be her luck. If she were being honest, she was having a pity party, and since it was a party of one, it was so much worse.

Another friend from college had gotten married this past weekend, and while she adored Michelle and her new husband, Skye couldn't help the little pinch of envy that stung each time. Not that long ago, everyone assumed she would be the first to marry. Now, all of her high school and college friends were getting married, buying homes, and having babies while she sat on the sidelines, watching their new lives start as hers passed by.

Still, she'd rather remain alone than settle into a loveless marriage, filled with long nights that would make her feel more lonely than she was now. She'd had enough of that during her childhood and knew enough about what she wanted in life to know she hadn't found it.

Skye finally lifted her head off the soft fabric and glanced around the open-concept room, taking in the hardwood floors, the clean butcherblock countertop in the kitchen, and the cabinets that matched the sage exterior of the house. A variety of plants in painted terracotta pots held positions throughout the room, the only thing she trusted herself to keep alive at the moment. Though some of the smaller plants did look a bit wilted. Skye promised herself she'd water the plants just as soon as she could gather enough will to convince her body to move from the comfortable position.

The cell phone beside her vibrated against the seat cushion, sending tremors through the soft fabric. She pushed herself up onto her elbows and watched the screen, groaning at the name flashing there. The phone continued the ring and vibrate while Skye ignored it, letting voicemail deal with the caller. A few seconds later, the voicemail icon blinked, and she played it on speaker. Leaving her phone on the reading chair, she padded to the kitchen to pour herself a glass of water and deposit the multitude of stainless-steel cups she'd brought home from school. Honestly, the number of thermoses she had was ridiculous.

"Hello dear," her stepmother's irritated nasally voice rang out, loud and shrill in the otherwise quiet home. "Your father and I wanted to speak with you, but you haven't been by the house."

Censure marked her tone, something she never failed to express in regard to Skye. Gayle had come into Skye's life not long after she'd been born, her biological mother passing away from complications only moments after she'd named her infant daughter. Skye's relationship with her stepmother had never been what Skye hoped for and despite promising herself otherwise, some intrinsic part of Skye still strived to meet her approval. Even now, it hadn't taken Gayle all of ten seconds to start her ridicule, possibly a new record speed for her disapproval.

"I know summer school let out today." The disdain for Skye's job dripped from her voice like honeyed poison. "Dinner will be on the table at five o'clock sharp. See you shortly."

"Goodbye to you too, Mother," Skye muttered, fighting the urge to roll her eyes at the sheer audacity her stepmother exuded, expecting Skye to drop any plans she may have had and attend a family dinner. The fact that her plans had involved a dinner for one and watching bad reality television in her pajamas was beside the point. She couldn't help herself as her eyes drifted to the clock on her phone that read 4:30 p.m.

Crap!

Skye raced to her room, cursing herself for her spineless inability to stand up to her parents. To simply *not* answer their summons. She'd done so once before and paid the price, though she couldn't say she regretted her decision. She peeled off the t-shirt she'd worn to work. The cheesy, "Get your Cray-On" saying in bright, bubbly lettering always made her laugh, but her parents wouldn't appreciate it like she did. In its place, she chose a more sedate option from her closet, a turquoise tunic with a black breast pocket. Skye slipped the shirt over her serviceable white cotton bra, left on the dark denim skinny jeans she'd worn to work, and threw on a pair of black ballet flats in place of her multi-colored tennis shoes. As for her long, tangled honey-blonde hair, she did the best she could, tossing it up into an artfully messy bun at the back of her head.

Skye hurried to her older model silver compact SUV where she'd parked it on the curb.

The drive across town took all of five minutes, yet that all too familiar panic rose each time she glanced at the clock. Fifteen minutes had passed. Technically, she was making good time. That fact didn't matter to her heart rate, which sputtered erratically, or her breath, which seemed content to stay permanently locked in her lungs. Her fingers strummed on the steering wheel frantically, and her left foot kept rhythm on the floorboard. Each mile passing at the lawful thirty miles per hour seemed to last an eternity.

Skye made it to her parents' grand house with about ten minutes to spare. Rationally, she knew this, but it didn't stop her heart from hammering in her chest, forcing her to spend another few minutes in the car, working to ease its beating back into a normal cadence.

As her heart calmed, Skye's gaze drifted beyond her parent's well-manicured lawn to the awful and sterile poly fence that demarked an unofficial dividing line between Shiloh Hills's upper-crust and everyone else. Typically, Skye did a decent job of ignoring that fence when she answered her parents' summons. But maybe her vulnerabilities and insecurities had overridden her better sense because her eyes were drawn to that space between property lines. That particular fence hadn't always been there. At one point it was open, sporting two rows of painted wood nailed to neat square posts.

She'd been only five years old when she heard the word rabble spat from someone's mouth in her parents' patio garden. She didn't understand exactly what or who a rabble was but she spent many days studying the fence the person indicated, wondering if clues were present in the wood grain or the way the white paint clung to the splinters. The grasses that waved in the breeze, the wildflowers that danced around the posts, were the same on either side of the fence.

The crooked For Sale sign on the other side of the fence, maybe that was the rabble? Or was it the family that moved in not long after that garden party? Maybe it was the little boy who ran around in dirty bare feet and torn jean shorts.

Skye's eyes drifted from the cold fence that mocked the memories she held dear, though they made her heart ache with sadness. She forced her eyes away and back to the opulent home her parents occupied. The idea of going inside made her stomach roll again and she couldn't help but seek some level of comfort by glancing one more time at the place she'd spent such happy times. The way the fence had changed through the years stood out, a stark comparison to those good memories and the corners of Skye's mouth turned down as that ache in her chest grew. Not every memory made at that fence had been positive, not all of them promised hope and companionship.

Graduation day held so much promise for Skye, not because of the numerous scholarships and school acceptance letters she'd received like the crowd seemed to think. The principal's list of her achievements went on forever and Skye slowed her steps to ensure the man had plenty of time to finish before she reached the podium. She made it through her Valedictorian speech, reading the words she'd written without emotion. The heat of too many bodies pressed in on her and she tried to focus passed the pounding headache she'd developed. Not a single individual in the large school gymnasium saw her accomplishments for what they were. Chains.

It took far longer for Skye to escape the congratulations and well-wishes from fellow townsfolk than she would have liked. She breathed the late spring air deep into her lungs, relief lightened her chest and for the first time all day, she let herself feel that hope she clung to.

Her sandaled feet raced through the soft grass, passed the lilac bush whose blooms were fading in late May. Excitement lit her eyes as she searched for a hint of him but the only thing waiting for her at that horrible sterile fence was a thick stack of papers, wedged between two slats. That hope she'd carried with her crashed to the ground in a heap of splintered dreams. Skye pulled the tri-folded paper from the fence and opened it, her hands shaking with that familiar sinking feeling that crept into her chest and stopped the breath in her lungs.

The words, typed in an official font blurred before her eyes. Blinking several times, Skye struggled to absorb the words before her, her mind refusing to comprehend. She recognized the name on the paper, Matthew R. Raden. Then, a horrible sense of finality overcame her as the words United States Army came into focus. Skye crumpled to the ground, lost, heavy. All of those chains finally weighed her down.

Skye swiped at her cheeks, the wet tracks there surprised and frustrated her. She jerked her head away from that fence and yanked the sun visor down, exposing the mirror to her salt-stained face. Sniffing, Skye dabbed under her eyes and hurried to hide the evidence of her weakness, frantically brushing at the reddened skin of her face. Her efforts were in vain and she eventually growled at her image. Slamming the sun visor shut again, Skye took a steading breath, ignoring the way it shuddered through her and focused on something, anything, else that would distract her from the memories that threatened to crush her heart.

Her eyes landed on the other vehicles in the driveway beside her own.

The concreted circle driveway held three cars and her trusty SUV. Two of the brand names she recognized as expensive. The other she didn't know, but she had no doubt it was every bit as lavish. Her SUV seemed like a cheap knock-off toy compared to those vehicles, and it took all her strength not to flush with embarrassment.

She alternated between hurrying toward the house, determined not to be late, and wishing she could turn around and flee. Years of avoiding disappointing her parents and operant conditioning won out, and she found herself rushing up the opulent stone steps.

The doorbell clanged the same as when she lived there, and she fought against other memories that tried to drag her under. As proud members of one of the oldest families in Shiloh Hills, Max and Gayle Wellington exuded perfection in every facet of their lives, except for the ones behind closed doors. From the outside, Skye's parents were perfectly put together and socially acceptable. She often wondered if her father had ever been happy with Gayle, who had been her stepmother for as long as she could remember. While her parents would never leave each other legally, they'd given up on happiness a long time ago.

The door swung open and revealed Gayle Wellington, second wife of Shiloh Hills's mayor. Her hair was a warm cinnamon color from the roots to the tips—not her natural color but the result of expensive taste and a well-trained hairstylist. Willowy thin but proud, she coifed her hair perfectly, not a strand out of place or root left untouched, and accentuated her figure in a pink plaid suit jacket and pencil skirt. Rubies dangled from her ears and rested at the hollow of her throat. As she opened the door wider, her disapproving brown eyes slid over Skye and dismissed her. She always expected Skye to show up and be less than. Silently, Skye followed her stepmother into the house.

A staircase lined the wall on both sides, curving elegantly toward the second floor. They passed under the obnoxiously grand, crystal chandelier, Gayle's daringly tall heels clicked loudly against the cream marble tiles beneath their feet. She led Skye through the foyer and past the expansive library to the formal dining hall at the back of the house. One entire wall consisted of windows that provided a gorgeous view of the extensive backyard and endless woods beyond. Skye's father sat at the head of the needlessly long, dark-wood table. The cream-cushioned seat to his right, pulled out slightly, waited for Gayle to take her seat again.

Across the table from Gayle, where Skye typically cowered, another guest stood and angled his body toward her.

"What are you doing here?" Skye could have smacked herself the minute the words flew from her mouth.

Gayle paled and sputtered while her father's face soured to an unholy shade of red.

Dylan cracked a furtive smile, the mockery of pleasantness didn't reach his eyes. "Skye, it's been a long time."

About four years actually. Not nearly long enough.

Dylan Santoro was not someone Skye would have willingly dined with ever again. She hid her clenched fists behind her back; she not only despised his presence at this family dinner, but also what it might imply. They'd briefly dated in college at the behest and urging of her parents. Considering she had royally disappointed them by changing her major to education, Skye had agreed to a first date with Dylan. His father was a state senator, a powerful ally for power-hungry couples and small-town politicians like Max and Gayle.

Apparently, Skye had been the only one to think their relationship was obviously going nowhere because he'd proposed to her after only a few dates, the ring a spectacular show of dazzling wealth and influence.

She doubted he would forgive her for turning him down, not that his smiling face spoke of any ill will today. But despite his waving blond hair and crystalline blue eyes, something behind the pretty-boy facade made her skin crawl. Skye slid into the chair Dylan pulled out for her, noting the pristine Armani suit he wore and rolled her eyes. She slid closer to the table and took a healthy swig of the red wine already in her crystal glass. This was going to be a long night.

Chapter 3

Rabble

Rabble spent the next two days organizing the specifics of moving Catherine, now Bekah, to Shiloh Hills, down to the last detail. Much of that time was on the phone, coordinating the pieces and parts of the relocation plan to keep her safe and give her the tools she needed to start over. He had to admit the amount of time he spent on the phone was beginning to annoy him. With face-to-face communication, truths and lies were easier to decipher and harder to hide. Long ago, he'd accepted these alternate methods of conversing, email and phone calls, but that didn't mean he had to like it.

If he were being honest though, his mood had plummeted steadily since they'd decided to spend the Independence Day holiday in Shiloh Hills. Since that conversation, he'd thrown himself into work, desperate for any distraction. He spent hours going over new government contracts, updating previous client details, and generally completing busy work that kept his brain numbed. Still, a part of Rabble looked forward to seeing some of his favorite places, like the quiet library where he'd spent a good amount of time while his mother worked at the diner on the other end of the town. He missed the old mill, the faded murals painted on the sides of red brick buildings, and wondered if Mr. Jack still worked at the mom-and-pop pharmacy on the corner by the railroad tracks. Rabble hoped not. Mr. Jack had been ancient before; the man deserved to retire. His chair groaned as Rabble leaned back, folding his hands over his stomach.

Rabble frowned, his mood dropping further, his mind straying to so many other elements of the town he'd rather never see again. He had spent years avoiding thoughts about anything remotely related to that town, so much so that he committed a grave sin he needed to rectify during this trip. In the years since he had left, he had never returned to visit his mother's grave, to the tree beside his dilapidated childhood house where he had placed a homemade cross to remember her. That was all he could give her at the time. The longer he thought about it, the sicker he felt until he rubbed at his chest to soothe away the ache that had taken up residence right over his heart.

Thinking about the tree where he lovingly buried his mother's remains conjured images of the fence rows just behind it. The fence and that giggling, curious little girl who stared at him that first day, when he'd moved to town. The fence rows Skye peeked through, her young face alight with a child's nosey nature. He had years upon years of wonderful memories with Skye beneath the fence, ones where they shared their thoughts and dreams and others where they simply lay in silence, basking in each other's calming presence.

When he'd walked away from his hometown, he'd never intended on returning, hadn't planned to ever see that girl again. She'd gone off to an Ivy League school long ago, though he had left before she'd chosen which prestigious university she'd attend. Without him around to distract her from her goals, he wondered just how far she'd travelled, how much she'd achieved. He comforted himself with the knowledge that, even though he'd been cleaved in two, he'd freed Skye to become all she could be.

A wave of solemn acceptance threatened to swamp him and Rabble found himself typing with more force than necessary as he readied and emailed Declan and Dash the final plans for Bekah's relocation, powered down his laptop, and packed it away. He spent long minutes shredding documents, correspondence, even the stack of menus they'd gathered since they'd opened the security firm. His procrastination tactic may have continued to work, had he not run out of reasonable shredding material. He frowned at the pile of tiny squared paper in the bin and finally gave up on avoiding the inevitable.

The rest of his things were already in the truck, waiting for him to gather the nerve to set course for Shiloh Hills. He slung his backpack over his shoulders, the weight of the laptop inside settled against his middle back. After one last walk-through of the building, he flipped the light switches, killing the florescent overhead bulbs. A final glance around had him considering spit-shining the toilets, just to evade Shiloh Hills for a few moments longer. With a defeated huff, Rabble programmed the security system and stepped into the hallway.

"Quit stalling, big baby," he chastised himself aloud, shutting the door to the office space and locking it. He turned away from the door, a sense of finality weighing heavily on his shoulders. Grudgingly, Rabble took the stairs down to the main level and ambled out the front doors.

He dragged himself across the parking lot, swiveling his gaze from side to side, taking in as much of his surroundings as he could. After he reached his truck, Rabble stood at the door, his hand on the handle, his mind wandering as a row of little black ants marched by on the hot pavement at his feet. The whisper of the summer breeze through the still growing trees planted out front of their shared building drew him into memories he'd long ago buried.

An old truck, orange and brown from rust, sat stoically beneath the huge tree by that damned fence. Mama said Matthew wasn't supposed to say damn, but she wasn't there, and his dad didn't care. He didn't care about anything, and Matthew supposed he shouldn't care either. He slipped his head beneath the fence, his eyes staring at the tiny cracks in the aging paint. She was already there, studying a line of tiny ants marching silently by. With his head next to hers, he tried to banish the vision behind his eyes, of one of those small bugs crawling in his ear. He shivered, and Skye looked at him knowingly. She'd never laugh at him, but she couldn't help that twinkle in her eyes either. They stayed together, under the fence, the massive oak tree and flowering bush keeping them company.

They didn't talk, and Matthew kind of liked that part. He didn't have to lie or pretend with her like he did at home and school. She didn't judge him when salty streaks rolled down his cheeks after a day from hell—another word Mama didn't like.

But the fence was his safe place. It had been since the first time Skye dragged him under the wooden rows when they were five years old. She'd taken one look at his scraped-up palms and oversized dirty shirt and asked him, "Are you Rabble?" He hadn't been sure what that was, but her smile revealed nothing but kindness. If that's what she said he was, he supposed it was true, and he'd been Rabble ever since.

The ants continued to march by, unbothered by his presence and completely unaware of the turmoil threatening to consume him. He stood at the tipping point, and the sensation of swaying gingerly on the edge of a sword overcame him. One way or the other, he was going to fall. All it would take was the right gust, and he would be destroyed. Determined to stop that train of thought, Rabble shook himself, rolled his neck, and convinced his muscles to unlock enough so he could climb into the cab of his truck. Dumping his laptop bag in the passenger seat, he gathered the heather-gray vest he kept there for emergency client meetings and shoved it into the backseat with his other bags.

As he methodically slid the key into the ignition, Rabble listened to the rumble of the engine come to life and made up his mind. He may be returning to Shiloh Hills, but that didn't mean he had to let the town, or the people in it, get to him. His job and spending the holiday with his family were all that mattered, nothing more. That mindset lasted until he rolled past the welcome sign at the edge of town, heralding his arrival to Shiloh Hills. After his mom passed away and his father left him alone for all intents and purposes, he would walk to the edge of town, take a seat beside the blacktop, and stare at that sign. He dreamed of leaving so often, when he finally did, it hadn't seemed real. Even then, the relief he thought he would feel hadn't come, too burdened by what he left behind.

Sometime in the years since his mother passed, the old fence between the properties had finally rotted into worm food. He couldn't pinpoint exactly when that happened, having not been near the property divider in what felt like a lifetime. Skye's parents had sprung to replace it with a new one, tall vinyl planks stabbed into the ground, one right after another. Some days he thought, if he pressed his face to the fence boards, would he catch a glimpse of that flowering purple bush Skye loved so much?

That new fence, so cold and imposing made a statement and he received the message, loud and clear.

Rabble sat beneath the oak tree, studying the fence with red and heavy eyes. A lead stone sat where his heart should have been and he wondered if his ability to feel had finally disappeared. His mind filled with words he wanted to say, and never would. Words that went unsaid in the days, months, years, following that fateful night when she'd kept him from being consumed wholly by the darkness, when she'd stood up to her father, for him, and paid the price for her defiance ever since.

He missed his best friend, missed spending more than a few passing moments with each other in the school halls. Plenty of moments had come and gone where he simply wanted her there, by his side as she had been since they were children. He longed to speak with her, to lean into her when his father had reached new lows, tossing his mother's ashes to him in a cardboard box, no better than garbage. He wished she could have stood by him as he took a shovel from the shed and buried that box in the most peaceful place he knew, right beneath that towering oak tree.

Skye was graduating today, the decorated princess of the town. Rabble chose not to attend, despite the principal's look of disappointment. Nothing new there. He wouldn't walk across that gymnasium floor, the local charity case and a loser to be gawked at.

He rose from his seat beneath the tree and tucked the tri-folded packet of papers he held between two of the sturdy, unfeeling vinyl planks. Swallowing back his sorrow, Rabble turned from the fence and walked away.

Rabble's spine went ramrod straight as he passed that welcome sign, a bit faded with age but still the same. The town itself looked almost exactly as he remembered.

Deep-red brick buildings, the color of blood and chalky rust, lined Main Street and bordered the courthouse town square on three sides. Beyond the main square, the oldest homes stood tall and proud, a testament to when craftsmanship mattered more than convenience. Each street beyond that featured a mix of brick ranchers and cottages, until the very edge of town—where he'd grown up.

Lost inside a town established by the same five families who still ran things, Rabble was an outsider. Always had been. Always would be. Even the moments when he felt like he'd belonged were now wrapped in the same dark memories that haunted his every step. No matter how much regret and pain he had in abundance, they wouldn't carry him through life, not anymore.

Driving down Main Street, Rabble noted the subtle yet vital changes made during his absence. As people strolled by and customers entered and exited shops, a sort of quiet tranquility and eager, barely controlled excitement danced together to create a strange feeling of youthful age. It sang in the breeze that blew through the red, white, and blue banners hung outside several storefronts.

Rabble took a deep breath and let the feel of the town settle over him. *Just a job. Just a job. Just. A. Job.*

Parking his truck across from The Wild Bride, he took a moment to assess Elyza's renovations. The shop, built of traditional brick and aged wood, displayed large glass windows and antique double doors at the entrance. Behind the glass, mannequins in an array of poses wore varying lengths of white fabric. Perfectly placed bright lights made the crystals and beads shimmer. The cynic in him wondered how Elyza's security system held up as he mentally calculated how much money sat exposed in those huge front windows.

He let the truck door fall open, propelled by the light shove he'd given it, and took a moment to assess the strange feeling that welled in him when his boots touched the ground. An odd mix of disquiet, relief, and anticipation. The first he expected, the other two took him by surprise and set him on edge. His eyes drifted toward the southside of town, as if he could see clear passed the buildings, beyond the trees, to the outskirts of polite society, where the privacy of the high-browed met the poverty of the riff-raff. Scrunching his eyes shut, Rabble pinched the bridge of his nose between his thumb and forefinger. Those old memories awakened a thrum in his chest, one that felt an awful lot like regret.

He strode to the bridal shop, pushing open the door and let the pleasant jingle of a bell announce his arrival to Elyza.

He arrived earlier than his friends. While Declan picked up Bekah from the airport in St. Louis, Dash had gone to the rental cottage she'd be using and installed an assortment of security measures to keep Bekah safe in the event her psycho ex-husband decided to show up.

Elyza came running from behind a rack of white dresses hanging from rolling carts, "You're finally here!"

Rabble straightened his shoulders, willing his negative mood to roll off him. He gave her a crooked grin and winked, "Of course I am, and you'll notice, the cool brother showed up first."

She giggled, a girlish laugh that brightened Rabble's mood just a bit. Rabble had the pleasure of meeting the twins' sister only a few times, despite that, they still considered each other family. Several months had passed since he'd last seen her, and he studied her with a brother's watchful eye.

Her rich mahogany hair, a shade or two darker than her brothers', fell in thick waves down her back, held away from her face loosely by some sort of clip. Her eyes, emerald green to her brothers' hazel, tended to shine and sparkle when she smiled.

"How've you been?" he asked, accepting her embrace as she raced toward him, her long tanned legs eating up the distance.

The strength in her arms as she held him with genuine warmth impressed and reassured Rabble. Her hug settled into him, easing some of the tension that coiled there.

Before she could answer, the bell above the door jangled again, admitting Declan, Dash, and a pretty young woman with straight light-brown hair. Elyza repeated the exuberant welcome she'd given Rabble with both of her brothers, ribbing them good naturedly for taking so long to visit. She shook Bekah's hand, her genuine smile seemed to loosen something in the other woman's shoulders and she relaxed ever so slightly. Rabble suppressed the desire to lift his brows in surprise. Elyza's quiet welcome showed a level of restraint he hadn't known she possessed.

"I'm Elyza," she introduced herself to the young woman, whose eyes held a weary type of watchfulness Rabble recognized all too well. Behind that though, a flash of curiosity, of interest in her surroundings.

Good. That interest meant surviving and overcoming. They could work with that curiosity

"Cath—Bekah. I'm Bekah," the woman hurried to correct herself, her cheeks going pale and pink all at once.

Elyza smiled reassuringly, no stranger to her brothers' work, "It takes some getting used to."

Rabble noted the way Bekah's shoulders relaxed a bit more, how her eyes conveyed a type of gratitude for Elyza's gentle understanding.

Pride welled in his chest, for Elyza's easy acceptance, for Bekah's terrified determination. Maybe he didn't have a right to feel anything for either of them, but here were two strong as hell women. They reminded him so much of another strong individual who haunted his sleeping and waking dreams.

Declan and Dash took turns bumping the side of their fists against Rabble's in acknowledgement.

"All good?" he asked, curious how Bekah's initial home visit had gone.

Declan had already shown Bekah her rental cottage where Dash played the dedicated technician and explained every instrument at work on the property, from locks to sensors. The rental cottage and Elyza's home were only a block from the bridal shop, an added security aspect they hadn't bet on, but appreciated nonetheless. Having grown up with brothers like hers, Elyza herself was a force to be reckoned with when necessary.

Elyza's green eyes caught on Bekah's wary chocolate brown gaze as she cast them toward the ground, "Bekah, how're you feeling about all of this?"

Bekah's head whipped up, a startled expression marred her face, "Oh, this is wonderful. It's all wonderful."

Rabble's bullshit detector pinged, but it was Declan who stepped nearer to her.

"Bekah," he said, his face gentle and open. They waited in the quiet for her to answer truthfully.

"No, it really is wonderful. The sensors alone are a welcome relief. I just—." Bekah frowned, searching for words she couldn't quite conjure.

"It's going to take some time," Declan said and Bekah nodded, withdrawing slightly from them.

Rabble frowned, knowing Declan was right. What she'd been through wasn't something people just recovered from overnight. He hoped that the brothers' expertise and Elyza's steady optimistic nature would eventually provide a sense of ease and reassurance to Bekah. Already her shoulders dropped from around her ears, inch by inch.

Declan's flash of a bright white smile contrasted with Dash's quiet peace in their sister's presence as she babbled, the drone of her steady voice a comfort all on its own. Rabble sat back, observing the three biological siblings, enjoying their banter and only inserting himself when asked a direct question. With watchful eyes, Rabble saw the way Bekah's gaze darted between the siblings as well, taking in their conversation, the air they exuded, and measuring it with her own subdued aura.

The three MacAlister siblings looked enough alike that no one could mistake their relation to each other. As the youngest sibling, Elyza still lived at home with their mother when the twins enlisted in the military, but that hadn't damaged the strength of their bond. If anything, the twins' absence made their connection stronger. Rabble's chest constricted with gratitude for their family's acceptance. They welcomed him without a second thought, creating the kind of familial bond he'd always dreamed of having and never believed he would.

"—had a favor to ask," Elyza smiled winningly at them, including Bekah. No matter what she was going to ask, she already knew they wouldn't tell her no, especially not Declan or Dash.

Rabble refocused on the conversation and raised an eyebrow. *This ought to be interesting.*

Elyza exhaled, hurrying to finish her sentence in a single, long-winded breath. "I sort of volunteered to be the lead for organizing the town's floats this year."

"Sort of volunteered? How do you even do that, El?" Dash scoffed.

"What does that entail?" Rabble cocked his head to the side, trying to dislodge the slight pounding that started behind his right temple.

Elyza picked up three folders from the counter behind her. "Well, clarification: It's not the whole parade exactly. There are just three floats, and only two of those are technically for the town."

"Do none of the council members do anything?" Declan grumbled. He already knew they didn't, but Rabble appreciated his refusal to give up hope.

Elyza handed Declan the folder labeled Historical Society in bright pink gel pen. He flipped the manilla folder open and waded through illustrated examples of her visions and small samples for each part of the float. Dash got the folder for the library, and he too opened it to review the internal documents, while Rabble took the last folder. His eyes skimmed over sketches and pictures of bouquets and faux floral samples.

Rabble made a note not to underestimate Elyza's creative prowess. He could clearly see what she had planned for each float and was positive the final product would be nothing short of spectacular.

"Please help me." She pouted and clasped her hands together as a mock plea for their assistance.

Rabble considered his options. Elyza would rope the brothers in no matter what. As an honorary family member, Rabble was likely already on the hook too, and the thought made him break out in a cold sweat. His eyes shot to Elyza's pleading ones and he swallowed roughly.

Her eyes studied him, no doubt he had become as pale as he felt, the thought of standing on display in front of the entire town spurred the same reaction that being in an enclosed space did. The same people he'd stand before were the ones who judged his mother for staying with an abusive drunk but did nothing to help. They were the same ones who watched him fall apart at the seams after his mother's passing and sneered at him instead of extending a friendly hand to a destroyed teenage boy. The thought of performing for them now, he'd rather face a firing squad at point blank range.

Elyza must have read between the shadows in his eyes and the lines around his mouth because she backtracked quickly, "On second thought, I think I really only need two grooms and the center bride will shine all on her own."

Rabble contemplated picking her up and twirling her around in his relief but his knees felt a bit unsteady and he settled on a strained smile that he hoped conveyed his appreciation for her subtle ability to read him and the fears he despised.

Declan and Dash shared a deep groan, their eyes rolling in unison. Elyza took their reaction as an answer and did a little jump before pulling each one in a tight hug. To his surprise, she came up to him and squeezed her arms around his middle again. Two hugs in one day; Rabble was going to end up with a complex.

"I have the perfect person already lined up to help you work on the float, Rab!" She practically vibrated with energy.

He envied her ability to see the bright side in almost any situation, to turn rainy days into opportunities for fun. He wanted to learn that trick. Maybe someday.

"Who is it?" he asked, tilting his head skeptically.

Elyza grinned back at him. "Oh, you'll love her!"

At Rabble's side Declan's amused snicker filled the air. To his other side, Dash smirked quietly, his eyes conveying his mirth.

Great, she's playing match-maker.

Chapter 4

Skye

Exhaustion pulled at Skye's shoulders, weighing them down and bowing them beneath the fatigue. She could not recall a time she'd felt quite so drained, mentally and physically. She tossed and turned throughout the night, her nightgown twisted around her, furthering her irritation. Every tick of the clock on the wall grated against her frayed nerves, and the groans and creaking of the house settling echoed in her ears.

Dinners with her parents were, on a normal day, tedious. Discovering her ex-boyfriend sitting at the dinner table added an entirely different level of difficulty to the meal. The entire evening became a trial, determined to test her limits and ability to sit still in her seat without fidgeting uncomfortably.

Because Dylan belonged in the same circles as her parents, they spent the entire evening discussing politics at local, state, and federal levels;

bills; and laws. The topics of conversation mixed into a muddled pile in her brain. None of it interested her, but the way the conversation was going, she doubted she needed to be present for it anyway. Skye practically bolted from the table at her first chance, making feeble excuses to escape into the humid summer night.

She spent the drive home, brief as it was, in silence, the lack of noise and voices a balm to her overstimulated brain. If only she had the strength to tell her stepmother no, to stand up to them, to refuse to come to dinner, or to ignore their condescension toward nearly every aspect of her life. Not for the first time, she mentally kicked herself for being weak. Too weak to stand up for herself. Too inept to go after what she wanted.

In her life, she could only recall two instances when she gathered her strength to form herself some kind of backbone. To stand against her parents and speak up. They'd both cost her. Once when she returned home from college for the first time and notified her parents of her degree change to elementary education. Their negative reaction and beratement had sent her fleeing back to the campus before the end of the first night.

The other time made her heart hurt when she thought about it, so she spent a good amount of time avoiding the memory altogether. Still, in her morose mood, Skye tumbled into the sweeping memory.

Rabble Raden was going to be the death of her. She took a blanket and her textbooks down to the fence every day where they studied together, not that he struggled with school any more than she did. Mr. Raden, as Principal Smith called him, was doing better than her. But he hadn't been to the fence in three days, and Skye was ready to pull out her hair. Even the mild scent of her Mamaw's lilac bush in the early spring didn't cheer her. A bad feeling swirled in her gut, slowly creeping up to her chest to seize the oxygen in her lungs.

Skye stared at the peeling paint on the fence and waited. Darkness fell, making shadows stretch across the yard. Rabble's lanky form emerged from behind the rust-bucket old truck. Specks of starlight gathered at the corner of his eyes and fell down his face like droplets on a windowpane. Even from a distance, Skye felt the devastation that held his whole body taut. She rushed to him, leaping over the fence in a bound, and took him in her arms. Rabble's shoulders shook as the dam burst, and he broke apart in her arms. She gathered him as close as she could, as if her arms alone could hold him together while his soul spilled out of him and lay dead in the dirt.

His mother. His sweet mama. Gone.

Her smiles, tired as they were. Her quiet humming when she danced around the local diner where she worked, taking orders with a smile. Always with a smile.

Gone.

Rabble fell to his knees, cracking them on the pretty stones they'd collected and stashed near the fence through the years. Skye refused to release him, to let go of what was left of him. Even when her father hollered for her to come inside, she stayed and let him stalk back into their home. She'd deal with the fallout later. Always, she stayed.

After that, Skye lost any sense of freedom she'd possessed. Her father's fury knew no bounds and she became a prisoner in her own home. Her parents hauled her from the house when they needed her to play her role as doting daughter but beyond that, she spent her days at school and school-sponsored activities. The rest of the time, she spent in her room, watching the fence line for any sign of the broken boy beyond it.

Skye cringed, those painful memories bursting through as she lay in bed, refusing to move. Light peeked through her dainty floral curtains, and she gave up trying to sleep, dragging herself out of bed with a determined sigh. No matter how badly she wanted to stay beneath her covers and mope, she knew that would only make things worse in the long run. Forgoing the more comfortable choice of black leggings and an oversized shirt that would do nothing to draw her out of her funk, she instead chose a pair of denim shorts, sandals, and a soft T-shirt with tiny yellow bumble bees zipping across the cream-colored fabric. The v-collar exposed more of her tanned chest than typical, just enough to push her to the edge of her comfort zone but ensure she didn't feel too awkward to leave the house.

A glance in the mirror told her all of her efforts were in vain. The purple smudges under her eyes spoke to her sleepless night, and the lines around her mouth showed her utter frustration lingering from the night before. Stepping outside, Skye inhaled sharply, immediately bending at the waist to throw her tangled honey-blonde hair into a messy high ponytail, leaving on the ends to trail over her neck. The humidity hung thickly in the air, coating her skin and making her clothes hug her body a little more. Summer in Shiloh Hills was gorgeous, but the humidity alone could make a person cranky.

She started her silver SUV and waited impatiently for the air conditioning to kick on. After several moments, she finally felt the tickle of the cool air from the vents brush across her arm. Though she didn't necessarily feel like socializing, Skye drove toward the local grocery store on the opposite side of town, waving politely to those braving the summer heat to walk along the well-maintained sidewalks. The trip was quick, more of an excuse to force herself into public when she would have preferred to wallow in self-pity on her couch. The boxes and pouches of pre-packaged foods fit inside four of her reusable bags, which she settled into the cargo space beneath a mesh covering.

Skye sang along to the radio absently, parking along the curb at the courthouse, across the street from the Brick House Cafe. Brick House Cafe served great coffee, sweet pastries, and juicy gossip, depending on what interested the patron. Kellyn, one of Skye's dearest friends, owned and operated the cafe and caught Skye's eye through the front glass windows. Before she'd even walked through the door, Kellyn had the supplies gathered to prepare Skye's preferred beverage. Skye smiled, her chest tightening at Kellyn's thoughtfulness.

She ordered a second latte, this one for Elyza, a mutual friend who worked further down, on the adjacent street. Skye decided to walk, despite the oppressive heat, and kept a loose but secure hold on the drinks as she made her way toward The Wild Bride. She gave herself the luxury of letting her mind wander as she strolled by other shops, admiring the way the relatively new concrete sidewalks sparkled in the bright sunlight.

Outside The Wild Bride, Skye balanced the lattes in one hand, swung the door out with the other, and propped it open with her hip as she entered. The bell above the door jingled merrily.

"Hey girl, I —" The words died on Skye's lips as her eyes lifted from the floor and landed on a pretty, petite woman and three of the biggest men she'd ever seen in her life.

Each had turned toward the door the moment the bell signaled, and suddenly Skye found herself the center of their attention.

The woman stood on the end, her slight frame tucked behind one of the broad-shouldered men, her light-brown hair and smooth olive complexion bore no resemblance to any of the others in the room.

Skye's eyes widened, her mouth popping open into an O, while her brain tried desperately to reconcile the sight in front of her. Each man was well over six feet tall, and their navy blue cotton T-shirts stretched tightly across their chests, hugging well-defined biceps and highlighting their muscled arms.

Two of them, to the left and right respectively, were almost identical. Both had mahogany hair, a shade or so lighter than Elyza's, that matched one's short stubble and the other's neatly trimmed beard. While the man on left had a shorter haircut, the other's scrapped the tops of his shoulders in thick wavy locks. The man with the cropped hair and shadowed jaw had a smirk plastered to his face, almost as if that was his usual expression. The other one appeared more serious, his eyes roaming over her and then moving away to finish assessing the rest of the sales floor.

But the man in the middle... He shook her to her core.

His hair was the same deep soil brown she remembered, still thick and tousled from running his hand through it—a habit he'd had since adolescence. Those eyes, like storm-darkened clouds under straight eyebrows, were the same shade as her favorite color.

She'd know his face anywhere.

In front of her now though, that face belonged to a man, not a boy, not like the last time Skye had seen him.

Peeking around the man on the right, Elyza hurried over to Skye. She could have kissed her friend for the way the pressure seemed to begin dissipating from the air, at least, until Elyza spoke.

"Skye!" She smiled hesitantly, picking up on the hum of tension hanging heavily around them. "You've never met my brothers."

Hearing her name snapped Skye out of her thoughts, and her eyes darted to Elyza's brilliant green ones, safer territory than looking at almost anything or anyone else in the room.

"I, I didn't know you had...brothers." Her voice shook as she stuttered.

Elyza took the two paper coffee cups from Skye's fingers, which suddenly seemed frozen in place.

"She doesn't talk about us much, but who can really blame her?" The man on the left sauntered forward, smiled charmingly, and grasped Skye's hand in a kind but firm handshake.

"What with our ugly mugs, she's probably afraid people will think there is a family resemblance," the man on the right said, stepping forward to take Skye's hand smoothly.

She might have laughed if she didn't feel like she might be sick all over the floor.

"Don't listen to them; they think they're funny." Elyza pointed at each in turn. "Declan, Dash, this is Skye Wellington." Pointing behind her, Elyza added, "And this is the brother we adopted, whether he wanted us or not, Rabble." Elyza smiled affectionately at her brothers, including Rabble in her look.

Skye's back went ramrod straight, her breathing shallow and the awful feeling of panic swelled in her chest. Her head shook back and forth, tendrils of her honey-blonde hair escaping her ponytail to catch on the damp skin by her ears. *No. No. No.*

Those eyes. They crashed into hers, sparking with recognition and smoldering with something Skye wasn't prepared to acknowledge. She choked.

What was that emotion there? Was that...anger? Why would he be angry? What right does he have?

Annoyance and her own rising anger slowly took over the panic flooding her, blotting out the frantic feeling that threatened to pull her under. She could barely form a coherent thought now, her temper climbing.

"Mr. Raden," Skye said, pleased and surprised her voice came out even when nothing about her felt as centered as she sounded.

The look of apprehension that passed between the three siblings spoke volumes. Skye hadn't spoken of her past with Elyza, or with anyone else for that matter. Based on the startled expression the siblings shared,

Rabble must not have mentioned anything either. The tension built between them and hung in the air like a wet blanket.

This was too much. Seeing him, the memories that came with him, everything he represented. It was all too much.

Skye had been doing a decent job faking her energy level for the sake of those around her and her pathetic attempt to manifest a few molecules of dopamine, but now her strength wanned. She was done. She barely managed to force herself outside today, let alone deal with the emotions that wrecked her every time she thought about Rabble and their time together. That final year together. That last day.

With a small, shaky wave of her hand and a smile that felt more like a grimace, Skye did an about-face and rushed out the way she'd come in.

The bell's chime didn't sound nearly as merry as she yanked the door against it, the clanging sound sawing at her nerves. She gritted her teeth, barely keeping herself from breaking into a full run right there on the sidewalk, settling instead for something between a sprint and a canter. Her focus went entirely into putting as much space between her and Rabble as quickly as possible.

"Skye! Skye, wait!" Elyza shouted behind her.

A part of her wanted to keep going, to ignore her friend, and just make it back to her SUV. If she could do that, she could easily drive home and hide forever under her blankets. As a teacher at the height of summer break, she didn't need to leave her house for the next several weeks. The darker part of her, the part that did everything in her power to avoid disappointing anyone, the part she tried so hard to hold back, demanded she slow to a stop beneath a large shady tree and wait for her friend while her chest heaved deep breaths in and out.

"Hey girl, what the hell was that?" Elyza caught up and clasped her shoulder, spinning Skye around to face her.

It took Skye a moment to lift her eyes to Elyza's face, expecting anger or judgment. Instead, all she saw was deeply rooted compassion and a desire to help. Elyza's attitude toward the entire situation took Skye by surprise, considering her friend seemed to love Rabble like a brother, and Skye just took a mad dash out of the bridal shop to get away from him.

"S-sorry." Skye cursed herself silently. She still sounded breathless, even to her own ears.

Elyza's grasp fell to Skye's upper arm, and she smiled slightly, "No need to be sorry. They can be a lot. Do you want to talk about it?"

Did she? Absolutely not. Should she? Skye wasn't so sure. "There's just a lot of history there."

Skye smiled in what she hoped was a reassuring manner, but she was positive she looked like she was going to throw up.

Elyza seemed to consider if she would push the issue or leave it be. Discussing the history between her and Rabble would take a while and expose wounds that still festered, even eight years later. Thankfully, she didn't press for details. Minutes passed in relative silence, the shrill screaming of cicadas in the trees the only real noise to interrupt the contemplative quiet. Elyza lingered with her friend for several minutes while the summer breeze swirled around them, rustling the leaves on the branches above them.

"Look," Elyza said, her voice soothing, like she was speaking to a frightened animal.

Maybe that's exactly what Skye was.

"I want to make sure you're okay," Elyza said. "Truly okay."

Skye nodded, her lips twisting up into a semblance of a smile. "Yeah, I'm fine. Go on back to the shop. I've got to get going home anyway. Laundry won't do itself."

She'd hoped Elyza would laugh, chuckle, or snort at Skye's ridiculous attempt at humor, but she didn't do any of those things. Instead, she pulled Skye into a hug, the kind that seeped into all the cracks she hid and did its best to heal, and waited for Skye to pull away first before releasing her.

They parted ways with Elyza heading back to The Wild Bride and Skye to her car, determined to fold and put away some laundry now that she'd used it as an excuse for escape. Getting out of the house had been the plan, and she succeeded in that journey. Now, it was time to go back to the comfort and safety of her own space, where there were no unexpected events to occur, no unwanted old acquaintances to run into.

Alone on the sidewalk, Skye mourned the loss of her coffee that would sit in the bridal shop and grow cold while she drove home and tried to function on three crappy hours of sleep. No way could she survive the rest of the day without liquid energy or a serious nap, but the idea of going back into The Wild Bride to retrieve her cup sounded even worse, so she silently said farewell to her drink.

"Skye."

She stiffened, her body freezing at the lulling baritone of his voice. The gravel there was much deeper and more assured than when he was a boy. The fear of the future and pain of the past didn't seem to hang in his words like they used to. No matter what had transpired between them, Skye nearly sighed in relief, thankful he'd found something that made life worth living. Even if it wasn't her.

She turned as Rabble approached, her coffee in his large hand.

He studied her, his eyes seeking out her soul as only he seemed able to. Whatever he saw there must have puzzled him and he frowned, though his eyes softened with everything once between them. Skye's muscles tightened, her traitorous body igniting at his nearness, his intense gaze. She refused to acknowledge that feeling low in her belly and shook her head slowly as she walked backward a few paces before hurrying away. Maybe that's what they'd always be to each other, just pieces of their past that didn't fit anywhere in their present.

Chapter 5

Rabble

Rabble watched, eyes wide, as Skye practically ran down the street, away from him. His first reaction was shock, it knocked the wind from him, frying his veins and sending static through his brain. That was immediately followed by a thought that horrified him.

She wasn't supposed to be here. What the hell was she doing here?

Eight years felt like an eternity when the days slogged by without a heart, but presented with that missing part of him, the part that belonged to her, those years really weren't that long in the grand scheme of things. Seeing her immediately transported him back to that warm spring day when everything had well and truly gone to hell. Rabble could almost pinpoint the exact moment he and Skye had fallen apart and any chance they had disappeared like the evaporating dew on new spring leaves.

It wasn't something he liked to think about, the choices he'd made, how they'd plagued him in their years apart. In the weeks after he'd left

Shiloh Hills, during those long days of the intense hellscape of basic training, his mind drifted to her often, the silken gold of her hair, the light blue eyes that sparkled when she laughed. Images of her haunted him in his sleeping and waking hours, leaving him exhausted and vulnerable. It was that vulnerability his commanding officers honed in on and hammered like steel in a blacksmith's forge, until it became a tool in Rabble's arsenal, it became the strength of his will and the determination of his body. After that, he still thought of her, but with a resolute acceptance that kept him moving forward.

Had those moments tormented her as well? Did she wake in the middle of the night, as he did, sweaty and panting from dreams of what had been and never would be again?

He'd never tell Skye what prompted him to enter that recruitment office or sign the papers that meant leaving her behind. She didn't deserve the shitshow of his life, so he'd taken it with him.

Confronting her on the sidewalk had not been his smartest move, but he couldn't stop himself from following her. Since the day he enlisted, he imagined what he'd say if they ever saw each other again, but the moment he had the chance, he'd choked on words that refused to leave his mouth while she'd paled like she'd seen a ghost.

Rabble returned to The Wild Bride, anticipating at least one of the three siblings, or maybe even Bekah, to grill him on his strange encounter with Skye. He wished someone would yell at him, curse him, or do something, anything, to wipe the pity off of Elyza's face and the look on Dash's that said he saw more than Rabble wanted.

Only Declan didn't stare at him with a mixture of emotion that made Rabble's stomach churn but only because his friend was busy showing Bekah around the boutique, pointing out exists and hiding spots and anything that might work as a weapon if she ever needed one. Declan's words echoed in the otherwise quiet space. Maybe they were having an odd conversation at a potential workplace, but for someone in Bekah's situation, the men at Rabble & Bros. Security agreed they would encourage their clients to adopt proactive measures and self-defense. They took their duty seriously; they didn't shy away from the fact that they stood at the border of life and death, nor did they pretend these cases were anything other than what they were, situations that could go to hell in a handbasket at any moment.

Rabble took a breath, centering himself. He was in no way prepared to answer the questions brewing behind Elyza's curious and loving eyes as she sidled closer to him.

"Elyza," he said quietly, "I really don't want to talk about it."

She pursed her lips together, her face taking on a semi-apologetic expression, "Okay, Rab. But I have bad news. Skye is the other half of your team for the float."

Rabble's heart stopped cold.

Damn. When was he going to catch a break?

He forced a small smile of acceptance. "Doesn't matter, little sister. I told you I'd help; I got your back."

Rabble tucked his hands into his pockets and left the siblings standing at the retail counter to catch up while Declan and Bekah wandered around the bridal shop. The comfortable atmosphere suddenly grated at his nerves, so he shouldered his way outside, needing a moment alone.

On the sidewalk, he took a deep breath of humid summer air and glanced around the familiar scene. Though new concrete pads made up sidewalks that no longer sank unevenly along the path, he could still picture the old cracked and broken places he'd traced years ago. Patches of flowers bloomed along the path, fresh dirt and mulch mounded up around them to keep weeds at bay—so different from the dried, dying grass he remembered from his long walks between the school and his house.

He had grown up on the outskirts of town where the nicely maintained houses gave way to the countryside and the poverty that was an unfortunate reality for some, like him. Skye had been his only neighbor; a field bordered the other side of his property line. The school bus didn't bother driving down their street, a narrow gravel path that counted as a backroad. Instead, the driver stopped at the top of the road to let him and Skye off. Her father always picked her up, leaving Rabble to walk every dusty step back to the rundown trailer home he lived in.

Outwardly, Shiloh Hills looked to be making a noticeable effort to reclaim some of its former glory; glory that had faded long before he'd moved in. He wondered if their efforts would be in vain, if the rot in certain parts ran too deep, remained too ingrained, for the town to ever be truly lovely again.

Rabble wandered down the new sidewalk, alternating between staring at the fresh light gray stone and taking in the slowly maturing trees planted equidistance from each other between the road and the narrow pathway.

What was Skye doing back in Shiloh Hills? Was she here for the Independence Day celebration or some other reason?

No matter the answer, it looked like he would be seeing a lot more of the girl who had always been there for him, always stood beside him. That is, until he stepped away, leaving her and all of their plans in the dust of a Greyhound bus.

At the end of the street, Rabble turned around and walked back to his truck where he'd parked it in front of the bridal shop. He climbed in, determined to focus on work instead of getting stuck in his head and obsessing over the situation he now found himself in. Driving through town, he noted the differences, the changes for better or worse. Several older buildings appeared abandoned with plywood covered windows and amateur graffiti gracing the red brick. In other areas, buildings restored to their former glory now heralded the beauty of architecture gone by, or their renovations fit a more modern style altogether.

He nearly sighed in relief when he came upon one of his old familiar haunts and took in the well-maintained grounds, the way the flowers bloomed welcomingly. The Sunny Morning Trellis was Shiloh Hills's only bed and breakfast—and the only place for an out-of-towner to stay, as no local motels or hotels existed nearby. Originally known as The Greer House, the house had once been one of the largest, most grandiose homes, belonging to a long-ago wealthy businessman who built the home for his wife and their children. Painted a fresh white color, wood board-and-batten siding reflected the sunlight. Intricate lavender detailing added elements of charm to the exterior and complemented the various types of blooming plants around the grounds. The smell of freshly cut grass in the air soaked into Rabble's soul and made him smile; pulling up to the house felt like coming home.

The Sunny Morning Trellis bed and breakfast belonged to Mrs. Sylvie Basket, an older woman who had lived in Shiloh Hills her entire life. Widowed at a young age with no family to speak of, Mrs. Basket hadn't known Rabble when she'd saved his life, hadn't thought anything of the protection and care she provided to the poor teenager she found pawing through the leftovers thrown out by the local grocery.

As if she saw something in him, something good that no one else ever had, she'd approached him as she might a wild animal, carefully and with a soothing tone. Instead of charity, which she'd somehow known he'd never accept, Mrs. Basket hired him to do all manner of manual labor around the bed and breakfast after school. In exchange, he had a safe place to hang out and, at minimum, one nutritious meal per day. Rabble owed a lot to certain members of the Shiloh Hills community, and Mrs. Basket was at the top of the list.

As Rabble parked his truck on the one-car gravel pad outside of the bed and breakfast, he noted where the paint was fading and peeling on the façade. Although in relatively good shape, the building showed its age more now than he had ever seen before.

Grabbing his bag, he started toward the large house. Rabble's long gait ate up the short, paver-stone walkway, but he took the four stairs onto the wrap-around porch one slow step at a time, savoring each step, each breath of sweet-scented wind. He pushed open the familiar door, its decorative glass casting prismatic slashes of light across the porch, and stepped into the front room.

"Be right there!" a young voice called from further inside.

Rabble dropped the experienced duffle bag at his feet and waited, taking in the cream and navy floral wallpaper and the dark-stained wooden chair-rail that dressed the lower third of each wall. Though the windows remained shut to keep out the summer heat, someone had drawn back the sheer curtains, allowing the natural light to illuminate the space. The bed and breakfast boasted four bedrooms, three on the second level and one on the first, two shared bathrooms and two common gathering spaces, the living area and dining rooms respectively. Even though their stay included breakfast and lunch, Mrs. Basket always made enough dinner to share with any of her guests.

After a minute or two passed, a teenage girl hurried from the direction of the kitchen, her ginger red hair falling free of her braid and tangling in her face. She brushed it away with an impatient hand and rushed to the rolltop desk that sat against the wall.

"Checking in?" she asked, carefully rolling back the top of the desk and grabbing a pen.

Rabble snorted. Based on the number of pens inside the antique desk, Mrs. Basket still preferred paper to any form of electronic management system.

"Yeah, three rooms if you have them. We'll pay by the night, but let's start with four," he said, pulling out his wallet.

Rabble grabbed his driver license and the company credit card, then stood still and silent while the girl tallied the cost per night. When she gave him the number, he handed over his cards.

"Where's Sylvie?" he wondered aloud.

"Who? Oh, Mrs. Basket? She's around here somewhere." The girl worked while she spoke, keeping her eyes focused on the papers before her. "She still wants to be involved in everything, but I try to make her take it easy when I can. Last I saw, she was hanging a load of sheets out to dry."

The girl smiled as she spoke about the older woman. That someone cared for Mrs. Basket as much as he had warmed Rabble's heart.

"I'm Olivia." The girl held out her hand for him to shake. "I'm around every day after 3:00 p.m. and in the morning on the weekends. If you need help with anything housekeeping-related, I'm happy to help when I get out of school."

Rabble shook her hand and returned her smile. "I'm Rabble. The other two rooms are for Declan and Dash MacAlister; they'll be here later."

Olivia handed Rabble a key to the Green Room and said she'd be cleaning the first floor for another hour or so if he needed anything. After thanking her, Rabble took the steps up to his assigned room. She would never know his thanks were less about the room and more for the care she showed Mrs. Basket while he had run off to the ends of the Earth.

The Green Room was aptly named, and Rabble couldn't help but chuckle at the décor. When Mrs. Basket had been redecorating, she'd asked his opinion on colors and furnishings. Being a teenage boy lost in his own angst, he honestly hadn't been able to muster enough energy to care about wall coverings or paint colors. Later, he wished he'd had the heart to tell her that there was such thing as too much green.

The emerald rug centered under the four-poster dark-wood bedframe marked just the beginning. She'd chosen bed sheets and pillows in differing shades of forest and army, while the walls were a printed pattern of dark leaves on a sage background. The heavy wood furniture and the burlap wall prints barely made a difference in the overwhelming sea of green. Rabble hoped he could catch the look on his brother's faces when they arrived. Declan and Dash would be equally confounded by their rooms, each similarly decorated in shades of blue and orange.

Throwing his duffle on the bed, Rabble set his laptop on the desk, pulled up the file on Bekah's relocation, and reviewed the details, recommitting them to memory. Declan and Dash had set up alarms and other sensors at the rental. But despite Bekah's desire for safety in her relocation, she had drawn lines at too many security measures, albeit politely, but they would continue to monitor her situation and make updates as necessary until a predetermined amount of time had passed without contact from her ex-husband.

As Rabble reviewed the rest of her plan, trying to root out any flaws or loopholes that might have slipped past him, he rubbed his eyes and shut the computer down. The words blurred together, and his eyes strained against the harsh blue light of his laptop.

Despite his fond memories of the bed and breakfast, he felt antsy and trapped, but outside—well, that might be worse.

Seeing Skye had been an unwelcome shock, one he hadn't prepared for, assuming she'd left Shiloh Hills in the dust as surely as he had. Instead, he found her, a woman in her own right now. Her long hair a bit darker than it had been, her eyes a bit more wary. He'd taken her in, like a man starving at a feast he couldn't touch or taste. She'd been beautiful before, all heart-shaped face and forgiving grace. Now though, she moved beyond beauty, embracing the years with a radiance that shone around her.

Thinking about Skye grew his agitation and Rabble changed into gym shorts to run through a grueling regime, stretching and working his muscles to release some of the tension he'd built since arriving in town. He was still counting push-ups when heavy boots sounded outside his room, nearby doors opened, and matching muffled expletives sounded through his closed door. The twins had arrived and were now experiencing the wonder of the Sunny Morning Trellis bed and breakfast.

Chapter 6

Skye

Skye gripped her sloth-themed thermos firmly in her hand as she tested the doorknob on the heavy white metal door. It twisted easily, and she let herself into the warehouse. As the unofficial meeting place for citizens of Shiloh Hills, the warehouse hosted odd get-togethers and gatherings, including the fall festival and winter markets when the weather turned bad.

In the summertime, the warehouse became a hotbed of activity for Independence Day parade float committees. The cavernous space stored the trailers in the weeks leading up to the holiday, providing complete coverage for decorating committees to work in all weather and all hours.

Shutting the door behind her, Skye scanned the trailers of varying sizes and designs that sat scattered throughout the space. Sheets of white paper hung on each one, labeling the trailer's owner or business.

The citizens of Shiloh Hills considered the parade floats a point of pride. If a business or an individual chose to participate in the Independence Day parade, everyone expected a level of commitment and flare. Skye had seen more dedication to these floats than some marriages, not that anyone talked about that. Without fail, businesses began planning changes and upgrades immediately following July Fourth for following year's festivities.

In the past, Skye had never dedicated herself to any particular float or committee, knowing full well her stepmother presumed she would work on the one for the mayor's office, her father's office. She hated it. Not only did she loathe the lack of creative license because glitter and bright colors apparently jarred her father's nerves, but she also detested anything that had to do with politics. Unfortunately, as the mayor's daughter, people always assumed it was in her blood. Skye would rather walk barefoot through the streets than work on his float.

Thanks to the extra responsibility that came along with summer school teaching, she had doggedly avoided her stepmother's questions over the last several months and thought she might skip the parade planning this year, a welcome change of pace, until Elyza called nearly in tears. Like Skye, Elyza had a tendency of over-extending herself and her resources and had promised to help both the library and the historical society with their floats. So, Skye offered her services for the bridal shop. She couldn't resist the way the lights sparkled off the jewelry and the crystals decorating the beautiful dresses, and she relished the way the silks and satin fabrics brushed softly against her skin. For once, helping would be fun—and a great distraction from thinking about Rabble.

Seeing him had been a jarring experience. Skye tried desperately not to think about the days since Rabble's mother passed away, the days when he should've been there but wasn't. Especially that fateful day, the one caused her physical pain to think about, that had changed everything. She'd hurried home from the graduation ceremony, skating passed friends and faculty trying to congratulate her on her speech or her scholarships to the most prestigious schools in the country. She'd run to and from her car, her bag packed and hidden beside the fence, but Rabble wasn't waiting for her. Her entire world unraveled like a ball of yarn dropped down a flight of stairs.

His return to town shook her, rattling the mostly solid foundation she'd established. Though she knew it was a lie, Skye told herself daily that he didn't matter, their time together meant nothing beyond the friendship and dalliances of two lonely and scared kids. Each lie she told herself, her heart sputtered and whispered, "liar" over and over. Skye thought back to Elyza's shop, trying to draw forth the features of the others with Rabble from her memory bank but it failed her. All she had seen, all that mattered, was him. Was Rabble.

Nope, I'm not thinking about him.

Working her way toward the left side of the warehouse, Skye glanced at each sign until she found the one for The Wild Bride. A black-framed 16-foot-long trailer with a newly replaced pine wood floor waited to be dressed up for the whole town to see.

Skye smiled and rolled her shoulders, letting the stress flow from her body. She pictured the tension leaving her through her feet and left it on the concrete floor, far away from the area where she'd be working. Anticipating a sweaty afternoon, she'd worn her rattiest pair of jeans and a tank top with paint splattering the chest, and she'd twisted her hair into the messiest bun she'd ever managed, with paintbrushes tucked into the knot like individual peacock feathers. Whether or not she would use paint today, Skye had been around children long enough to know she should plan for chaos and dress accordingly.

She wasn't sure what time Elyza's brother would arrive, or which one, but she was eager to lose herself in the process of making her friend's artistic vision come to life. She wanted to create beauty in her world, which sometimes felt colorless, as if all of her creativity and joy had been leached from her over the years.

Frowning, she hauled a deep breath into her lungs. She hadn't always been so bland and broken, had she? Then again, she couldn't exactly recall a time in recent history when she'd done something spontaneous. Spontaneity required leaving her comfort zone and leveling risk against reward. She wasn't comfortable with either of those, and a part of her hated that.

Setting her coffee down on the metal fender well of the trailer, Skye took in the light-colored wooden boards of the trailer deck and the long, black-painted metal frame. Sylvie Basket's legendary 1940's robin-egg blue truck, with white wall tires, would pull the entire float while Mrs. Basket rode shotgun and her assistant, Olivia, drove.

Skye stared at the printout Elyza shared, which primarily included rough sketches and color swatches. She alternated looking at her paper and studying the trailer until the pieces of the plan fell into place, and Elyza's vision came to life. Skye couldn't help but cave to the eagerness that lit her from the inside.

The sound of heavy footsteps startled her from her thoughts, and Skye whipped around. Instead of finding one of Elyza's brothers, Rabble stood before her, his hands tucked into his jeans, his eyes darker, the lines around his mouth deeper. He looked apprehensive, like he had been worrying over what type of emotional turmoil might have been waiting for him today, like how she felt every time she approached her parents' house.

Emotions welled in her chest. Her gut churned, and a sick feeling crept through her as she took him in. With his simple T-shirt tight against his muscled arms, Skye hated to admit it, but he looked good but also...weary.

But why was he here? "What are you doing..."

"Elyza asked us to help."

"Oh."

Neither spoke for a long moment, unsure what else to say. She wracked her brain, searching for any topic that might be safe territory but came up empty. Desperate to end the silence, Skye fell back on the familiar and blurted out simple directions as if she were talking to her students.

"Okay, so let's get started. If you can build the platform, then I can focus on the piecing together the accents." Hearing herself, she winced, hoping he didn't think she was purposefully being condescending.

Rabble nodded, accepting his duty without complaint, "Aye, aye captain."

Skye rolled her eyes and hefted the box of crafting supplies Elyza had given her, onto the platform. She popped the top off of the tote, hearing a long, low whistle from where Rabble had climbed up on the trailer bed.

"What?" her eyebrow quirked.

"That's a lot of shit."

Skye snorted and shook her head, "Just ... get to work."

He bent at the waist, giving her a mocking bow before turning to assess the pile of supplies that had been left for them. Skye turned in a circle, searching for an outlet on one of the many pillars that held the roof above them. Finding one near the ground, she bent, glue gun in hand. A subtle clearing of a throat had her whipping around, Rabble stared at her, jaw clenched.

"What now?" She huffed.

"It's just ... there's an outlet over here," he pointed toward the post nearest him, "it's higher off the ground and closer to the trailer."

Skye's brain blanked and her cheeks heated at the assumption she'd jumped to. Of course he hadn't been checking her out. Why would he? He had no lingering interest in her.

"Uh, thanks."

They worked near each other, their relative silence hanging a bit awkwardly in the air, neither willing to address that strange feeling between them. Skye focused, stringing and gluing flowers together with an intense concentration that went beyond the task at hand. Rabble likewise poured his attention into his task, the hammer in his hand swinging and banging against the framing posts with finality.

For a while, they worked quietly, each wrapped in their thoughts. As time wore on though, the increasingly awkward silence drove her batty. More townsfolk arrived to work on their respective floats, and someone unlocked the giant garage doors to allow in fresh air and sunlight. The routine sounds of hammers, laughter, and general conversation filled the air, but even that could not penetrate the hush that surrounded her and Rabble.

Grimacing, Skye did the one thing she told herself she wouldn't do. "What do you do for a living?" Her voice cracked as her words left against her will.

The stunned expression on Rabble's face almost made her snort with laughter. Had she not been so surprised at her own question, she may have.

Rabble stood, lowering the hammer to his side, like her question had caught him off guard, "Uh, I work security. With Elyza's brothers."

"Isn't that dangerous?" Skye asked, keeping her eyes cast on the glue gun and little string of flowers clasped in her hands.

"Potentially, but usually no. We're good at what we do."

"How did you fall into that?" She couldn't help the genuine curiosity that overtook her. It was simply a natural part of who she was.

When Skye thought about particular moments in their past, she could see how Rabble belonged in a field like security. He had always had a soft spot for the downtrodden and less fortunate. Those years in high school, when he had been so lost, Skye feared he'd fallen into such a pit of all-consuming despair that his future ceased to matter. He constantly got into trouble with someone either at school or around town, and few people believed in him as a person when it finally came time to graduate.

Which aspects of his life had led him down this path? Had more happened to him since he left town, more than added to the hopelessness she remembered? Had his work given him a sense of purpose? Did he find satisfaction in his work?

Rabble gave a small smile and set his hammer down, reaching instead for a drill and a box of screws. He straightened, lifting his shirt to wipe at the sweat beading on his forehead. Well defined abdominal muscles peeked out from under the cotton fabric and Skye turned away, fighting the urge to fan herself. A blush flaming on her cheeks, her mouth suddenly dry.

Rabble's face relaxed, a faraway expression settling in his eyes, like he was no longer in the warehouse with her but somewhere in the past, lost in a memory that helped shape him into the man in front of her. "The three of us met in basic training. We make an—let's say—interesting team. After making our way around the block a few times, there was a darkness—"

He swallowed heavily and shook his head as if to clear the thoughts that had settled there. "Well, anyway, we decided collectively that something had to give. When reenlistment came up, we went out for a beer, which turned into several pitchers and maybe some harder stuff. Honestly, the only thing I remember is that the tab was ridiculous, and we came to a decision that night. Two days after we got out, we met right back at that same bar, and Rabble & Bros. was born."

Skye decided to ignore the insane gaps in the story, though her interest nearly got the better of her. All these years later, she still wanted to know everything he'd been through since leaving town, leaving her. The man working beside her now was definitely not the man she expected if he'd continued down that self-destructive path. She told herself she'd made her peace with his leaving, with the pain of his rejection, but that sting stayed with her, fighting her desire to learn more about this man, the one who had once been her most trusted and beloved friend.

This is not the same boy I remember, not the young and broken one, not the teenaged and angry one, and not the one who left me here. How do I figure out who he is now?

Her thoughts whirled as she tried to reconcile the Rabble from her childhood with the man who worked alongside her.

A twinge went through her, sharp and ugly. A part of her had wanted to be the cure to all his pain. That he had gone off and found a life worth living without her, even though she was happy for him, still stung a little.

Skye thought to that petite woman with light-brown hair from Elyza's shop, standing among her brothers, her family. Who was she to Rabble?

Had Rabble found a life with her? If he had, their relationship must be serious for him to bring her home to Shiloh Hills.

Before Skye's better nature could zip her mouth shut, she blurted, "Who was that woman with you at Elyza's shop?"

Her face heated and she kept her head down, grateful for the glob of glue that stuck her fingers together and gave her a less cowardly reason to avoid his gaze. She pulled a rogue flower off her skin while she waited, breathless, for Rabble's reply.

"The woman? Oh, Bekah. We know her from the city, but she just moved here. Declan, Dash, and I are helping her out while we're here."

"Oh," Skye said, her voice coming out louder than intended. As she glued together two more white flowers, her brows furrowed. Were they helping her like a friend? A client? Something else?

Gah, why does it matter?

As she studied Rabble out of the corner of her eye, more questions swirled around in her mind and waited at the tip of her tongue. Skye opened her mouth to ask another, but something in his eyes stopped her. Behind the self-assured projection he gave the world, a jaggedness lurked. Any question she may ask, he would likely answer, but what would it cost him? She wasn't prepared to find out. Plus, they didn't know each other well enough, not anymore.

Rabble's muscles rippled as he sank a screw into the two-by-four board he held. "What about you?"

That slightly unsettled feeling that had been with her all morning welled up again. Everyone who knew her growing up judged her because her chosen profession was so far off from what she'd planned, or rather, what others had planned for her. Even though she'd received acceptance letters from the most esteemed schools in the country, scoring above average on her ACT in math and science, that Skye—the one who would have ended up in the family business simply because that's what her family wanted—she didn't know anything about life or heartache.

But he had been honest with her…

"I'm a kindergarten teacher at Shiloh Hills Elementary."

Chapter 7

Rabble

A teacher.

Rabble's brain short-circuited the minute she said the word kindergarten.

A teacher.

She studied at one of the most sought-after universities...to become an elementary school teacher.

He'd been ready to follow her to whichever school she chose, albeit at the community-college level, maybe, and support her goals. He had been prepared to work as many jobs as necessary, whatever hours needed, if it meant she could focus on her studies and achieve everything she wanted.

And yet he immediately saw her surrounded by tiny humans with dirty hands, messy grins, and a thirst for knowledge they didn't understand. It suited her and felt significantly more natural than a political career. Rabble had always struggled picturing her stuck behind a big desk and pushing papers on someone else's behalf.

He felt her gaze lock on him as he worked through his thoughts. Could she see it delighted him that she'd gone with her gut and not the career her father had pushed her toward all her life? Not that Rabble had the right to feel pleased. He didn't have the right to feel one way or the other.

Still, he recognized that familiar pressure in his chest, especially when it came to her. Pride.

"Do you enjoy it?" he asked, his voice light and low.

Skye blinked, once, twice, and a peaceful smile graced her face. "I love it."

His answering smile was unstoppable, even as he read the emotions that flitted across Skye's expressive face: puzzlement, confusion, and something else. Something like joy. Honestly, that felt about right to him. Skye's quiet defiance had always been one of his favorite traits and here she was again, throwing him for a loop.

"So, you came back after you got your degree, to teach?" He'd always wondered which of those fancy schools she'd decided on, if she enjoyed the pomp and circumstance. When she had only a week left to decide, he was already gone.

Digging into a bag of fake flowers, Skye shook her head. "No, I stayed here and went to community college."

The screw he held poised between his fingers clattered to the wooden boards beneath his feet, and he gaped. *She hadn't gone? Why?*

Skye's eyes took on a subdued impish glint, like she wanted to surprise him but didn't have the heart to play. Would she gain a sense of satisfaction by completely throwing him off? If so, she'd succeeded.

He lapsed into silence, letting Skye off the hook for more conversation despite the burning questions swirling in his head, causing his head to pound behind his temple. What had changed her mind? Why hadn't she gone off to one of those fancy universities or even one a little further away than fifteen minutes down the road?

They worked in silence for a few more moments before Skye muttered, "What, not even going to ask me?"

Rabble turned back toward her slowly and drawled, "Do you want me to ask?"

"Maybe it wouldn't hurt if you did."

"Why didn't you go, Skye?"

A contemplative look stole over her, and her gaze became unfocused. "You were gone. Maybe it's silly. We were only eighteen after all, but it seemed like the very reason I pushed myself was suddenly missing. I didn't care if I pissed off my parents anymore. And I kept dreaming about those early days when we first met and just thought if more people had been there for you, maybe things would have been different. I wanted to be someone who could help kids like you. And me. Someone they could trust to care for them without any ulterior motives."

He heard what she didn't say. *Maybe he wouldn't have left.*

Rabble would be damned if his entire heart didn't shatter into a million pieces right there in the middle of the warehouse with townspeople making loud noises all around them.

"And your parents were just okay with that?"

"I started school with political science as my major and almost immediately changed it." A beautiful determination set her jaw. "Oh, Dad was mad, but I just stayed away as much as I could until he could be civil again."

His jaw flexed, and he clenched his molars as irritation flashed through him. Skye was a dreamer, and that had always been an issue for Max and Gayle Wellington. They didn't want a dreamer for a daughter; they wanted someone who would be worth something to society, at least, something that matched their idea of worth.

The little girl who lay near him, their faces parallel on either side of the fence, their cheeks almost touching beneath the six-inch gap, saw animals and shapes in the puffy clouds that floated by. Her imagination had baffled and bewildered Rabble, but the stories she'd tell got him through the days and nights when his mother worked long hours. He clung to those stories, memorizing every detail, reciting them to himself as he fell asleep.

Yes, he could definitely see her as a kindergarten teacher, and he bet she was a damned good one at that.

He tilted his head and leaned against the post he'd just secured to the trailer. "What's your favorite part of teaching?"

She straightened, her eyes widened in surprise, and studied him curiously. "No one has asked me that before."

Seriously? Rabble fought the growl that rose in his chest, threatening to spill over and out of him. He had many choice words for her parents and none of them were nice or anywhere near cordial. Their daughter was following a career she was passionate about, and they couldn't be bothered to ask her about her work. He supposed there were different types of abuse and neglect, and while Skye's parents may never have laid a hand on her, the damage they'd done ran just as deeply as his own.

A softness replaced her surprise, and her eyes went distant. "My students. I know that's the cheesy answer, but it's true. In kindergarten, they're just learning how to be their own person, what they like, what they want. I start the school year telling them a story about making friends with someone who may be different from them. Watching how they embrace that and the friendships that develop throughout the year is always a blessing. Some of the most interesting pairings have come out of my classroom."

She met his gaze knowingly, and a surge passed through him, striking his chest and traveling through his body as he froze. She told *their* story to every student that came through her door.

How am I supposed to respond to that?

Looping a garland of flowers around her body, Skye climbed onto the platform, kneeled down at the base of the post, and focused on her project as if she hadn't just completely tilted his entire world on its axis.

His chest felt tight, like his heart didn't have enough space to pump, and his lungs refused to take in enough air. He wasn't used to the feelings roiling around in his head, and each time he tried to grasp onto the end of one thought, it would skate away from him and tangle with the others again. It was enough to drive him crazy.

"Skye." His voice hushed, but she tilted her ear toward him, listening. If only he could hide the anguish that worked its way up his throat and choked him. "Thank you."

She lowered her glue gun and locked eyes with him, those clear blue depths conveying so many thoughts she wouldn't say aloud. Skye glanced away first, releasing him and providing him the space he needed to breathe, to process. Shrugging, Skye turned back to her work, "Nothing to thank me for."

He kneeled down beside her as her long dainty fingers worked to untangle the floral garland. Tenderly, Rabble slid his hand over hers, stilling them as he stroked his thumb over the backs of her knuckles as he waited for her to pull away, to jerk out of his touch with disgust.

When she didn't, he whispered, "All I ever wanted was someone to stand up for me, for someone to see me through the poverty and dirty clothes. You always did, and now you're making sure no child who enters your classroom feels the shame that comes with being from the wrong side of the tracks. Thank you."

A pretty blush graced her cheeks, and Rabble brushed a featherlight kiss over the smooth, pink skin.

He stood, putting distance between them, hoping the tension would dissipate and release the vice grip on his heart. Neither of them spoke again, hammering nails, gluing and stringing garland in a tentative truce for the next couple of hours. She must have been lost in her thoughts the same way he was in his, and neither was prepared to share. Mechanical sounds filled the space, providing mind-numbing clamor for their deep thoughts. If she appreciated the background noise as he did, Rabble wasn't sure, but he was thankful for the chance to focus on the storm raging in his head. He could hardly sift through the static and thunder to form anything that might resemble a coherent sentence.

Several hours later, Rabble leaned against the warm white metal siding of the warehouse, the ribbed edges digging into his back while he stared out at the gravel road. He flipped a pen between his fingers, fidgeting the way he used to with his lighter, before he'd given up cigarettes.

Skye had gone home a long while ago, leaving him to finish up his project for the day and clean up their tools. He couldn't shake the uneasy feeling that his whole life, that the entire world he had built for himself, was teetering on a ledge. What would happen when it finally tipped? And what would be left when the dust settled?

Chapter 8

Skye

Skye barely focused on placing one foot in front of the other. If not for the new sidewalk, she could easily have tripped and broken her ankle with how little attention she paid to where she was going.

Rabble'd still been working diligently when she'd called it a day, unable to erase the feeling of his lips pressed sweetly to her cheek. Any hope she had of being marginally successful for the remainder of the day had fled at the brief touch. When she realized her focus was truly shot, the garland in her hand having been threaded and rethreaded three times, Skye organized her supplies and hurried away from the still-crowded warehouse.

She needed to clear her head, a difficult task considering his scent lingered in her nose, the smell of forest and summer rain. She opted to walk through town instead of heading toward her cottage, hoping some of the rose-tinted clouds would drift out of her consciousness and allow her to think clearly.

Given how lonely she's been, she was eternally thankful for Elyza's friendship, but what in the world had her friend been thinking, pairing her with Rabble for the parade float? Granted, there was no way Elyza could have known about Skye's complicated background when it came to that particular subject. She had done her best to suppress that part of her past, and though aspects of it still seeped into her daily life, she preferred to ignore them. Thinking about when Rabble had been a reassuring constant in her life made her long for things she had given up hoping for, like adventure and a lifelong confidant. They'd spent years planning the places they wanted to see, the things they wanted to do, with only the lilac bush and the shade tree as witnesses to their childish dreaming.

All these years later, Skye still thought about when she'd find Rabble already lying by the fence, waiting for her. He would spend hours upon hours out there, breathing in the scent of peace. Skye didn't ask questions; she let him decompress for several long minutes until he was ready to speak. Did Rabble know he provided the same peace for her that she did for him?

Thoughts like those made her shake her head to clear them away. What good did it do her? They promised each other they'd leave Shiloh Hills together on graduation day and never look back.

Well, Rabble had left, alright. But he didn't bother to take her with him.

Why on earth did he join the army? Why had he run away … from her?

In all of their long conversations, their daydreaming and planning, he'd never mentioned that path as one he might want to pursue. Had he, maybe she could have made him understand, could have showed him that she didn't care where they went, what they did, as long as they were together.

In those days, when Skye looked to her future, there wasn't a single scenario where he wasn't right by her side, sharing in every moment, every triumph and trial, with her. When she let herself think about their days together under the fence, the days when they learned to love and hurt together, the thought of being without him tore at her very soul, at the core of who she was.

Remembering those long-ago conversations and broken promises did nothing for her mental health, and if she was going to get through the next several days working alongside him, she needed to see Rabble as a man, as a friend of a friend—not the boy who forgot her. Besides, she was different now too.

Despite telling herself to stop that line of thinking, Skye commenced a full-blown pity party by the time she reached the end of the street. Fortunately for her mood and unfortunately for her waist, Brick House Cafe was open for business, and several colorful pastries lined the inside a pretty little glass case. Skye wondered which pastry went best with heartache and painful memories.

Chocolate. It had to be chocolate.

Inside the cafe, a long counter separated the small but functional kitchen from the seating area. Glass topped cake stands housed sweet treats in a fantastic array of flavors and colors. Muffins and brownies, cake pops and some other fluffy pastries, each arranged artfully on the trays and along the short glass dome beside the register. Several wrought iron bistro sets dotted the chalky black and white checked tile floor. Exposed brick reached from the floor to the open HVAC and steel support beams overhead. The place had *cozy industrial* written all over it, not to mention the warm and inviting atmosphere. Skye immediately felt her shoulders ease as she slid into one of the bistro chairs.

Like Elyza, the owner, Kellyn, was a transplant to the town, but she moved to Shiloh Hills and opened the cafe several years ago. She worked behind the counter, whipping up specialty coffees and hot drinks and using a pair of dainty tongs to place soft pastries on several tiered dessert stands and behind the domed glass. Flour dusted the pockets of her black apron, and a smudge of whipped topping sat on her cheek, beneath her multicolored glasses frames. She wore her signature red hair piled high atop her head, and a black bandana separated the artfully messy bun from the choppy bangs that hung over her forehead.

Skye smiled. Kellyn never failed to cheer her up, partially because the woman looked like she just stepped out of a Rosie the Riveter poster, if Rosie wore black denim and leather and carried a frosting bag instead of a wrench.

Before Skye could lift her hand in greeting, Kellyn turned to her, eyebrow raised, and immediately picked up a chocolate donut with hot pink frosting swirled on top, plated it, and slid it onto the table in front of Skye.

A moment later, a white chocolate mocha joined the plate, and Skye found herself struggling to hold back tears. "How do you always know?" She sniffled, willing the pressure behind her eyes to subside. That was all she needed to break down and blubber like a crazy woman in the middle of the local cafe.

Kellyn gave her a secret smile, revealing straight white teeth. "I work in mysterious ways."

"Elyza called, didn't she?"

"—and Elyza called." Kellyn's smile turned sheepish, and she slid into the opposite seat.

Skye should have known; Elyza worked faster than the emergency call service in Shiloh Hills. If someone needed something, you could bet Elyza would have that item procured within a few minutes. Unfortunately, the talent seemed to extend to news about her friends as well. Skye couldn't complain too much. Elyza meant well.

Chuckling with defeat, Skye took a bite of the pastry to stall their inevitable conversation and groaned with appreciation as she savored the chocolate treat that never lost its pillowy center.

"Should I expect her to show up too?" Skye contemplated licking the remaining icing from her fingers. In the end, she grabbed a napkin and cleaned off her hands.

A rush of hot air swept over them as the door opened and in walked Elyza, her forehead dotted with sweat from the trek over, even though her shop and the cafe were both on the same block, just opposite ends.

A giggle escaped Skye, and she shoved her hand in front of her mouth to keep from spewing crumbs everywhere at Kellyn's knowing look.

Skye was thankful for these women, more than she could ever express. After Rabble, Skye struggled to make friends, always throwing up a wall between her and whoever tried to get closer. Holding everyone at arm's length was easier, but it made for a lonely existence, especially as her college friends went off, got married, and had babies.

Kellyn and Elyza were different though, and they both seemed to adopt her as their own. Sometimes the best part of their friendship was the silence they allowed to lapse between them; it was so much like the reflective quiet she'd enjoyed with Rabble, and her friends seemed to understand her needs. She loved them for that, the unspoken understanding and acceptance that went into everything the three of them did. Even now, with both of them most likely dying to find out about Skye's issue with Rabble, neither of her friends would push the issue until she was ready to talk. She needed to be the one to open that line of conversation. After that though, it was fair game.

Taking another bite, Skye chewed thoughtfully, searching her memories for a good place to start. Summing up her history with Rabble would be complicated and messy. Parts of their time together, like the night his mother died, belonged solely to them.

Deciding what to tell them was harder than she anticipated, and she ended up sitting back and finishing her donut while Elyza and Kellyn made small talk. The chocolate worked its way into the cracks of her heart and soothed the jagged and painful edges. Explaining who Rabble was to her was like explaining the Sun in relation to the Earth, a vital element that could both heal and scorch. It wasn't an easy thing to describe, how intrinsically they had been linked, only to have that connection sundered so completely.

When the last of her pastry was gone, Skye cleared her throat, and her friends turned toward her, their conversation forgotten as they sat, ready to listen and be by her side, no matter what.

"I've known Rabble since we were children. He was my next-door neighbor. But...he was so much more than that." Skye kept her voice as even as she could and waited for the explosion.

Chapter 9

Rabble

The next morning, Rabble, Declan, and Dash sat around the dining table at the bed and breakfast, which had not changed since as long as Rabble could remember. The table had been built by Mrs. Basket's husband, Charlie, the winter after they'd married and held the honored position as their dining table for their too few years together. Imperfections aplenty marked up the wood—discolorations in the stain, indentations, and scratches. For every scar or mark though, Mrs. Basket had a story to tell, lovingly running her fingers over each mark as she spoke. Rabble had heard those stories repeatedly while working at the bed and breakfast. Whenever she echoed a certain story, Rabble never let on, allowing Mrs. Basket to relive the memories when she'd been happiest with her husband.

Now, the table seemed smaller, casework files spread across the wooden surface and three large men perched on the questionably rickety chairs. Breakfast platters piled with eggs, bacon, biscuits, and skillet potatoes sat on the buffet table against the wall, empty except for a few crumbs. No one would doubt that the three of them could put away a decent amount of food on a good day, but when Mrs. Basket made everything from scratch—well, it had been a long minute since any of them had enjoyed a good homecooked meal.

Seeing Mrs. Basket again had nearly brought Rabble to his knees. Logically, he'd known she would age, but the increased wrinkles that pulled at her mouth and crinkled the corners of her eyes when she smiled almost bowled him over. Just as beautiful as ever, she was the closest he had ever come to having a grandmother. He'd asked about her health and hobbies and had a hard time not inquiring after every detail of her life while they caught up. He'd missed her. Giving up Shiloh Hills had come with its downsides, and missing out on time with Mrs. Basket was one mistake he would never be able to undo.

Rabble checked his watch again, noticing the late hour, and tried to hurry their morning meeting along, knowing Mrs. Basket and Olivia would be in soon to clear away breakfast and prepare for lunch.

"She's definitely made the place into a home," Declan said, reporting on how Bekah was doing. Claiming the house as her own, decorating and creating a home, was a small but vital part of the process as far as Rabble was concerned. If the client never felt comfortable enough to settle into their new accommodations, they wouldn't be able to pull off staying away from their old life for long.

Declan tapped his pen against the table. "And she seems genuinely excited about starting work with Elyza."

Rabble hoped Shiloh Hills suited Bekah well. The small town had some level of commerce that kept it from falling completely off of the map, but it was one of those hidden gems people didn't tend to find unless they were looking for it. The fact that Rabble could distance himself enough from some of his worst memories to view Shiloh Hills as promising spoke volumes about the town as a whole. Bekah should be able to live a quiet and safe life there if she wanted to.

Rabble caught Declan and Dash glancing at each other again, the fifth time in half an hour. Admittedly, his brothers had waited longer than he thought they would, and he commended their restraint. Regardless, he could tell they were growing weary of his vague answers and half-truths about the woman from The Wild Bride on their first day in town. He was also tired of tip-toeing around the topic of Skye, but how did he tell his brothers he had never been man enough to go after the only woman he ever truly wanted?

He was happy with his life now, wasn't he? They had plenty of work coming in and helped people who needed it. He worked with the two best friends a guy could ask for and had relative peace. So why had coming back to Shiloh Hills made him feel sick inside? Why had the thought of seeing Skye made him so nervous and frustrated? And why couldn't he stop replaying the kiss he'd brushed against her cheek?

He knew why. Rabble just didn't want to say the words out loud. The moment they knew, Declan would probably tell Rabble exactly what he was thinking while Dash would stay silent, his disapproval showing in his eyes.

Was he being a coward? One hundred percent yes. He didn't doubt that. Still, he had never been cagey with his brothers before, and he wasn't necessarily interested in starting now. "I've known Skye since we were children. She was my next-door neighbor."

His sudden announcement hung in the air as silence fell. The twins gave Rabble their full attention and respect as he outlined the basics of his time with Skye. He didn't get into too many details about his father, mother, or childhood, only that Skye had been an anchor in his otherwise stormy life.

"She was my sanity for the longest time, the only part of my life that made sense after my mom died."

Silence.

Rabble tried to swallow past the lump in his throat. "But her dad is—well, he's a jackass. When she broke their house rules to stay with me, they forbade her from seeing me again, even though we lived next door to each other and went to the same school. They finished convincing her she wasn't worth anything unless she was perfect, and I made promises I didn't keep...especially when she needed me most." The disgust was evident in his voice, and admitting his failure aloud made his stomach churn.

He glanced unseeingly at the reports in front of him. Instead, he saw her standing behind the school building, the early morning light painting the sky in purples and pinks while he promised they'd go somewhere far enough away to leave behind the pain and anger of Shiloh Hills. She'd been so radiant, so hopeful, looking at him with eyes full of trust despite the trouble he'd managed to get into in the last few years.

"That was then," Dash said quietly, his deep voice rumbling, filling the space.

Rabble's gaze snapped to him; he didn't speak often, so Rabble listened when he did.

"This is now." Dash shrugged.

Confusion rippled through Rabble. "So?"

Uncharacteristically serious, Declan answered for his brother. "I think what he's trying to say is that you were both still kids then. You aren't kids anymore, so what's stopping you now?"

Dash cocked his head to the side incredulously. "That's exactly what I just said."

The twins left Rabble sitting at the dining table, warring with himself. On one hand, he wanted to go after Skye, wanted to chase the dreams they'd had when they were those lovesick kids. On the other hand, how could he face her, knowing how fantastically he had let her down, and ask for a chance this late in the game? He hadn't been a major part of her life since they were eighteen, and a lot of time and history had passed since then. Their lives had diverged, and their experiences had shaped them, molded them, into different people.

And yet, even though Rabble considered himself a fairly smart person, he felt like the biggest idiot in the world. In some ways, he was still that eighteen-year-old kid who knew nothing of the world or himself.

With his mind spinning, Rabble quite literally felt dizzy. What in the world was he doing? Eight years. Eight damn years. Wasted.

Think, he chastised himself, forcing back the self-loathing to focus on his current problem.

He was a planner; that was what he did for work every day. He solved problems and developed solutions that benefited every party involved. Applying the same process to himself should come naturally, right?

Something that felt oddly like hope flickered in his chest.

Yet each time he thought about talking to Skye, about bringing up the past and the promises he broke, something inside him shrank away from the pain he knew it would inflict on both of them.

Mind occupied, Rabble left his truck keys in his room and hurried down the stairs. He pushed through the screen door at the back of the bed and breakfast and soon found himself on the sidewalk. With his hands stuffed into his pockets, he lumbered toward the warehouse where he planned to meet Skye again. By the time he reached the building, he needed his thoughts organized, or he would quickly put his foot in his mouth. That was inevitable.

As he neared the warehouse, he'd worked up a decent sweat. He hadn't considered the heat, the distance, or the fact that jeans were not the best choice of clothing for a long summer walk. At least the multiple garage doors were wide open, letting sunlight and a summer breeze stream in. The massive space was busier with more parade trailers parked inside and outside on the grass and gravel. Townsfolk milled about, chatting and trading equipment; the sound of power tools and sporadic laughter built into a cacophony of noise that drowned out all thought and reason.

Damn. The loud banging and constant hammering made him wince.

He glanced around, seeking Declan and Dash, each working on their respective floats. They'd moved their trailers outside, as far onto the grass and away from the loudest sounds in the warehouse. Rabble once again had to acknowledge how smart his partners were. The freedom and fresh air they gained from their distance to the building was well worth the lack of electricity that far out.

His eyes scanned the back wall where Elyza's trailer was truly stuck in the warehouse. Trapped. His heart hammered in his ears, and he swallowed thickly. Stealing himself, Rabble made his way through the tangle of air hoses for a variety of compressors running power tools, around trailers and large props for the parade, and through the crowds of people moving about their projects. The noises bounced around the echoey space and made him jumpy.

Spotting Skye took longer than he liked. With a paintbrush in hand, she sat atop a turned-over bucket at the back of their trailer and traced tiny, delicate lace patterns on the posts he'd put together yesterday. He paused and watched as she focused on her task. A cute little crease dipped between her brows as they furrowed slightly in concentration, and she silently mouthed the words to whatever song blasted from a large speaker across the room. The care she gave each detail was remarkable. *She* was remarkable.

As he got closer, Rabble made enough noise so she could hear him over the din. Grimacing, he thought of the times someone had come up behind him without warning. Those memories were not some of his more pleasant ones.

Skye turned and asked, "Is something wrong?"

"What? No, why would anything be wrong?" he stammered.

"You're frowning, again." She gave him a pointed look, daring him to argue with her use of the word *again*.

Instead, he gave her a strained smile and opted for honesty. "The noise. I wanted to make sure you heard me coming so I didn't sneak up on you. Not so good when it happens to me." He grimaced, hating how vulnerable the admission made him feel, how exposed and weak.

Skye must have read what he wasn't saying in the strained lines of his face and nodded, dropping the issue and returning to her tiny lace markings. Rabble gave a silent sigh of relief. That was a conversation he desperately didn't want to have with her. Not yet.

He left her to her details and turned his attention to the low platform where the three *brides* would stand during the parade. He let his mind wander as he constructed each of Elyza's ideas for the float, Skye painting the entire time, pausing only to mark off each project from the checklist provided to them by Elyza.

At one point, Rabble practically begged Skye to take a short break and scarf down the sandwich Elyza delivered, along with a heap of praise for the work they'd done. She'd agreed reluctantly, proceeding to eat faster than anyone he'd seen before, including his time in basic training. He'd be lying if he said he wasn't impressed, both with the speed in which she finished lunch and the dedication she showed to each minute detail she included on the posts.

Dusk had fallen by the time Skye stood, slowly, arching her back to stretch the kinks out of her muscles. Rabble tried, he truly did, not to let his eyes wander over her form as she reached toward the ceiling on her tiptoes. His self-control slipped when her shirt pulled up, exposing a thin strip of bare skin at her waist.

Skye came out of her stretch and turned to greet several of her previous students who had come with their parents and were leaving for the night. The smile that lit up her face took his breath away, and he was moving before he knew what he was doing.

Rabble grasped Skye's hand lightly and watched surprise and wariness war in her eyes. "Can we talk?"

Chapter 10

Skye

Skye wasn't sure if she should panic or be angry. Maybe both? Everyone knew "can we talk" was the line somebody said right before they broke bad news. Rabble wasn't someone she would consider *everyone* though. He'd never operated on society's standard of normal.

Her hand settled against his warm, rough skin as he entwined their fingers, and Skye let him lead her out of the warehouse, under the glow of the building's security lights. The crowd had dissipated throughout the day, many of the families having headed home within the last several minutes. Only a few dedicated stragglers continued working and would stay late into the night. They were relatively alone among the crickets and other singing bugs that made homes in the grass and trees behind the warehouse.

He rubbed the back of her hand with his thumb, in soothing circles. Skye didn't know if it was more for her or himself.

She felt the shift, a subtle change during their conversation the day before while working on the parade float, something almost companionable between them. His soft lips against her cheek as he brushed a kiss there had solidified her confusion and left her feeling like a silly schoolgirl. This though, felt different even from that. The urgency to his movements set her heart racing and made her stomach clench in nervousness.

"Skye…" He dropped her name from his mouth like he wasn't prepared to speak at all, and he seemed to struggle for the right words.

His throat bobbed as he searched for the vocabulary to convey his dismay. "Dash and, well, I suppose Declan too, made me realize something this morning. It's eight years too late, but I, I'm sorry."

Skye sucked in a breath and held it like her life depended on it, her heart thudding painfully beneath her chest, but she stayed quiet as he went on.

"I let you down. I left when you needed me, when we needed each other, and I can't ever take back these years of doubt and everything that could have been different, but I want the chance to. I mean I hope, maybe I might get the chance to." He cringed as his words rushed out, desperate to be spoken and yet wished they'd remained unsaid.

Skye found his fumbling endearing, but what was she supposed to say to that? She had loved him since childhood, had probably always loved him in truth. She'd been waiting to hear him say those words for so long, but too much history divided them. Too much to start fresh? Could they use the broken blocks of their past to build a stronger future? Was she a fool for wishing they could?

She stared at her hand, linked with his. "I think I'd been holding out hope, maybe you'd just been held up with something. Maybe you were just running late. I wanted so badly to believe you still planned to run away with me, that you hadn't left me behind. But when I found your enlistment papers," her voice cracked and she swallowed, disentangling their fingers to distance herself, "I felt like my world finished crumbling completely. All the freedom we longed for was gone. The only person who knew how I felt, gone. It *hurt,* Matthew."

Skye watched the blow land when she used his given name, the way he flinched and blanched at the same time. She didn't say it to hurt him. Even though telling him the truth sounded selfish in her ears and unshed tears blurred her vision, he needed to understand how deep her wounds went.

His eyes darkened in the fading light of dusk, but she could read pain in the lines around his eyes and the tightness of his mouth.

"Did you think I couldn't handle going with you? That your career choice might scare me away? Did you not think I was strong enough to be there to support you through trainings and deployments?" The vulnerability in her questions made Skye

cringe.

She hated feeling so exposed but there was no other way to convey the way he'd hurt her. "I would have given anything to stay with you, no matter where that path led." All of the hurt and confusion bubbled back to the surface, and Skye felt like the eighteen-year-old girl she'd been, betrayed and alone. Scared.

"No! I knew you would go with me. But you had your heart set on college and—." He swallowed roughly, his warm hand following the path of her jaw to caress her cheek as he rushed on, "

I couldn't be the reason you didn't chase your own dreams. I couldn't take you away from all of that."

Skye sighed, suddenly exhausted, and pulled away from him to sag against the rough siding of the building. "What a pair we are. I was looking to you for freedom, and all you saw were the chains you thought you represented. I wanted you, Rabble. Just you."

He closed the distance and leaned in, cupping her face with his huge hands and smudged his thumb across her jaw. He dipped his head, his lips grazing the shell of her ear before he pulled back and met her eyes with an intensity that awakened some long slumbering part of her. "I don't deserve to ask this of you, I know that." Leaning his forehead against hers, his soft breath whispered passed her ear, "Would you give us the chance to find out what we missed, Skye? Let me show you how truly, devastatingly, miserable I am without you."

The silence that followed was thick with tension, hurt and fear yawned like a chasm between them.

"I...I need to think," Skye murmured. She wasn't sure who she was speaking to, maybe Rabble, maybe herself, maybe even the universe.

If she hadn't known him so well, she may have missed the minuscule way his face fell, but the flash of pain in his eyes disappeared immediately. He nodded but didn't speak, as if he couldn't quite trust his voice.

She stared intently into the steely gray depths of his eyes. "Just give me the night, Matthew, please."

He nodded again and pulled back, offering his hand and a sad smile. "Let me walk you to your car."

After Rabble saw her safely tucked inside her sensible vehicle and heard the doors lock, Skye watched him walk away in the beams of the headlights. By the time they finished speaking, they were alone, the last of the others having wandered off at some point. Rabble refused a ride when she offered and a part of her was relieved. Admittedly, she needed time alone to reel and think and probably cry, but she would have waited if it made a difference in his safety.

Rabble's form disappeared into the night long before Skye put the car in gear and began her short commute home. She spent the drive on autopilot, stopping at the red light automatically, driving between the yellow lines marked on the asphalt because it was habitual.

Even putting her key into the lock and letting herself into her house felt automated.

She threw herself onto the reading chair with a groan, her mind drifting as she closed her eyes against reality. She'd been in love with Rabble ever since that For Sale sign next door came down and the dusty, shaggy-haired little boy appeared beneath that wonderfully tall tree. He had been her confidant in all things, and anytime she had something to celebrate or cry over, she ran directly to their fence, always to Rabble who waited for her.

Skye knew, in her heart, Rabble loved her, had always loved her as no one else ever had before or since. Her head however, liked to throw around her insecurities, letting them hurdle through her mind like a bouncing ball. Did he truly love her? Or had she simply been a convenience of the time, another lonely person looking to escape the confines of the small town. Did he love her now? Or was she once again, a convenience for the time being. With her heart and head constantly at war, was it worth the risk of finding out which was right?

Skye's head spun as she weighed years of history and strife against wishes and plans that had never come to fruition. He had broken her heart in ways that were ultimately hard to repair as they were such an integral part of who she was now. Her parents, despite their controlling manipulation, could never have crushed her the way he had, whether he meant to or not. That type of heartache wasn't easily forgotten.

Skye glanced around her house. It was small, sure, but it was hers, and it was solid and steady and everything she wanted from her comfort zone.

But we don't grow in our comfort zone do we, Miss Wellington? she heard herself in her head, as clearly as if she were speaking to her students. She said something similar to a little girl from the previous year who had been afraid to try out the monkey bars.

At one time, Rabble had been her comfort zone... Was it worth it, the probability of heartache if she took the leap and let him back in?

Skye moved aimlessly about the cottage, starting a load of laundry, washing the few dishes that sat in the sink, folding the blanket that graced the back of the couch—anything to put off the inevitable. She jumped in the shower, taking extra time washing her hair, scrubbing every inch of her skin, and shaving her legs to perfect smoothness. The water turned cold before she finally shut off the spout, wrapped herself in her fluffiest bath towel, and stepped out of the tub. With a second towel, she tied her hair up in it, letting the cloth pull the extra moisture from the long strands, and sat on the edge of her bed, her towel dampening the sheets as she laid back, lifting her phone in front of her.

She shot a text message off to Elyza before she could second-guess herself, and a few minutes later a ten-digit number appeared on her screen. She saved the number to her contacts and opened a blank message. The cursor laughed at her, mockingly blinking at her. She typed a few words, then deleted them, and the cursor kept blinking on and off, a bleak reminder that she had yet to write a single word worth sending, nothing that reflected how she truly felt. Good lord, she felt like a teenager again!

Inhaling deeply, Skye gathered her courage, typed the one word she could manage, and hoped he understood who it was from and what she meant.

Chapter 11

Rabble

Rabble fully expected Skye to ignore his question and leave him waiting for her reply. They hadn't exchanged numbers and he regretted that now more than ever. A short-sighted mistake made on his part, fueled by the myriad of emotions that swamped him each time he saw her. His brain ceased working in her vicinity and he did good to form coherent thoughts at all.

He waited outside of view until her car drove away from the warehouse, then took the long path back to the bed and breakfast, hoping the hushed night noises would soothe some of his anxiety over her lack of answer. He wanted to shout at the dark sky, but he finished his walk, letting the cool night air breathe life into him. Whatever she chose, he would respect it, even if her rejection tore him to pieces.

Returning as late as he had, he missed out on Mrs. Basket's formal dinner but found a sandwich and bag of chips atop a tray on the table with his name scrawled across a piece of white printer paper beside it.

A sealed manila envelope also sporting his name waited next to the plate.

Grabbing the dinner tray and envelope, he hurried up to his room, sat down at the small desk, and practically inhaled the turkey sandwich and plain potato chips. Then he turned his attention to the envelope.

Tearing at the flap, Rabble pulled out the final documents from the title company, detailing the purchase of his parents' old property. He'd met with the realtor in the city before he'd left, signing the paperwork and officially accepting ownership from an older man who purchased the land at auction after Rabble's father passed away. He shoved the documents into his laptop bag, knowing he'd need to review them at some point but not willing to let thoughts of his father and his life on that property weigh on him.

After showering and dressing in a loose pair of cotton pajama pants, he switched off the lights and laid down on the bed, his feet dangling slightly at the end, and snorted, picturing how far Declan and Dash's feet hung off since they were both several inches taller than him at just over six-foot tall.

He pulled out his phone, the bright light shining strongly in the dark, temporarily blinding him as he squinted at the name that appeared. His breath hitched at the unknown number. One word, that was all she'd messaged, just one word. But Skye had said yes. Sleep evaded him after that, his mind spinning with all of the possibilities open to them now. Tendrils of doubt tried to worm their way into his thoughts. They couldn't pick up where they'd left off as kids, too much had transpired in their lives since their idealistic days of dreaming of running away together. He'd been to war; his body and mind bore the scars of that. But she had too, a different sort that wore on her heart and soul. Would they fall into the same familiarity that felt so natural when they were younger or had life changed them so irrevocably that they couldn't find middle ground? Rabble avoided those thoughts, trying to squash them as they arose to focus instead on what he could do to make Skye smile.

Just the mental image of her smiling face lightened Rabble's mood, the weight that normally sat on his chest, eased. Her shining face appeared behind his eyelids as he closed his eyes and drifted. The picture blended Skye's appearance throughout the time he'd known her. Her face lit up like it had as children, the excitement of learning something new with him or her laughter at a silly joke he told, but her eyes belonged to that of the woman he was becoming reacquainted with. There was sadness there, a loneliness he understood and hated, and a sense of hopelessness, of being trapped in a cycle that never ended.

As he drifted off to sleep, he vowed to steal that sadness, the loneliness, the hopelessness, and help her create a life that reflected the dreams they'd chased all those years ago.

***

Rabble spent the entire next day feeling like he was walking on air.

He woke early, momentarily forgetting he and Skye weren't meeting to work on the parade float. They'd made plenty of progress staying late the previous two days, in part to remain on schedule and because life had a tendency of getting in the way at the least opportune times. He also had work obligations during his time in Shiloh Hills, and Skye had a home to maintain and a job helping Elyza during the summer.

With the hot sun still low in the sky, Rabble threw on a pair of basketball shorts and went for a run.

She'd said yes!

His brain pretty much stopped comprehending anything else and played that thought on a loop. He wanted to take her out immediately, somewhere fancy, something nice, one of the places he'd always thought about taking her to when he was just a poor kid without a dime to his name. Even then, she'd deserved to be treated like royalty. He contemplated several restaurants, mentally debating their merits and pitfalls. Ultimately, he ended up tossing each one he'd considered. He worried his lip, coated with perspiration, as his brain raced through different date ideas, ones that wouldn't end up a complete disaster or with Skye changing her mind and telling him to completely fuck off.

They'd been apart for a long while. Maybe she'd changed significantly. Although from what he'd seen so far, it didn't appear like she had at the most important levels. She was still the big-hearted perfectionist with horrible self-doubt he'd loved forever. Her core personality, the things that made her Skye, remained the same. Everything else—well, he'd enjoy the opportunity to learn about her now, as a woman; what she liked and disliked, what she did for fun, and what she wanted for the future.

For the final two miles of his run, Rabble pushed himself as far as he could until the sun rose high enough to heat the air unmercifully and the humidity became oppressive, like he had a wet towel pressed across his face. By the time he returned to the bed and breakfast, he was dripping sweat.

When he moved to swipe a piece of bacon from the buffet in the dining room, Mrs. Basket waddled in and swatted his hand with her wrinkled one. Her soft blue eyes were still as sharp as ever as she admonished him. "Rabble Raden, you get your hind-end upstairs and shower. You know better than to come to my table smelling like a pigsty."

Grinning, he gave her a quick kiss on the forehead before she could stop him, and her feigned scoff of disgust followed him up the stairs and into the bathroom. By the time he came down dressed in jeans and a faded black T-shirt, his hair still wet from his shower, Declan and Dash had joined Mrs. Basket and Olivia at the table, and each had a plate piled high with breakfast. Rabble took a clean china plate from the buffet and filled it with bacon and eggs and biscuits with homemade jam. He groaned with pleasure at his first bite, his eyes rolling slightly.

Declan grinned mischievously from across the table. "Do you need a moment alone with that biscuit, Rab?"

"Don't you dare flip him off at my table, Rabble Raden," Mrs. Basket said, her eyes focused on her plate.

Rabble slowly lowered his hand back to the table and blushed. How she knew exactly what he would do had always been a mystery to him, but she'd done the same thing when he'd been a teenager.

Breakfast passed in companionable discussion. Even Dash joined in the conversation when Mrs. Basket or Olivia asked him a direct question, and Rabble smirked at his friend's discomfort. Conversing was like pulling teeth for Dash.

"How's our Skye?" Mrs. Basket asked, her question pointed directly at Rabble.

He ducked his head and tried to rein in the grin that wanted to break free. "I think she's good."

Mrs. Basket's sharp eyes found his, "You *think*, or you *know*?"

Rabble chuckled, long and low before settling back into his chair, "Let's just say, we're taking a chance on us."

The reasons he'd left Shiloh Hills and Skye behind no longer held sway over him, he'd grown, matured, and now, nothing and no one would stand in their way of the life they'd always dreamed of.

Mrs. Basket smiled back at him, and gripped his arm with a comforting hand, "I think that's a chance worth taking, dear."

He nodded, his eyes going distant as his mind traveled back to Skye for the umpteenth time that day, "Me too."

"Did you know she goes out to see your mama every month?" The older woman used her fork and knife to slice through a thick cut of cantaloupe on her plate before lifting a small bite to her mouth to chew.

Rabble's muscles locked up, and the eggs in his mouth turned to ash. Suddenly, the food on his plate and settling in his stomach didn't seem so appetizing anymore.

Mrs. Basket had no qualms seeking out the things that burdened his soul and laying them bare, though he wished she'd waited until they were alone. That had never been her way though. She always said there was no time for beating about the bush.

Olivia excused herself politely, sending a sympathetic look his way. He appreciated her gesture, but hated it just the same. Dash picked up his plate, still full of breakfast, and nudged his brother to join him. They pushed through the backdoor and sank into the rocking chairs on the porch to finish their morning meal.

"You sure know how to clear a room, Mrs. Basket." Rabble's laugh was tight, strained.

She set her cutlery down and grasped his hand in both of her smaller ones, her skin soft and thin. He frowned with worry at the obvious signs of her age.

"Baby boy," she said, her southern twang becoming more pronounced as she settled into the surrogate grandmother role, "you need to go see your mama."

A chill crept into his bones, and he tried to staunch the tremors that stole over him. "I...I'm not sure I'm ready for that."

"It's been eight years, son." Mrs. Basket gave him a sad smile. "I'm sure she's missin' her boy."

He tried to pull away. If he could escape, he wouldn't have to face what she was saying, the pain that it drudged up. Her grip was surprisingly strong, and he quickly found himself clinging to her hands like a lifeline.

His voice broke. "Skye goes to see her?"

She nodded. "Every month, baby. Every month."

Pressure built behind his eyes and nose but he refused to acknowledge it, even in front of Mrs. Basket, who had shown him such kindness and care when she didn't have to. Instead, he closed his eyes and let the emotions wash through him while he focused on taking deep breaths.

He shouldn't have been surprised Skye would do something so selfless. That was just the kind of person she was, always looking out for others and seemingly able to root out the pain a person kept closest to their heart. He was thankful Mrs. Basket told him; Skye certainly never would, not thinking about it as anything more than exactly the kind of thing a person would do. Except they wouldn't. Most people would have left his mother's makeshift grave alone, left to be buried under years of leaves and debris. Instead, Skye visited her, spoke with her, and cared for her, even when he'd run away.

"Thank you for telling me," he choked out, his voice a tad nasally as he fought back the tears.

She nodded sagely and leaned over to kiss him on the forehead, the same way she'd done when he had a particularly rough day at school and needed to know someone out there cared for him.

"Now, clean up this mess," she joked. "These old bones are too tired to clean up after you three big men!"

Rabble sputtered a laugh and agreed to clean up the dishes. Declan and Dash didn't stay outside much longer, the heat forcing them seek out the cool breeze of the air conditioning. Neither of them spoke a word about his conversation with Mrs. Basket, and Rabble appreciated that more than he could express. Setting aside his feelings about his mother, about Skye, Rabble focused his attention on reviewing Bekah's security measures and discussing the email Dash received from a contact in California who kept an eye on Edward Elnor's movements for them.

"If Elnor is on the move, which I honestly think he is," Declan said, the light of his laptop flashing in his eyes as he scrolled, "we should be able to track him. We can also look into tightening the little security Bekah is allowing."

Rabble detected the barely concealed annoyance in his friend's voice. Likewise, Declan had voiced his frustrated with Bekah's level of security. Even though Rabble agreed with them, they would try their best to work within her approved constraints. She was just now free of a man known for being cruel and controlling; the last thing she'd want was men placing more restrictions on her, no matter how well-intentioned those restrictions were.

"What is Bekah up to today?" Rabble asked. "Think she'd be open to a little chat about our concerns?"

Frowning, Dash ran his hands through his long, wavy hair. "Elyza's snatched her and Skye up for the day. They're taking a road trip into the next town to check out another bridal shop and size up the competition. I know, I know. Elyza shot me a text after they were already on the road."

Well, that makes keeping an eye on Bekah harder. Even if Elyza didn't know the extent of her new friend's situation, Bekah did. They needed to talk to her sooner rather than later about the risks she was willing to take.

Rabble winced as another realization hit him. *Dang. There go my plans with Skye.* "What about tonight?"

Despite his obvious irritation, Declan grinned. "Oh, the ladies are having a book date night or something. It's an excuse for them to read smutty books, drink booze, and stay over at Bekah's. Elyza, Kellyn, and Skye will all be there too."

Rabble's eyebrows rose. "Smutty books?"

Declan wiggled his eyebrows while Dash gave an uncharacteristic smirk. "Yeah, smutty books."

Despite his best efforts, Rabble's dedication to his work didn't stop his mind from wandering to Skye and the reading material she'd be curled up with tonight. What did she enjoy reading? Did the romance in the novels come anywhere close to showing how he wanted to be with her? Did she imagine . . .

No, no. Focus.

He shook his head but those distracting thoughts stayed, playing out like a movie in his mind. He ground his teeth. If he didn't focus on something else soon, he'd need to head upstairs for a shower cold enough to freeze the images in their place.

He concentrated on work, on Bekah's situation, and the tension slowly eased from his body.

Waiting to speak with Bekah wasn't ideal, but their talk could wait until tomorrow. Given they'd all been working hard between The Wild Bride and the various floats Elyza assigned them, they deserved a night off from the chaos. Their date would just have to wait one more day.

"Our information doesn't say Edward has left California yet." Rabble twirled a pen between his fingers. "How much trouble can a few women get into?"

Chapter 12

Skye

Clutching the forest green shopping basket tightly, Skye meandered down the snack aisle at the local grocery. The store wasn't nearly as large as the bigger box stores in the city, but it was serviceable for regular grocery shopping. She perused the aisles, making sure she scanned each shelf with care. For her first ever girls' night, she didn't want to mess up her snack selection and be booed out of the house.

Skye forced down the rising nervousness that threatened her enthusiasm for the night. While other kids had been spending their days and nights together, having sleep overs, and get-togethers, Skye's experience consisted of spending long nights studying some subject, practicing some talent, or staring at the fence where it denoted the property line. Outside of school functions, Skye had become a prisoner in a pretty cage. Friends were a commodity she'd given up, and she'd do it again without hesitation.

Now, Skye tumbled in a riot of emotions, unsure of herself and anxious that she would somehow do something wrong or say something odd. She was a kindergarten teacher after all, her days tended to be filled with teaching basic skills to young minds.

She would probably throw up before she arrived at the gathering. Her nervous terror was completely irrational, but that didn't stop the butterfly circus spinning around in her stomach.

Her eyes caught on the bright red, blue, and yellow packages that contained her favorite comfort junk foods. Skye'd been avoiding as much junk food as possible, trying to watch her weight and be healthier, but not a single part of her planned to bring a vegetable tray to her first girls' night.

When she'd been littler, Skye would sneak the packages of chunky chocolate chip cookies down to the fence after school to share with Rabble. He always savored every bite, even licking his fingers clean of the melted chocolate and crumbs.

Did he still savor sweet treats in that way? Or had life taught him a different lesson, to devour without pausing to take in the quieter parts of life.

Another facet of Skye's anxiety, the response she'd spent minutes mulling over before finally pressing send. Her thumb hovered over the send button until it cramped. The finality of recognizing his desire for a second chance mirrored her own drudged up those old memories that pricked and pulled at her heart. Not to mention the potential town-wide fallout if her parents were to find out she and Rabble were finally, officially, an item. Skye shuddered to think of the octave level her stepmother's voice would reach when she found out.

After careful consideration, Skye picked crinkly plastic containers of crunchy and chewy chocolate chip cookies off of the shelf, deciding neither deserved to be left out of the basket. With unhurried steps, she headed toward the alcohol aisle, determined to let loose a little in the safety of her friends. She'd never been much of a drinker, having missed all of the parties where people chose their favorite alcohol. Still, Skye peered at the bottles, trying to pretend like she knew what she was looking for. Trying, and failing, not to feel like an imposter.

The air around her grew warm and uncomfortable. A moment later, an arm snaked around her waist and tugged her backward. She landed against a hard chest with a muffled "oof" as the air escaped her lungs and that palm roved across her waist, eliciting a queasy response in her stomach. The shopping basket banged against her legs as Skye whipped around, shoving the basket between her and the owner of that seeking hand. Smirking, Dylan slowly extracted his arm and slid his fist into his pants pocket as if he had no cares in the world.

"Dylan," Skye huffed out. The relief of recognizing who the appendage belonged to quickly gave way to boiling-hot rage at his presumptuous touch.

"What are you doing over here, Skye?" His muddy-brown eyes perused the assortment of colorful bottles on the shelf behind her. "I didn't think you were much of a drinker?"

"I'm not." She gritted her teeth, straining to maintain a civilized appearance.

His smirk remained firmly in place. "For a wedding, I recommend a nice red, or something a bit more bubbly."

Skye frowned. "Yeah, sorry about dinner the other night. I had no idea my parents were planning anything. They know we left all of that in college."

His eyes seemed to dim and harden, and his smirk transformed into something a bit more sinister. The uncomfortable feeling in the air intensified, and a shiver ran down her spine.

"Of course." He inclined his head briefly. "Who knows? People do things for unknown reasons all the time."

Dylan grabbed a bottle of red wine by the thin glass neck and set it in her basket. "Have a good night, Skye."

She watched him saunter away, no basket in hand or cart to push. Breathing deeply through her nose, she exhaled through pursed lips, willing her heart rate to return to normal and refusing the need to shudder. She pulled the bottle of wine out of her basket and examined the Pinot Noir. For a moment, she flashed back to the college party where she'd first experienced that discomfited feeling, so like alarm, around Dylan. Why did that type of wine ring a bell? Feeling mildly ill, Skye put the bottle back on the shelf, mindful of the slight tremor in her fingers. The last thing she needed was to knock a row of glass bottles to the floor with her shaking hands.

Skye quickly paid for the few things in her basket, sticking with the tried-and-true drinks she knew and loved. If the ladies gave her trouble for showing up with a bottle of sparkling grape juice and a quart of apple juice, she'd just take it. She had no doubt their jokes would be only a good-natured ribbing, free of actual judgment.

With the bags safely tucked in the backseat of her car, Skye glanced around the parking lot, the sense of being watched lifting the tiny hairs on the back of her neck. She scanned each row of vehicles, but beyond an elderly couple holding tightly to each other, the man gently helping the woman bent with age into their car, no one else was in the parking lot.

"That's it, Skye. You are losing it," she whispered.

She waved to the man on her way out of the lot and turned toward Bekah's. Having friends in the same neighborhood was nice and though she didn't know really know Bekah, if Elyza and Kellyn got along with her, Skye knew she would too.

Despite being able to walk to Bekah's rental from her own cottage, Skye enjoyed the freedom her car afforded her, the ability to drive where she wanted, to leave if needed. Pulling up to the rental, she parked along the curb, noting the other cars already in the short driveway.

She'd been the last to arrive. It wasn't because she would secretly rather be anywhere else. At least, that's what she told herself as she left her car and grabbed her groceries. Even though she loved her friends, she still wished she'd come up with some excuse to stay home, tucked in under mounds of blankets.

Elyza and Kellyn ambushed her at the door, pulling her into the lightly decorated living room, and slammed the door behind them. Early 2000's pop music came from somewhere near the kitchen where Bekah did her best to dance while stirring what looked like homemade pasta sauce. The scent of tomatoes, garlic, and herbs filled the air, and Skye relaxed into the atmosphere.

Bekah may have been in town for only a few days and her house may not have many personal effects, but something in the air spoke of coziness, protection, and peace. The living room evoked images of long nights curled up on the couch under a soft afghan blanket and freshly baked chocolate chip cookies. It felt like a home. Though she was new to town, Bekah had managed to create an atmosphere of peace and tranquility, something Skye still wasn't convinced she'd accomplished, even after owning her cottage for several years. The tension flowed from her shoulders, and she smiled for the first time all day.

Skye kicked off her shoes by the door and padded to the kitchen barefooted. The smell of some red-sauced pasta dish cooking nearly had her groaning.

"It smells so good," she hummed.

Bekah wiped her hands on a frilly pink gingham apron tied around her waist and hurried to intercept Skye, a hesitant smile on her face.

"You're Skye, right?" The slight-framed woman held out her hand for Skye to shake. Skye took Bekah's smaller hand in her own, noting the stormy blue eyes that observed her with the caution of a prey animal. Skye hated that for her, wished she could take away this woman's demons, though they'd just met. A gentle air surrounded the woman, her presence a calming one despite her background.

"I am, we met at the bridal shop, briefly. What brings you to Shiloh Hills?"

Bekah's eyes turned dark and her slight smile drooped, "Just needed a change of scenery."

The half-truth hung between them but Skye decided not to pry. The woman deserved her privacy. Though a troubled quality stuck in Bekah's eyes for a while, Skye already decided she liked her. Bekah's energy fit right in their little girl gang and Skye smiled.

Within an hour, the ladies were seated on the floor around the coffee table, plastic bowls full of penne noodles, red sauce, and loads of mozzarella cheese with garlic bread on the side. Out of the corner of her eye, Skye watched Elyza push the pasta around on her plate, eating a few bites before pushing the plate away. Before she could muster the words to ask Elyza if she wasn't hungry, her friend had pasted a pleasant smile to her face and engaged Bekah in conversation. Skye frowned, pushing her concerns to the back of her mind for the night. Tonight was about the girls.

Between the four of them, they'd brought enough books to keep them busy throughout the night, though instead of settling down to read, they took turns reading spicy scenes aloud, some of made Skye blush while others made them all cackle with glee. At one point, Kellyn gripped her chest and fell completely to the floor in hysterics. Skye wiped her eyes dry and tried to rein herself in. She was hungry, but every time she tried to take a bite, Bekah or Elyza would say something that made her start laughing again. If she wanted to actually eat, both women needed to stop talking altogether.

After dinner, they worked as a unit to clean up the dinner dishes, their conversation turning to more mundane topics.

"I've got a new competitor going in across town," Kellyn scowled, "Of course, his coffee is nothing but sludge and I heard he buys his pastries from a source down in Grand Rock."

Skye, along with the others, appeared properly appalled and they commiserated with Kellyn's frustration.

"Bekah," Kellyn asked, "how do you know Elyza's brothers?"

Bekah blanched, going a sickly pale color for a few moments before shaking her head. She kept her voice low as a whisper before saying, "The officer who saved me that last time," she gulped, "he recommended them. Said there were no better men or protectors in the entire world. He gave me money for the plane ticket and everything."

She left the other women to read between the lines. Knowing the work Rabble and Elyza's brothers did, Skye pieced enough of Bekah's puzzle together to know, her ex-husband was a piece of filth.

"That is one dedicated officer of the law," Elyza whistled and the others agreed from where they lounged around the living area.

Girls Night came to an end with a rom-com that had Kellyn and Bekah throwing popcorn at the television screen when the main character professed his undying love. Even though the characters overacted and the dialog was a tad ridiculous, Skye still wondered what it would be like to have someone profess such profound love for her. Love that suggested a man would simply expire on the spot if she did not return his affection. A gloominess stole over her and she fought back the morose feeling that threatened to sour her mood as images of Rabble floated through her mind.

The text she'd sent him terrified her and she hated the way it left her open to disappointment more than anything. She'd hedged all of her bets on him once before and fell drastically when he'd failed to follow through with their plans. Despite the carefully constructed wall she'd built to protect herself, she planned to turn right around and let him through without further hesitation.

What was he doing tonight? Was he getting some extra rest or was he spending time in front of a desk, working, always working. What thoughts raced through his head and were they anything like the ones that kept her up at night, nightgown and sheets twisting around her thighs.

Skye shook her head, feeling the blush staining her cheeks.

As the credits rolled on the rom-com they'd watched, Bekah yawned, her slender hand covering her mouth before announcing her departure from the room as she sought her bed.

"It's past my bedtime," she joked and Skye grinned at her, recognizing one of her more common sayings, typically uttered when she'd stayed up too late reading.

Elyza and Kellyn followed her upstairs to the guest room where they would fight over who got to sleep on the bed and who got the futon.

Skye wasn't interested in fighting over either; the sofa in the living room was comfortable enough.

"I'll never walk again if I sleep on the futon." Kellyn's slurred complaint drifted downstairs as she disappeared from Skye's view.

With a chuckle, Skye settled onto the soft cushions, nestling down and burying herself under the throw blanket and assorted pillows. Yeah, the couch would work just fine.

***

It felt like only moments had passed when Skye's eyes popped open. The sky beyond the windows still a deep midnight blue, urging her back toward sleep. Instead, she lay perfectly still, careful to keep her breathing even and her limbs still, though the need to twitch grew persistently as her muscles protested the tension straining at them. She waded through the remaining fog of sleep, back to full consciousness as she struggled to work through what it was that had woken her, what felt off. Because something was definitely wrong.

A soft thud sounded in the kitchen, and Skye's heart stopped in her chest. She flipped back her blanket and tiptoed cautiously toward the kitchen, her toes a mere whisper over the rug and the hardwood floors. "Kellyn? Elyza? Is that you?"

Shadows played across the ground, cutting through the limited light of the waning moon streaming through the window on the backdoor. Scanning the room, Skye could make out the dark shapes of the dining table, the chair legs, and another lanky shadow, one that moved about, too tall and broad to belong to her friends.

Her eyes widened, heart hammering excruciatingly loud in the quiet. The owner of the shadow turned toward her and Skye spun, an earsplitting scream erupting from her chest as she sprinted toward the stairs.

The others are still asleep upstairs. I've got to warn them!

A light in the stairwell came on, and one of her friends shouted, though Skye wasn't sure which one. A hand gripped her upper arm in a bruising vise, yanking her backward and away from her goal. Skye went weightless, flying through the air before colliding painfully with the coffee table, a sickening thud sounding in her ears. Her head swam with vertigo, and she closed her eyes, letting the cresting waves of dizziness pull her under.

Chapter 13

Rabble

Sleep eluded Rabble. Entirely too occupied with an intense game of cards, neither Declan nor Dash opted to turn in either. Rabble didn't understand the objective and was fairly certain their game wasn't even real but rather some strange concoction of their own design.

They continued lounging in rocking chairs along the back porch of the Sunny Morning Trellis bed and breakfast, each moving at a pace that matched their moods. He gazed at the backyard where the fading half-moon cast shadows and the darkness played with the soft glow of the porch lights.

A girls' night at Bekah's house stood between him and Skye. But it also likely kept him from making a complete fool of himself, and he was happy she was having fun with her friends. Bekah, although new to town, seemed to fit right in as a fourth member of their elite group. Elyza called it a book club, though he did question how much they actually discussed books and how much of the time was dedicated to sampling gossip on the rocks.

Regardless, he was thankful they included Bekah and that Bekah was open to hosting, whether or not they actually talked about books. Relocating clients always went over better when the town they moved to welcomed them with open arms. That Bekah had already made friends ticked several more sensitive concerns off of his list. They just needed to convince her to come around to the extra security measures Rabble and the guys devised earlier in the day.

Despite the relative peace of the night, caught himself bouncing his leg with a tension he didn't understand.

"Rab, you want us to deal you in?" Dash asked.

Rabble shook his head but moved his chair closer to them. "Absolutely not. What is this madness?"

Declan put a hand to his chest in mock offense. "Excuse you, sir. This is a game of princes."

Rabble snorted, and Dash dealt him in anyway.

Three rounds later, Rabble was one hundred percent certain the guys invented the game, given the rules seemed to change depending on who was winning. With a groan, Rabble rubbed his temples, and Dash gave him a rare amused smile which quickly fell from his face at Declan's phone ringing and vibrating on the side table. Its piercing siren ringtone penetrated the otherwise tranquil night, making Rabble cringe against the shrill noise. Rabble checked his watch 2:30 AM. That wasn't good.

Declan's brow furrowed as he swiped to answer. "It's Bekah."

That really wasn't good.

Alarm bells rang in Rabble's head, and he shifted forward into a half crouch on the edge of his chair. Dash mirrored Rabble's move, his face a mask of calm.

While Declan pressed the speaker to his ear and listened intently, sounds of hysteria carried through the phone into the open air. The moment Declan pushed to his feet, Rabble and Dash were right behind him, their heavy boots pounding the wooden boards beneath them. Rabble said a short prayer of thanks they were still dressed and awake at the late hour.

Rabble's truck keys were in his hand in an instant, the remote start starting the engine with a deep rumble. They scrambled for the truck, Rabble behind the wheel, Dash riding shotgun, and Declan practically throwing himself into the backseat while keeping Bekah on the phone. The truck tires spun before Declan slammed the backdoor shut.

Rabble desperately wanted to bombard Declan with questions and only rigorous training kept his mouth closed over gritted teeth. Based on Declan's responses and the muffled bits of conversation Rabble heard, he worked out what he could. Every second that passed made Rabble's heart beat faster, his blood nearly a fever-pitch in his veins. His knuckles turned white as he gripped the steering wheel, thoughts of Skye, of Elyza, and the others being in danger flooded his imagination. He could just see Skye's face in his mind's eye, desperate, pleading and he drove faster.

They arrived in the cottage district within a few minutes. Thank God for small towns like Shiloh Hills with minimal traffic stops, practically no one on the road, and no additional police presence to stop him from going twenty over the speed limit in a residential area. The only law enforcement in the entire town parked sideways on the street outside Bekah's rental, firmly declaring the area restricted. The red and blue strobe lights flashed blindingly, leaving stars sparking behind their eyes.

A young officer stood guard at the front door, like a bulldog. He wasn't the sheriff, but some other version of what passed for the law in the small town. Probably some temp sent from the county to assist the sheriff. Rabble would have admired the man's dedication to his position had he not been standing between them and the women inside.

Declan's signature smile slid into place as he tried to explain to the officer their relationship to the four women, that one was a client, one was their sister, and the other two were good friends. Surprisingly, it was Dash who grabbed Declan's shoulder, restraining him, when the officer snorted and mumbled, "Great job keeping them secure."

Rabble would have continued arguing had the officer not finally stepped aside and let them by. When they pushed through the doorway and into the living room, Rabble wasn't prepared for the sight that greeted them.

Granted, he needed more fingers than he had to count the number of times they'd seen worse. But the splintered and broken coffee table wasn't what nearly broke him. It was the women perched on the edge of the living room sofa, each showing various stages of adrenaline dump, and the feeling of fear that drenched the air and soaked into his skin. It was Skye sitting in a kitchen chair, a jagged red and weeping cut descending from her hairline to just above her eyebrow. It was her wincing when the paramedic dabbed at the wound with an alcohol swab and the confusion in her beautiful cornflower eyes that overwhelmed and silenced him.

Declan moved inside with authority, methodically searching the rooms one at a time and giving the all clear while focusing not only on safety but also on anything that looked out of place. Dash, always keeping a level head, took one look at Rabble's clenched jaw and proceeded with securing the information they needed from Bekah. His voice took on a surprisingly soothing tone, and he positioned himself in a way that made him seem as non-threatening as possible. What happened? Did anyone see anything? Was anything taken? On and on the questions went. Elyza seemed the most capable of answering and leveled her gaze at her brother, careful to keep her eyes on him and not across the room where Skye's head wound had yet to stop bleeding.

No one had seen the intruder's face. Skye had been the only one downstairs at the time. Pure unadulterated rage bubbled beneath Rabble's skin, slowly stamping out the fear that had taken up residence around his heart. He willed his eyes to move, away from Skye, to take in the room around them.

Declan returned from his full sweep of the cottage and sat on the arm of the couch, just to the right of Elyza, and directed discreet questions at her while Dash spoke with Bekah and Kellyn.

Beyond the coffee table, not much appeared out of place. The rug at the base of the hardwood stairs was peeled back at the corner, as if someone had tripped. That must have been where the intruder grabbed

Skye and tossed her backward. The image of her slender body flying through the air like a rag doll and colliding with the low-lying table burned behind his eyes and threatened his rationality. He prowled to the conjoined kitchen and dining room, taking in every detail. Four wine glasses sat by the sink, the keys and mail intermingled in a bamboo bowl on the dining table. All untouched.

"He stood over there," Skye's voice cracked, and she cleared her throat.

Rabble followed her pointed finger to the corner of the dining room. "How'd you know it was a man?"

He wasn't trying to be a jerk and hoped she could sense that. He just asked these questions all too frequently in his line of work.

"Tall. Strong. He grabbed me by the stairs and threw me across the room when I—I wanted to warn the others."

She hugged her arms around herself, and Rabble hated the look of self-depreciation that crumpled her face. He read her like an open book. No doubt she blamed herself for her injuries. Hell, she probably blamed herself that the bastard got inside in the first place, even though neither of those was remotely her fault.

"Do you think it was her ex?" Giving up on normal speech altogether, Skye settled into a nearly imperceivable tone that resonated with her mental state.

Rabble took in her clouded eyes, the barely discernable wince, and ignored her question altogether. "Why aren't you going to the hospital?"

"Because I'm fine. They said no concussion. Just a bump on the head."

As she moved her fingers toward the gash, Rabble shook his head slightly and grasped her hand tenderly before she could prod at the fresh wound. He frowned, the butterfly bandages showed how fun getting that "bump on the head" had been. If nothing else, she'd likely have a righteous headache.

He guided Skye back into the living room, urging her to sit between Elyza and Kellyn while Bekah paced in the corner and wrung her hands together, anxiety surrounding her like a shroud. With the same smooth coaxing Dash had employed, Rabble led his client back to the couch, and the four women wore varying shades of the same emotions. Fear was prominent, along with anxiety and shock. Concern for Skye and Bekah eventually took over, along with a bit of curiosity regarding who and why. But the storm of wrath building among the women both surprised and pleased Rabble. That rage would carry them through the fear.

Chapter 14

Skye

Skye wished everyone would stop talking. Her head pounded, and the jagged gash on her forehead stung when the air touched it, which was always. The gruff paramedic who tended her wound suggested stitches, but Skye declined as politely as possible. She had a thing about needles and barely got her ears pierced for her twenty-first birthday. She would rather handle a hideous scar than brave a needle piercing her skin. She'd keep her sewing to clothes, thank you very much.

Rabble, Declan, and Dash stood by, staring at Skye and her friends as they wilted into the couch cushions. Dash was the only who didn't look like he wanted to read them the riot act. That Rabble and Declan looked so disgruntled irritated her to no end. Head wound or not, she would screech at them like an angry hen if either said a cross word about any of her friends. They'd been through enough.

Bekah, seated at the end of the couch, vibrated with nervous energy. Her knee bounced a mile a minute, and the cushions shook despite the foam padding interior. Skye was willing to bet Bekah had chewed down every nail on her right hand in her nervousness. Elyza looked more ticked off than anything else, like she wanted to single-handedly track down the intruder and give him what for. With older brothers like hers, Elyza probably could have won a fight with the intruder. Not like Skye. The air hit her cut again, and she winced. If Elyza had been the one on the couch, would the lovely second-hand coffee table still be in one piece?

Kellyn, for her part, sat with her hands clasped in her lap and eyes downcast, oddly quiet. There was a story there, but it was Kellyn's to tell when she was ready. Instead of pushing for answers, Skye laid her hand reassuringly over Kellyn's cold fingers and squeezed. Kellyn returned her light grasp in acknowledgment.

Skye thought back, ignoring Rabble and Declan's glaring, and focused instead on what a memorable first girls' night she'd had. When she had come to, the intruder was gone, and every light in the house was on, including the exterior lights at the front and rear of the cottage.

Bekah and Kellyn had been fretting over Skye while Elyza had run to the backdoor where the sliding glass door stood wide open, the sheer white curtains billowing softly in the breeze. Elyza, still clad in her silk tank and shorts pajama set, had stormed out the back door onto the patio to search the shadows for any signs of the intruder. She must not have seen anything because she returned a minute later, slamming the sliding glass door shut and flipping the lock with excessive force. Seconds later, she was on the phone with emergency services, rattling off their location and situation in clipped and concise sentences. Admittedly, Skye appreciated Elyza's calm efficiency.

By the time Bekah's trembling fingers pulled up Declan's number, Skye had sat up and scanned her friends frantically until she was certain they were all whole. She didn't even realize she was bleeding until Elyza gagged. Apparently, she didn't "do" blood, and Skye had the absurd reaction to laugh, instantly regretting it. After that, everything seemed to blur together until she found herself seated beside her friends and wishing Rabble would stop glaring at her.

"Was it him? Was it Edward?" Bekah whispered, her voice wavering.

Skye fisted her hands beneath her thighs, letting her fingernails dig into her palms to distract her. She bit her lower lip, keeping it tucked tightly between her front teeth in an effort to keep the growing words of frustration from finding escape.

Declan shook his head, agitation wafting from him like a thick cologne. "Everything we have says he's still in California."

"We feared this was a possibility, but if he were on the move, we would have heard from one of our sources tracking him." Rabble's tone was hard and unforgiving. Though he hadn't necessarily called any of them out, his voice held a note that grated on Skye's nerves as he tapped his thumb against his front jeans pocket again and again.

"We need a different plan," Dash said matter-of-factly, his tone leaving little room for argument.

Rabble's frown deepened as he listened to his friend. Skye's head pounded, elevating her ire with each heartbeat that echoed through her skull.

They look at us like it's our fault someone broke in here. She ground her teeth together, clamping her jaw shut until it ached.

"Stop glaring," she ground out.

Rabble looked startled. "Excuse me?"

"You heard me, Rabble. Quit looking at us like we did something wrong." Crossing her arms over her chest, Skye leaned back while the others watched their interaction like a tennis match.

"Maybe you did. Are you sure the doors were locked? How much did you drink tonight?" He winced with immediate regret. Open mouth; insert foot.

At least he knows he messed up. "First of all," she said, her seething blatant, "how *dare* you."

"That didn't come out the way I meant." Rabble held his hands up like he was trying to soothe a wild beast.

Maybe she was one. She'd be roaring if the pulsing in her skull would subside just a little bit. "You've got about two seconds to explain what you *did* mean."

He sputtered, searching for words to help him out of the hole he dug. Skye marveled at the light-pink tinge that crept up his neck and stained his cheeks above his neatly trimmed beard. Was Rabble, blushing?

"Can we talk somewhere else?" Rabble stood and held out his hand for her.

She glanced at their friends. Each seemed overly interested in anything in the room that wasn't her or Rabble—everyone except for Elyza, who watched them intently, a contemplative, borderline-pleased expression on her face.

Accepting Rabble's offered hand, Skye let him lead her into the kitchen. The still-open containers of cookies and other sweet snacks sat on the counter, and she snagged a couple. She'd had a rough night, she justified, as she reached for another cookie.

In the kitchen light, Rabble carefully tipped her chin back with a finger, letting the bulb shine fully on her cut. His eyes lost some of their hard glint and took on a softer, more tender look.

"I've faced down many, many things that." He paused a moment and breathed in deeply. "I don't know if I've ever been as scared as I was when Dec got that call from Bekah. She's our client, and I care about her and the others, but my first thought was 'Skye is at Bekah's.'"

"Well..." She tried and failed to swallow past the lump that formed in her throat. "I forgive you for being a butt."

He arched an eyebrow, a slight uptilt pulled at his lips. "A butt?"

She shrugged, the motion sending another bolt of pain through her head. "I'm a kindergarten teacher."

"A beautiful and brave one at that." The deceptively light tone dropped from his voice, and a seriousness came over him, making her warm and fuzzy all over. "I'm glad you're okay, Skye."

She recalled another time, on different night, when their roles had been reversed and she'd taken care of him. The air hung heavily between them, pushing them toward a turning point, a precipice of change. Skye couldn't help but wonder what would happen if they both just jumped, without regard for a safety net, and let themselves fall.

She swayed into him. Rabble's fingers no longer held her chin. Instead, his hand slipped down to cup her waist, steadying her and lending her his warmth. She tipped her head, an invitation and question. Rabble dipped his mouth toward her in answer as he closed the space between them. The brush of his lips against hers sent a jolt of electricity zinging through her.

"— a plan. Oh shit, man. Sorry." Declan stepped into the kitchen and quickly turned right around, his hand covering his eyes like a child who caught his parents kissing.

Skye blushed even as Rabble growled at his friend.

"Okay, we're coming."

Declan retreated to the living room as quickly as his feet would carry him, and Skye couldn't help the snort of laughter that escaped her.

Skye stepped back, out of his embrace, immediately missing the warmth he provided. She took his hand in hers, giving it a reassuring squeeze before letting go, smiling. "I'm glad I'm okay too."

They rejoined their friends in the living room, the sense of doom having mostly dissipated. Skye grinned as Declan winked at her, which earned him a slightly-less-than-playful punch in the arm from Rabble.

"Alright, Rab. We've got a new plan." Dash slipped his cell phone into his back pants pocket. Skye studied his hard as granite face, the rage simmering in his eyes made her shudder. She wondered who he was more angry at, the intruder for breaking in and endangering people he cared for, or himself for the intruder getting passed his security measures.

Skye slid between her friends still sitting on the couch, though they'd relaxed into the cushions and slouched with exhaustion. Letting her head fall back, she closed her eyes, the deep rumbling of Rabble and his brothers' voices soothing in her ears. She listened half-heartedly as they planned a protection detail that now extended beyond Bekah to include Elyza, Kellyn, and herself, at least until they could determine if the break-in had been random or somehow connected to Bekah's possessive ex-husband.

When Dash announced the new living arrangements, Skye expected push-back from Elyza at minimum, but no one objected. Elyza and Kellyn would take two bedrooms at the bed and breakfast with Dash staying in his room. Declan and Bekah would leave town for a day or two, likely to Grand Rock, to put a little distance between her and anyone who might have caught wind of her past. That left...

Dash pointed at Rabble. "You and Skye—"

"I've got it," Rabble said, his gaze turning distant and making Skye wonder what he was thinking about.

She desperately wanted to go home and sleep in her own bed, but Dash made it sound like she would be staying with Rabble somewhere else—at least until the men of Rabble & Bros could come back during the day and do a complete sweep of Bekah's house and the property and review the sensors.

"Like we said, it was probably a random break-in." Declan's cookie-cutter tone told Skye everything she needed to know about how much he believed that. "We just want to be cautious."

He didn't repeat why. Even if Skye didn't know all the details about Bekah's ex-husband, the fact that the men now worried about Skye and her friends spoke volumes. She shuddered to think what lengths he might go to, who he might hurt, to get at Bekah.

By the time they secured the house, packed a go bag for Bekah, and cleaned up the remnants of their girls' night gone bad, the sun's first rays peeked over the horizon. Skye watched from the living room window as Dash, Elyza, and Kellyn left, stifling a laugh as he tried to fit his large frame behind the wheel of Kellyn's yellow Volkswagen Beetle. Declan and Bekah had left while darkness still lingered outside, hoping the night would give them additional cover. Skye offered them her car, and Bekah had hugged her tightly before letting Declan lead her outside, his hand resting in the small of her back. She hadn't been able to control the tremors running through her body, so Skye hugged her even tighter, the way she did with her students when they needed some extra reassurance.

Skye chuckled as the Beetle drove away, leaving only her and Rabble in the cottage. It took her a moment to realize there wasn't necessarily anything to be laughing about. Maybe the lack of sleep made her loopy, or maybe the excess adrenaline was finally draining from her system.

Rabble helped her to the truck and securing her in before returning to the cottage and locking the door. When he came back, he made sure she was buckled in and safe, then turned the key in the ignition and circling the block.

"What's so funny?" Rabble asked. He checked the side mirrors for the third time and pulled away from the residential neighborhood just waking up.

Skye rolled her neck toward him, and her head throbbed dully. "Just that for my first girls' night out, I hope we never top that."

Rabble smirked. "Yeah, let's avoid any future fun, okay?"

A gray vest rested on the center console and Skye settled her hand atop it, feeling the threads of it with her fingertips before pulling it to her, subtly sliding it under her nose to breath in Rabble's scent. It smelled of the sun and summer nights. A hint of something warm and seductive sang through her and she inhaled again, deeper. Rabble's quick glance over at her had Skye slowly setting the vest in her lap, using it as a cover. Wisely, Rabble chose not to comment and Skye relaxed a bit more into the seat at her back.

"Where are we going?" Skye asked, resisting the urge to lean her head against the window.

He was so still Skye wondered if he wouldn't answer.

"I bought...something..." Rabble's reluctant words immediately piqued her interest. "You'll see soon. Just rest."

She thought about challenging him, pushing him to talk about the things that pained him, that made him hesitate to let her know him. Even after eight years, he still feared people taking away anything he held dear.

The pull of sleep tugged at her insistently though. As her eyes fluttered closed, Skye took his advice to heart and rested.

Chapter 15

Rabble

He hadn't planned to show anyone what he'd purchased, certainly not Skye. Not yet anyway. Still, when Declan and Dash suggested that he take Skye somewhere safe, he'd already known exactly where they'd go. Hardly anyone knew he owned the place, and even fewer knew about his connection to the land. He turned down the short gravel road that led to a dead-end where two houses sat beside each other, an invisible diving line as tangible as the fence between the two pieces of property.

When the land originally went up for sale, Rabble wanted nothing to do with it. Maybe someone else restoring it would erase the stains of the past that infected the acreage. But the realtor, who had been friends with his mother before that drunk driver killed her, tracked Rabble down to let him know about the sale. He'd told her no during that initial phone call. He never wanted to return to where his father had spent so many years treating him and his mother like shit, but his desire to forget the offer warred with the underlying sense that he'd miss it. After all, that land was his mother's final resting place. At least, that's how he justified his rash purchase, not wanting to dive deeper into the baggage attached to those few measly acres. The title company managed to finalize the sale just a few days before Rabble and the twins left to spend the Independence Day holiday in Shiloh Hills.

Rabble pulled into the familiar gravel and dirt driveway. The strong oak tree still stood guard by the fence, which the Wellingtons replaced with tall vinyl panels, separating the two parcels of land with a finality that echoed in his chest. The mobile home he'd grown up in had long since been hauled away, and he wondered absently if they'd taken it away in one piece or in sections. The man who purchased the land after Rabble's father died brought in a single-room hunting cabin that he left behind. The simple cabin was small but serviceable, and Rabble appreciated its existence, especially now.

His truck crunched over riverbed gravel out front, the headlights shining against the hunter-green door and illuminating the short porch. Trees and brush grew tall around the building, disguising the piles of rusting metal and old tires that still lingered from his childhood. He took a few moments in the early dawn to let the memories wash over him, crashing into him like waves on the shore. The good ebbed and flowed into the bad, reminding him that no matter how much he hated the place because of his worthless father, he had good times here too, thanks to his mother and Skye.

He gently shook Skye's shoulder, coaxing her awake from where she'd fallen asleep against the window. She stirred, groaning as she stretched and brushed sleep from her eyes. Rabble jumped out and opened her door. She roused enough to take his hand as she got down. He held her steady on her feet and kept his arm secured around her as they ascended the two cinderblocks that stood in for stairs. Reaching into his pocket, he took out the key he received at the title office and slipped the intricately cut metal into the doorknob, turning the lock until it clicked.

Rabble followed Skye inside, feeling along the wall until he found and flipped on the light switch. A cozy warm light filled the space, brightening the studio-apartment room with a twin-sized bed pushed against one wall, a simple kitchen along the other, and a closed-off bathroom in the far corner. As far as hunting cabins went, this minimalistic one covered basic needs. Still, the homey feeling surprised Rabble.

"Not many know about this place," he said, noting the quizzical look in Skye's pretty blue eyes. "You should be safe here."

"I never doubted that for a moment, but—"

He waited; certain she had questions. Not a single part of him wanted to dive into the emotional background that would likely accompany any question she dredged up. He barely held back a sigh of relief when the inquisitive look left her eyes and she let the subject drop.

He glanced around the space again before locking the door and tossing his keys and wallet onto the countertop in the kitchenette area. Next, he pulled the curtains shut over each of the three windows, blocking the view inside the cabin. He smirked at the stereotypical lodge patterns of black bears, wild ducks, and deer that adorned the home-sewn curtains. He'd never been more grateful for the closing paperwork clause that stated the cabin came "fully furnished." He'd expected the furniture but not the full set of dishes and silverware, the blankets, or the toilet paper stored in the bathroom. He whistled long and low and shook his head with gratitude.

While Skye settled into one of the questionable folding kitchen chairs, he tracked down a set of linens for the twin mattress and threw several heavier blankets on the floor next to the bedframe. He also grabbed one of the two pillows from the bed and tossed it down with the blankets.

"Let's get some sleep, Skye." He ignored the early morning sun peeking through the sliver of glass that the curtains didn't cover and shrugged off his shirt.

Her blue eyes glimmered with something akin to appreciation, bordering on slight embarrassment and Rabble smirked to himself. Exhaustion pulled at her heavy eyelids but, despite her tiredness, if he wasn't mistaken, she was totally checking him out.

She didn't argue. Dragging her feet over to the bed, she flopped down, shoes still on and everything, the night's adrenaline having faded away. Her gaze stayed trained on him though, her cheek pressed against the sheets as her eyes followed his every move. Rabble chuckled silently and maybe he flexed a bit more than necessary, enjoying the way her cheeks pinkened. He helped her slip out of her shoes and socks, and after he threw the tan and green printed comforter over her, she shimmied off her denim shorts. Her eyes finally drooped and Rabble settled onto his blankets, an arm tucked under his head, and closed his eyes with a deep sigh.

For the first time since Declan received that phone call from Bekah, Rabble felt like his lungs could expand and he could actually breathe. His body demanded sleep, but his brain kept replaying watching Declan answered the phone, when the medic pulled that bloodied gauze away from Skye's forehead, when she looked at Rabble with pain in her eyes. He may be able to breathe now, but his heart still hammered. Taking another deep breath, he willed his body to relax.

She's safe. He chanted that to himself until sleep finally claimed him. *She's safe.*

***

He couldn't have been asleep long when Rabble jolted awake, disoriented and frantic. Nothing around him looked familiar, and a sense of dread welled up, squeezing in around his heart. He jack-knifed into a sitting position, eyes searching every corner until he was confident there was no immediate threat. Skye no longer lay beneath the covers on the bed, but a light shone from the bathroom. God help him if his eyes didn't stay glued to the door until she emerged, fresh from the shower.

Despite her hair hanging in wet clumps around her face, the dark half-moons under her eyes, and the jagged gash on her forehead, Rabble couldn't recall a time he'd ever seen Skye look more beautiful. She was adorably disheveled in his humble opinion.

"What time is it?" he asked, voice rough from sleep, a heavy tiredness in his bones.

"Around dinner time. You hungry?"

He hadn't noticed the delicious scent that hung in the air and made his stomach growl ferociously.

Pizza.

He frowned at the delivery box on the counter. *How had that gotten here?*

"Dash called while you were still zonked out," Skye said as she slid a slice of pepperoni pizza onto a paper plate. "He tracked your phone and brought us this, along with some clothes."

For the first time, Rabble took in the black athletic leggings and lilac tunic shirt she'd put on after her shower. Part of him wanted to be angry with his best friend for tracking them, especially considering he hadn't told Dash or Declan about the property yet. The other part though, the part that grumbled and growled at the smells wafting around him, thanked his brother for taking initiative and caring for them.

Rabble groaned as he got to his feet and threw his blankets on top of the bed. A long, life-altering stretch later, he felt mostly human. Despite being in his twenties, he was too damn old for this.

After emerging from the bathroom, Rabble smiled at the picture before him. Skye sat at the fold-out kitchen table in one of the two dubious folding chairs. Two plates of greasy pepperoni pizza and a couple bottles of water sat atop the flimsy table, and she held out one hand, indicating he should take the opposite seat. Her other hand gripped a slice of pizza like it might escape her. She paused, lifted the pizza halfway to her mouth, and waited for him to sit down.

As she tore off the end of her pizza slice with a moan, Rabble sat up straighter, the sound like music to his ears.

She chewed and swallowed before asking, "So what's the plan? I mean, we can't stay hidden forever. We all have jobs, and the Independence Day parade will be here in just a few days."

If he were being honest, Rabble would have locked all four of them up in a safe house and thrown away the key, but he suspected the women in his life would have something to say about that. And none of it would be complimentary. Rabble gestured for Skye to go ahead and eat while he spoke.

"For now, one of us will be with you until we can ensure this isn't connected to Bekah's ex-husband, and we aren't going to rule out anyone or anything else."

Skye lifted an eyebrow. "That's going to get old really fast, isn't it?"

Rabble shrugged. "Most likely, yes. Fortunately, it's summer, and three of you are frequently at The Wild Bride, which helps with security detail."

"Does this," she waved her pizza crust around in an all-encompassing manner, "normally happen with your work?"

After swallowing a large bite, Rabble tilted his head thoughtfully. "Mmm, I would say no. I mean, shit happens, right? But we don't have this kind of thing go sideways too often, especially with a simple relocation."

"I was pretty out of it last night, this morning, whatever." Skye grabbed another slice of pizza and bit into it. "But, did I recognize the house next door?"

"Yeah, I, uh, bought the old place. I don't want any reminders of Dad, but my mom's here." Maybe it was silly; he certainly felt ridiculous when he thought about his motivation. He didn't think Skye would laugh or tell him he was delusional, but if she did, he wouldn't let it hit him unprepared.

"Roll your shoulders, Rabble. I understand, and I think that's beautiful." Skye's voice was gentle as she reached across the table, her soft hands grasping his large, rough one.

Rabble did as she instructed, not realizing he'd tucked his shoulders in to ward off any verbal attacks, a learned behavior he desperately wanted to unlearn.

He spoke before he thought, sharing an idea that had been slowly taking shape in his mind since he'd purchased the land. "I want to do something in her memory here. I'm not sure what just yet. Whatever it is, I know your dad will hate it."

He wasn't sure what reaction to expect from her, but Skye beamed like a cat that ate a canary. "That will make it all the better."

Seated at the tiny card table, paper plates marred by pizza grease between them, Rabble felt like they were seeing each other clearly for the first time in forever. The hope surging through him was dangerous in the best and worst way.

Chapter 16

Skye

Skye couldn't remember a time she felt more content. Despite the circumstances, she was completely comfortable and relaxed hiding in the cabin with Rabble. Maybe the world was imploding around them. Maybe her head still hurt from where she'd broken the coffee table with her skull, but this time and this place with him, felt perfect. Almost like they'd drawn back the curtain of their past, allowing the natural light of simply being together come through.

Without much else to do, Rabble shared stories of his time in the military, though not many. He deftly avoided topics and maneuvered around subjects that brought up dark memories. Her heart ached for him. How could she not hurt for this man? He also shared funny tales about the twins, how he met them and Elyza, how he considered them his family, and what those relationships meant to him as he grew into this handsome, brave, albeit scarred, man.

When she asked about his security work, he delved into the topic with gusto, and Skye lit up as she listened to him speak about something he was passionate about. Unlike her parents and Dylan, Rabble didn't speak to her like she was a child incapable of comprehending the way the world worked and unworthy of honesty. Even though she couldn't care less about politics or the circles her parents ran with, she caught the looks of disgust among the politicians and Gayle when they threw around names that meant nothing to her.

Rabble returned the favor, asking what she enjoyed most about college, which were her favorite classes, and how she discovered she wanted to be a teacher. When he asked about her students, her heart melted; she loved talking about her kids. She also shared how she became friends with Elyza and Kellyn and how they fit into Skye's life. Everything that had happened to her or around her while they'd been apart came spilling out of her. The cracks in her heart filled with new details; like missing puzzle pieces, they fell into place. It was like they were talking under the fence again, sharing parts of themselves they often kept safely tucked away.

They talked deep into the night until Skye yawned, struggling to stay awake. When she headed to the bathroom to change and brush her teeth, she stared at herself in the mirror above the sink. Her plain blue eyes were tired and her honey-blonde hair stood on end with frizz. Smoothing the wrinkles at the corners of her eyes and the ones across her forehead, she sighed. She felt rejuvenated after lounging with Rabble, but fatigue pressed down on her, making her limbs heavy.

Skye left the door open after she finished, and Rabble took his turn while she busied herself arranging the bed linens and pillows.

"Rabble, I was thinking…" She could feel the hot blush building, creeping from her neck to her cheeks, and she hated it. Her gaze lifted to find him leaning against the doorframe, arms crossed and biceps bulging. His eyes sparked with awareness but he remained blessedly silent while she worked up the courage to voice her thoughts.

She averted her eyes, swallowing thickly as she searched for anything to focus on besides the way his cotton sleep pants hung on his hips, the thin trail of hair down leading from his bellybutton and disappearing beneath the waistband of his pants. Or how his stomach muscles clenched when she looked upon him. Skye's gaze landed on the mattress, and the air suddenly felt warmer.

"The bed is plenty big enough for both of us." She said, "You don't need to sleep on the floor." Ducking her head, she busied herself with fluffing the pillows for the third time.

His voice rumbled, sending shivers cascading down her spine and covering her arms in goosebumps. "Skye, I'm perfectly fine on the floor."

"I know," she mumbled. "I know that, but I…I don't want you to sleep on the floor."

"Skye…" Rabble rubbed his hand over his face, a war waging behind his eyes until his jaw set, and he nodded.

She blew out a breath with a sharp bob of her head, threw back the covers on the bed she'd just made, and climbed under the blankets without glancing at him, giving him her back. Several moments passed before the mattress dipped beneath his weight as he lay down beside her. The soft fabric of his cotton pants rubbed against her legs, which her own worn sleep shirt left bare. He rolled over and gently held her, careful to maintain enough space between them to keep her comfortable and allow her more than enough room to pull away. She sensed the hesitancy in his body as he strained to help her relax and avoid crossing any boundaries. She smiled softly; he really was a considerate man. In that moment, Skye knew, beyond a shadow of a doubt, he was still the same person she'd known before everything had gone to hell in a handbasket.

"Matthew," she said, her voice little more than a whisper.

Those same muscles that labored to keep from touching her tensed at his given name, the name she had used only a handful of times in her entire life.

Relaxing against him, she waited for him to do the same and felt his resistance crumbling and he finally settled against her back. The warmth of his large body curving around hers quickly lulled her closer to sleep. As she drifted off, she thought she felt him sigh into her hair, kissing her sweetly, tenderly.

When the sky was at its darkest, Skye awoke with a start, her heart thudding loudly. Her eyes darted around the dark cabin, searching for what had woken her from the deep sleep she'd been in. The hoarse cry sounded again, part anguish, part rage, all escaping the lips of the man lying beside her. She tried to turn over, but Rabble had wrapped his arms tightly around her. She struggled to maneuver over until she faced him.

His eyes, scrunched tight beneath the lids, flitted from side to side. A dream. A nightmare. He was trapped in a nightmare.

"Matthew." She ran her fingers through his hair and down his jaw, feeling the scruff of his beard against her palm. She traced a path across his brow, but try as she might, Skye couldn't break through the haze of sleep that held him in its grasp. So, she did the only thing she could think of that might calm him. She began to hum.

When his eyes opened into slits, they were haunted in more ways than one. She didn't ask about his dream; he wouldn't have told her even if she did. He had enough horror in his past that any number of things could have been plaguing him.

"You're humming my mother's song." His voice broke with emotion and disbelief. "You remember her song?"

"Of course I remember." Skye's lips tipped up at the corners.

Rabble's mom had been a sweet woman with a quiet voice that invoked feelings of sunny days and warm blankets. She'd drawn a short-stick sometime early in life and ended up with a hateful, abusive husband and a beautiful, burdened little boy. More than anything else, Skye's heart had broken for Rabble when that car crash took everything from him, but she'd heard Mrs. Raden sing her song to Rabble more than a few times over the years they'd been neighbors.

Skye tipped her head up, coaxing his chin down until she found his lips with her own. She intended a gentle, reassuring press of her lips to his, a kiss full of her love and compassion through that brief contact.

Before she could pull back, Matthew rolled over, pinning her with his hips. He took her mouth in a passionate, claiming kiss, one that spoke of hunger and longing as well as regret and pain. She relinquished complete control to him and his take-charge personality. She tangled her fingers in his hair, relishing in the silky softness of the strands. He kissed down her neck, and the scrape of his stubble on her sensitive skin made her shiver.

They matched each other, want for want, need for need.

Finally, finally, her heart chanted as they let themselves explore the fire that had burned between them for years without acceptance. He held her tightly through the night, his rough, reverent hands gentle on her skin. She felt safe. Cherished. Beautiful. Loved.

The morning sun rose, its warm light streaming through the curtains in thin shafts, dappled by the thick foliage of the trees surrounding the cabin. Rabble curled around Skye, his thumb rubbing soft circles on her hip as she drifted into an exhausted and sated, dreamless sleep, contented for the first time in years.

Chapter 17

Rabble

Rabble had no words for what Skye gifted him during the night, at least no words in his vocabulary. The time they spent just talking had been cathartic, cleansing old wounds that festered for far too long. They weren't quite healed, but it was a chance to start again. When Skye began yawning, Rabble knew they both need rest.

Sleeping beside her had never been the plan. He'd slept on the ground often enough; at least he had blankets this time. When she invited him under the covers, he nearly swallowed his tongue, and he barely contained the groan that rose in his throat at the warmth of her body next to his.

Sleep came more swiftly than he anticipated, but the peace he expected to follow their conversation didn't last. In his dreams, moments from his past blended seamlessly with fears for the future. The middle of a sandy, scorched battlefield where his friends lay in pieces. A car accident where he lay alongside his mother, her neck broken. Another crude cross he had to carve, her ashes carelessly discarded like her life had been. And Skye's attacker chasing her from scene to scene, a sinister shadow with no face or discernable features but who left her broken, bloodied, and lost to Rabble.

But then a low, calming sound drifted to him through the horrible dreamscape. It took a moment longer than it should have for him to recognize the haunting melody. The soothing notes drifted into his dreams, wrapping themselves around his soul. He hummed the same song when he had a particularly rough day with his father and escaped to the fence, hoping Skye would already be there, waiting. She never asked about the song, not that he remembered, but that melancholy tune freed him from his nightmare. That, and the way she'd whispered his name, Matthew.

The moment his given name passed her lips, he was gone. No one called him Matthew. He introduced himself as Rabble to everyone he met, and he was okay with that. He enjoyed it, especially since she'd been the one to give him that name all those years ago.

The sun, high in the sky, headed toward the western horizon when Rabble woke, feeling well and truly rested for the first time in years. Skye still slept peacefully in his arms, and he took a few minutes just to watch her breathing, the blankets rising and falling with her steady breaths. He wanted nothing more than to keep reality away for a little longer, to keep her here, safe and wrapped in his arms, peaceful by his side.

Tucking the sheets around her, he slipped from the bed and found his phone on the folding-card table. He unlocked the screen, which lit up with several missed texts from Declan and Dash checking in. Rabble fired off a quick response, letting them know he and Skye were fine. They planned to rendezvous for a late dinner at the bed and breakfast, giving him a few more hours with Skye.

His Skye.

After taking care of his morning routine, Rabble slid back under the covers and brushed Skye's bed-tangled hair away from her face. She shifted sleepily and wrinkled her nose before opening her eyes into slits.

"What time is it?" she groaned, stretching from head to toe, sheets slipping around her.

"Time to get up," he murmured, despite wanting to do the exact opposite. If only he could stay in this worn-out, twin-sized bed with her all day, tangled up in the sheets that smelled of them.

Thirty minutes later, Rabble hadn't stopped smiling since Skye finally dragged herself from the bed. She was a grump in the morning, which he found adorable. Equally, she found him annoying; she'd told him so, at least until he fed her a wild berry pop-tart and poured her a thermos of coffee. Rabble wished he had more to offer her, but the cabinets were bare, and he hadn't exactly planned on visiting when they made their early morning journey to the cabin.

As it was, he made a mental note to thank Dash for the supplies he dropped off, along with that pizza. His brother not only had the foresight to include a few basic groceries but he also had packed a few pairs of clothing for each of them. Admittedly, he likely needed to thank Elyza for the array of supplies.

Rabble locked the door behind them as they left, and set off into the woods behind the hunting cabin. He kept her fingers laced with his own as they dodged branches, vines, and thorns. A thick layer of leaf litter covered the ground, and Rabble couldn't help but chuckle as he lifted Skye over a fallen log and her feet disappeared in a deep pile of leaves on the other side.

"Where are we going?" she asked when they stopped for a break. She frowned, realizing her coffee thermos was empty.

Rabble passed her a bottle of water, warmth creeping up his neck. "As a child, there were two places I loved to go, under the fence and down here to the river. It runs across the back of the property and is beautiful year-round. When you weren't home and after, well, later, I came here."

He focused his eyes on hers and saw the moment she realized what he wasn't saying out loud, *why* he came down to the river when they could no longer meet under the fence; when everything in his life took a drastic turn downhill; when she had been stolen away, sequestered, like a pet in a cage.

They walked for another five minutes, dodging fallen trees covered in vines and wild rose thorns. Rabble was richly rewarded when they broke through the tree line and Skye gasped in delight at the sight before them. They stepped out onto an outcropping that hung over the river. Around them, the trees presented full, thick foliage in an incredible array of greens and browns. The river snaked by below, unhurriedly winding its way across the Earth without care, and the red sandstone and tan limestone of the overhang blended to create a seamless piece of natural art.

"When I came here, I walked out there." Rabble pointed to the far edge of the cliff, and Skye's eyes widened with shock, maybe a bit of fear and despair. "Back then, I didn't care if I came home."

Her brows slammed down, and he held up his hand, trying to stave off any of the dismayed questions she might lodge at him. The concern and sorrow in her eyes said more than enough of her thoughts about his admission; a secret he kept close to his chest his entire life, that he had spent many hours overlooking that river, wondering

"I was young. My mother was gone. You were gone, and my dad was... Well, he was what he was. There were days when Mr. Jack at the pharmacy was the only person who cared where I was. Later, Mrs. Basket joined the list. Eventually, I had a few people who cared that I came home, who expected something of me."

She was silent for a while, staring out at the cliff's edge. When she answered, she worded her response carefully. "I'm glad you don't go out there now."

"Me too."

They stood together, away from the cliff, but still watching the lazy river wind past them. Neither spoke, lost in their own thoughts and memories, their fingers intertwined as the summer wind blew around them.

Just before they turned to head back to the cabin, Skye tugged Rabble closer, brushing a kiss against his jaw, and whispered, "Thank you."

He swallowed hard and squeezed her hand lightly in his, careful not to put too much pressure on her dainty fingers. A current of emotion flowed through him, wreaking havoc in his chest and building pressure behind his eyes. There were a lot of words he wouldn't say, couldn't say to her, not here, not about what showing her this place meant. He trusted her perception though. She tended to see more than he wanted her to, always had. He loved her for that. It was *one* of the countless reasons why he loved her.

Back at the cabin, Skye dragged Rabble into the economically sized shower, claiming the water conservation was good for the environment. He seriously doubted they managed to save any water by the time they finally finished and were on their way to The Sunny Morning Trellis. According to the many missed text messages from Declan, everyone else was already waiting at the bed and breakfast and Rabble needed to "hurry his ass up."

When Rabble started his truck, Declan sent another message. "Do I have to send the local PD around for a well-check?"

Rabble's thumbs typed quickly, "Keep your panties on. We're on our way."

Three dots later, Declan shot back the middle-finger emoji. As Rabble barked with laughter and Skye smirked, he shifted the truck into reverse.

They arrived at the bed and breakfast less than fifteen minutes later. Entering through the dining room, they found their friends seated around the large wooden table. Fortunately, none of them looked any worse for wear, which Rabble was eternally grateful for. Judging by the way Skye scrutinized each of them after dispersing hugs to everyone, she had similar thoughts. Their late dinner was a fun affair, though notes of strain underlaid their attempts at upbeat conversation. Rabble and Declan entertained them with humorous anecdotes about their time in the military and since they'd opened the security firm. Dash rarely added anything to those tales, though he often smirked silently with mirth. While the others laughed and joked along, Bekah remained withdrawn and quiet. Her smiles were forced, and when Rabble wondered if he should say something to her, Skye reached over and grasped her friend's hand reassuringly. He watched them, a warm sensation spreading through his chest.

The rest of the evening passed in companionable conversation, an unspoken agreement to not mention anything negative and just enjoy each other's friendship.

Elyza, Kellyn, and Dash were the first to rise from their chairs, heading for their rooms upstairs. They would spend one more night at the bed and breakfast while Dash tested out the new security systems he'd installed at each of their homes, along with Bekah's and Skye's cottages. As long as he was satisfied with the results of his testing, they could return home the following day.

Elyza glanced back on her way up the stairs, pinning each woman with a stare. "Tomorrow ladies, 10:00 a.m. at the shop. Don't be late!" She wiggled her fingers in farewell.

Kellyn groaned quietly as she followed behind.

Elyza must have heard that because she shouted over her shoulder, "I have champagne!"

The groan turned into an appreciative hum, and even Bekah laughed as the dinner party broke up and she left with Declan. They would spend one more night outside of Shiloh Hills, allowing Dash to run his equipment tests without interference.

With their friends gone, Rabble mulled over taking Skye back to her cottage for the night. She would likely appreciate sleeping in her own bed, but he struggled to resist the allure of returning to the cabin and spending another night with her.

She made his decision for him as she, not so subtly, mentioned the merits of the cabin settled in the woods. "After all, it is far away from civilization. And Dash's new equipment testing..."

"Okay, I get it," he chuckled, walking her to his truck.

After parking outside the little cabin, Rabble left Skye sitting inside the truck and locked the doors. Looking disgruntled, she rolled her eyes at him when he told her to stay put, but he wasn't taking any chances with her safety.

As far as he was concerned, every shadow was a threat. He unholstered his sidearm and cleared the small space, checking behind furniture, under the bed, and in the bathroom. Maybe he was paranoid. He wouldn't be surprised if he was, but he'd rather be safe than sorry. He flipped on the light, then strode back to the truck and unlocked the doors, holding the passenger door open for her. She rolled her eyes again and slipped beneath his arm, pulling him behind her and into the cabin. Rabble smiled and followed her willingly, then locked the door behind them.

Chapter 18

Skye

No matter how many hours Skye put in at The Wild Bride as a part-timer, the beauty and elegance of the wedding gowns never ceased to amaze her. The way the rhinestones caught and refracted light appealed to the little girl in her who enjoyed playing dress-up, and the exquisite fabrics slipped sensually against her fingertips. She was a pauper lost in a princess's sparkling closet. Days when new shipments came in were her favorite. Hauling the brilliant dresses off the truck was a heavy but worthwhile job. She unzipped magenta-colored garment bags, admiring each dress's unique beauty, before moving them to the clear ones Elyza used to display the dresses on racks throughout the shop.

With Elyza's guidance, Skye laid out options for them to consider wearing for the parade. She admired the exquisite creations, and for the first time since high school, she could picture the face of the groom from her fantasies. It was the same face she'd imagined before, older now with life's experiences, but still the same at the deepest levels.

Bekah and Kellyn showed up together about fifteen minutes later, both expressing excitement and nerves at trying on wedding gowns. Nonetheless, their dedication to go through with the float lay solely in their trust in Elyza. She would never, ever, put them in a position to do anything they didn't feel comfortable with, but she would help push their comfort boundaries.

This event wasn't just another small-town parade. It was the pride and joy of every citizen of Shiloh Hills, even outranking the harvest festival and the winter extravaganza. Small businesses clambered for a chance to participate each year simply for the publicity that came along with it. Having a float or even a banner included in the parade was like a giant flashing sign that shouted, "We are here and open for business!" This would be the first year The Wild Bride participated with a float, and Skye was determined to do her part in making the experience everything Elyza dreamed of.

Skye finished pulling dresses from racks along the walls and hung them from a golden bar just outside the dressing area. The gowns came in all sizes, colors, designs, and lengths, and Elyza promised they could choose their own style so long as each showed off a variety of fabrics, embellishments, and designs. Bekah and Kellyn vetoed several dresses before finding two or three they would try on. Bekah found her dress on the first try, while Kellyn went through rounds before settling on one that made her feel like a queen.

While the other women sipped champagne from crystal flutes, Skye slid behind the ornately decorated divider to try on the two she picked out for herself. She listened to her friends chatting as she stripped off her leggings and T-shirt and reached for the first gown. The silky silver material flowed down her body like a waterfall. The gorgeous style didn't quite feel like her though and she carefully, she slipped the thin straps back on the padded ivory hanger.

I don't have the confidence to wear a dress like that.

The second dress brought a brilliant smile to her face. It felt natural around her, like another skin, one that elevated her from ordinary human to goddess. In the ornate wall-length mirror, her reflection gazed back at her; she hardly recognized herself.

Skye walked out from behind the decorative divider, adding a little extra sway to her hips as she did.

"Ow, ow!" Elyza hollered, wiggling her eyebrows comically in appreciation.

Kellyn whistled, catcalling jokingly to Skye.

Bekah clapped, "That's the one!"

They sat in a semi-circle a short distance from the dressing room, giving her plenty of space to catwalk back and forth in front of them. She couldn't help the grin that broke free and remained until her cheeks hurt. She felt sexy, desirable, and comfortable; the last being the most important of all.

Back inside the dressing room, Skye took a moment of quiet to herself, letting her hands trail over the fabric and across the details on the bodice that extended toward her waist. She bit her lip and shook her head quickly, ridding her head of the distracting thoughts swirling around in her mind.

Reverently, Skye slipped the dress back onto the hanger and closed the clear garment bag around it. She rejoined the others as Elyza passed her a glass of champagne, which Skye sipped slowly.

"Now then—" Elyza plucked a black tote from a nearby chair and promptly dumped its contents on the floor between them.

Elyza must have emptied the entire faux floral section at the local craft store, maybe the ones further away too. Long-stemmed flowers and tangled garlands of greenery mingled on the wood-imitation vinyl flooring. Amid the mess, sample pictures fluttered to rest on the floor, inspiration for Elyza's vision.

Skye took a healthy drink of champagne.

"We're making bouquets!" Elyza squealed.

Kellyn groaned good-naturedly. Skye couldn't stop the giggle that slipped from her mouth. She covered her lips with her hand, hoping to stifle the sound.

Fortunately, Elyza just stuck her tongue out at both of them and encouraged Bekah to take a seat on the floor. Among the shades of blue, red, and white flowers, Bekah looked like a little wood sprite.

Skye tucked her legs under her and eased down next to Bekah. Together, they worked on stabbing metal-cored, plastic floral stems into Styrofoam bouquet bases to build Independence Day-themed arrangements. Skye paused, taking a moment to sip from her champagne flute, and watched Elyza craft boutonnieres for the stand-in grooms, her friend wearing a serene expression on her face.

Skye smiled, realizing this is what Elyza lived for. She loved watching Elyza in her element, just as she enjoyed watching Kellyn move behind the counter at Brick House Cafe. Her friends had found careers they were passionate about, and though she didn't know Bekah very well yet, Skye hoped she would find something she loved to do as well.

As she thought momentarily of her students, melancholy swept over her. She appreciated the break in the summer months, but she missed the children and the satisfaction of helping their young minds make sense of the world. She quickly shook off the glum feeling, taking another sip of her champagne and centering herself in the moment again.

She glanced at the modern-industrial-style clock on the wall. In a few hours, she'd get to see Rabble, and he would help settle her while validating her feelings. He'd always excelled at reading her moods, and it seemed years apart hadn't changed that. He never made her feel silly or discounted her concerns when something bothered her, a stark contrast to her parents and most other adults from her childhood. It hadn't taken Skye long to learn to keep her concerns to herself, internalizing them until they gave her bellyaches and burned in her throat.

Two hours, multiple finger pricks from little needles, and a tiny sting-ing cut later, they had several beautiful bouquets and boutonnieres as well as arrangements they could tie to the float's corner posts. Gathering the scraps from their project, Skye threw them in the trash bag, let herself out the backdoor. As the door closed behind her, the telltale click of the lock snicking into place made her cringe. Her shoulders dropped and she tilted her head toward the blue sky above her with a heavy sigh.

"Shoot," she whispered. "Forgot about that."

A steel set of stairs connected the main floor companies with the ground on the backside of the sloping hill and Skye hurried down them, her shoes thudding dully on the diamond-plated metal. She heaved the trash bag over the edge of the large blue dumpster, and shut the heavy plastic lid as quietly as possible. It still slammed shut louder than she preferred.

Keeping her eyes on her feet, Skye trudged up the drive and around the side of the building. Loose gravel moved beneath her sneakers, threatening to trip her and send her reeling.

As she neared the front of the building, voices reached her, rising the closer she came to The Wild Bride. They were deep and rumbled with undisguised thunder, giving Skye the distinct sensation of standing outside right before a lightning storm, an electric tension hung heavy around those voices. As she inched closer, the voices evened out, becoming clearer, and her eyes widened with recognition.

Why is Rabble speaking with my father of all people? They hated each other.

As she identified the third voice, she furrowed her brow. *Dylan's here too?*

The hair on her arms rose, and unease snaked through her. She sprinted around the front corner of the long building to reach Rabble, barely comprehending the awful, hateful words spewing from Dylan's mouth like toxic sludge. When her father spoke, venom spitting in every clipped syllable, she skidded to a stop so quickly her bones protested. Incapable of moving, her breath seizing in her chest as the solid, reassuring bottom of her world fell out from under her.

Chapter 19

Rabble

Rabble took long, eager strides toward the bridal shop's entrance. He hadn't been apart from Skye for long, but he'd found himself glancing at his watch repeatedly, wishing the minutes would tick by faster. He wasn't confident in the picnic he put together for them, but he hoped Skye would enjoy herself on their first official date.

Hurrying up the walkway, he felt lighter than he was used to. His chest didn't feel as like a vise, and his shoulders weren't stooped with the weight of the world. After carrying that heaviness for so long, this new sense of freedom was an odd sensation, but one he could get used to.

He set his hand on the ornate door handle just as the reflection of two men appeared in the glass window panes to his left. Rabble heaved a heavy sigh and squared his shoulders, turning to meet them head-on with his face a mask of emotionlessness.

"Max." Rabble's rumbling voice concealed all the derision he felt as he met the older man's gaze.

The second man stood just shy of six feet, judging by the way he tilted his head slightly to look Rabble in the eye. Though a stranger, his self-confidence proceeded him like a wave, and he wore his suit like it meant something. His flawlessly styled blond hair didn't shift, stiff with product strong enough to stand up to the breeze. Rabble wondered if he held a lighter near that perfectly coifed concoction, would the entire thing go up in flames? He chafed at the man's self-assured importance, and a predatory stillness settled over Rabble as he prepared for a confrontation.

"This is Dylan Santoro," Max gestured, his oily politician's voice in full force.

Rabble's skin crawled.

Dylan extended his hand, a smirk set firmly on his smarmy face. A single glance at that polished hand, the manicured fingernails, proved Dylan had never done a hard day's work in his life. Rabble met the man's stare, ignoring the proffered hand and returned his attention to Max.

Determined to deal with this pissing match outside, Rabble stepped away from the door, away from Skye and anyone he cared about. They didn't need to hear this.

"What do you want?" Rabble kept his voice low, practically lethal with simmering loathing.

Max cleared his throat. "I thought we had a deal."

"A deal?" Rabble lifted an eyebrow and crossed his arms over his chest, the muscles flexing and stretching the confines of his shirtsleeves. He knew it was a defensive position, but he couldn't quite bring himself to care.

"Don't you dare play dumb, boy. You know damn well what I'm talking about."

"You had no right to demand what you did, then or anytime."

"Like hell I didn't. She's my daughter, and you were going to fuck up everything. You always did, and you still do. Ever since you moved into that dump next door."

Dylan remained silent, but the disgusted sneer on his face said enough. It seemed watching the mayor tear Rabble apart was more enjoyable than joining in the verbal lashing.

"As if you ever cared about Skye." Though Rabble's voice was deceptively calm, he held onto his composure by a thread.

"I've been planning her future since the day she was born. But then *you*," he spat the word like a curse, "wrecked everything. She may have squandered these last few years, but I won't let you ruin her future again."

Rabble felt the verbal blow like a slap across his face and took a bracing step backward. How this man always managed to find his insecurities and exploit them was as irritating as it was disarming.

Like a bloodhound on a trail, Dylan caught the scent of Rabble's momentary lapse in focus, and he sounded as revolted as his words made Rabble feel. "In college, I was her fiancé you know. We spent four years together. What did you think Skye was going to do? Move into your trash heap of a house with you? Pop out your bastard babies and waste away any potential she had?"

Skye almost married this man? This pompous self-important jackass? He didn't seem like her type with his expensive suit, product-laden hair, and politician snake-like smile.

Then again, maybe he'd misread her. Maybe the years had changed her. Maybe he'd pushed her toward a man like this prick.

He clenched his jaw but otherwise kept his face neutral. If he showed even an ounce of how deeply Dylan's words struck, this entire conversation would be over, and Rabble would be no better than the torn-down boy he'd been the first time Max cornered him and painted a grim picture of the inevitable path he'd lead. He still agonized over that grotesque vision Max convinced him waited in his future.

"Who did you say you were again?" Rabble asked, feigning a lazy boredom as he met the man's gaze.

"Dylan Santoro," he said, pride lacing his words. "My father is Senator Santoro."

As if Rabble was supposed to care who the man's father was? Dylan was a sleazeball of the highest order, that covered the knowledge Rabble considered important about him.

Rabble tilted his head, rapidly making connections with the information he had. "Senator Santoro. Isn't he one of the biggest supporters for your congressional bid, Mayor?"

The mayor smiled fondly. "He is. Dylan and Skye make quite the couple—a very striking, influential couple. Their children will be political prodigies."

Rabble felt sick. These men, her father being one of them, discussed Skye like she was nothing more than a prized breeding mare. Not like the gorgeous and caring woman he knew. Not like she was her own person. Like she was less than human.

"You're disgusting." Rabble's rough voice struggled to contain the rage simmering beneath the surface.

Mayor Wellington grinned, evil practically seeping from him like a dark poisonous cloud. "Maybe. Maybe not. Either way, Skye is part of a much bigger plan than a person like you could ever understand. Considering she's already wasted her potential, the least she could do now is give Dylan some children. Voters love it when their representatives have kids. Makes them more relatable."

Rabble stood taller, his fury roiling, spreading, and threatening to boil over. That Max and Dylan saw the profession Skye chose and thoroughly loved as a waste of potential spoke volumes on how little they knew her. How little they cared. Skye had a beautiful, generous soul; she'd give everything to anyone who needed it and more to those she loved. That these people, who held so much power in her life through the years, couldn't see that was beyond despicable. That roiling sensation pitched around in his stomach, making him nauseous.

Dylan curled his lip. "You need to pack up the band of riffraff you brought with you and get the hell out of town," he said, his voice menacing as he mentioned Rabble's friends, his brothers.

Rabble uncrossed his arms, though his fists clenched at his side. He pulled himself up to his full height and stared down at them. "Or what?"

Dylan opened his mouth to respond, but Max spoke first. "I paid you to get your ass out of Shiloh Hills and never come back. That was the deal. I suggest you keep your side of it."

Movement at the corner of the building caught Rabble's attention, flashing in his peripheral vision. His stomach plummeted and landed somewhere on the ground with what remained of his hope as Skye stepped into his line of sight. Ice filled his veins and a howling sounded in his ears as he turned, just in time to catch the destroyed expression on her face and the wrecked depths of her blue gaze.

Chapter 20

Skye

Skye's ears rang as she tried to process what she heard. Devastated didn't begin to cover it. The solid foundation of her entire world collapsed beneath her, and she free-fell into an abyss of swirling darkness. She always had a protective net, something to keep her from hitting rock bottom and never recovering, but any safety measure she'd constructed over time had snapped, leaving her flailing and screaming into nothingness.

She locked her eyes with Rabble's for only a moment. In his stormy gray gaze, she saw the same wreckage she knew her own reflected. How dare he have the nerve to look as crushed as she felt! He had kept this secret for years, to protect her. In the process, he completely and totally wrecked her. For years and years, Skye thought she was the problem, like she was the damaged and unwanted one. The one who would never be good enough.

Skye stepped back, tripping over her feet before turning and bolting away. She ran as far and fast as she could. She made it to the end of the street, the sound of angry voices following her around the corner as she ran toward the cottage district. She bypassed her cottage and let her feet carry her where they willed. Her shoes slapped against the black-topped road that led out of town until she couldn't breathe and her side pinched with pain.

Bending over at the waist, she rested her palms on her knees and gasped for air. She couldn't remember if she was supposed to bend over or lift her arms above her head. She didn't care. She was fleeing everything she thought she knew. She ran for the naive girl who still believed in fairytales and happily ever after; for the girl who had so much love to give and just wanted to be loved in return; for the girl who had cautiously lifted her head these last few days, hoping that maybe this was it. That girl now lay broken on the ground, right along with the pieces of her heart.

Skye's knees gave out, and she dropped onto a patch of grass to the side of the blacktop, continuing to take in great wheezing gulps of air and praying she didn't hyperventilate. What was wrong with her? Was she not enough? Was she not worthy of love? Had everything been a lie, their time together, talking late into the night, their lovemaking that was so full of passion and emotion that Skye had very nearly cried? Did Rabble truly not love her?

None of that felt right. Then again, how could she trust her heart to tell her what was right and wrong if the traitor led her down this path of grief?

She didn't know how long she sat there, gazing unseeingly at the tall waving stalks of wild grasses that grew along the road before finally struggling to her feet. Shadow from the reedy plants cast shadows on the asphalt. Several hours must have passed as she'd sat still, her mind a swirling mess of self-doubt, loathing, and heartbreak. Her limbs, her head, her heart, all of her felt so very heavy.

The walk home took much longer, her tired legs hauling her body forward one exhausted step at a time. Her strength flagged as she reached her cottage, unlocked the door, and collapsed onto her favorite reading chair, face down. Shoes still on, she surrendered to the blissful unconsciousness sleep would bring, which she desperately needed and wanted.

Early morning phone calls roused her from her chair. She slid her eyes open, the lids dragging and gritty. On top of the emotional pain curling inside her, Skye could barely move after sleeping in such an awkward position. The chair was perfect for reading but not so great for long nights of restless sleep. She groaned, lifting up onto her elbows, and squinted at the phone screen, still groggy from sleep. Apparently, her phone had a busy afternoon and night while she'd been busy drowning.

The majority of the missed calls and unread texts were from Rabble, a distressed plea in every single one. She listened to each voicemail, her own personal kind of torture. At times, she could have sworn his voice sounded choked and thick, that maybe he was on the brink of tears like she was. His despair seeped through the speaker, wrapping around her sorrow and adding to the weight pressing down on her.

Her friends had also left voicemails and dozens of text messages, some just asking for a sign of life. They each wanted to know how they could help and if she needed anything. She didn't have an answer for them though.

Skye created a group text to her friends and typed, "I'm not okay, but I will be."

Her fingers faltered as she pressed the buttons to send the lie. She wouldn't be okay. That simply wasn't possible.

Even Declan had called, though he hadn't left a message. Her mother had left several hateful voicemails mixed in with the entire mess, and Skye seriously contemplated pitching her phone in the trash can.

She peeled off her dirty clothes, dusty and sweaty from her impromptu afternoon run the previous day, and left them in a heap on the bathroom floor. The mirror above the sink reflected her blank and hopeless eyes back at her and she took in the heavy purple stains under her blue eyes. The way the previous night's tears left trails down her cheeks to the corners of her downturned mouth. Stepping into a scalding hot shower, she prayed the water would wash away the grime that to clung to her skin and soul.

With the water beating down on her, Skye sat under the spray with her knees pulled to her chest and let the tears spill over again, blending in seamlessly with the rivulets that ran down her face. Too soon, the water turned cold and goosebumps formed across her body. She toweled off and lay on her bed, clutching the terry cloth fabric to her chest. Breathing deeply, Skye stared at the ceiling fan as it made its never-ending circle above her.

Despite knowing how painful it would be, she wanted to see Rabble. With the anger and sadness firmly set in, she needed to speak with him, to hear in his own words what possessed him to make a deal with the devil, with her father.

Skye dressed in her comfiest pair of leggings and a favorite T-shirt, a tie-dyed souvenir from a charity 5k run she participated in years ago. The familiar shirt added a layer of comfort and security, and she finally thought maybe she could face Rabble without turning into a whimpering pile of mush. She brushed the stubborn tangles from her hair before she braided it back, feeling more like herself than she had since Rabble returned to Shiloh Hills.

Knowing she needed to speak with him turned out to be an entirely different monster than actually messaging him to set up a time to meet. She turned on her cleaning playlist and plugged her phone in, glancing at the screen intermittently as she tried to gather the courage to text him. Although she procrastinated, she justified taking her time by being productive, tackling the mundane task of washing dishes.

Was this the time to be washing dishes? Perhaps not. Did doing something simple like rinsing suds off of clean dishes feel good, steadying? Absolutely. And Skye needed that right now. She needed anything that could ground her, remind her she wasn't *that* girl anymore. She wasn't waiting for *that* boy to run away with her, to take her away from the house that had become a prison.

And Rabble was no longer that lonely boy who wouldn't have been a match for the snake that was her father. That man could lie and cheat with the best of them, and he would do anything to get his way, including bribing and threatening a vulnerable teenager.

Dishes washed, dried, and put away, Skye lit a floral-scented three-wick candle then straightened the pillows and folded the multitude of blankets on the couch. Putting off her conversation with Rabble could last only so much longer as she ran out of chores. A small part of her, the part that doubted his intentions despite his words, worried he would laugh at her, call her childish, and defend his actions. Another part, in the darkest recesses of her heart, felt ashamed that she ran away without asking questions or answering the many messages her friends and Rabble had left her. Ignoring every single one of them made her sick, but being a relatively private person, she couldn't stand the idea of her friends fawning all over her right now. She'd message them later tonight.

Once she finished cleaning every corner of the cottage, Skye spent too many minutes working up the courage to unplug her phone from its charging cord in the kitchen and call Rabble. It was time. She shouldn't, and couldn't, procrastinate anymore.

Skye dialed Rabble's number, ending the call after a second before it could ring through. Maybe this conversation would be best held in person, where she could look into his eyes and read his emotion in the gray clouds that resided there. Determined to speak with him face to face, she grabbed her phone and keys from the bamboo bowl by the door, then turned to the new alarm system. The illuminated blue buttons on the keypad mocked her with their simplistic complexity. Dash had explained how the alarm system worked. Skye stared at the keypad, willing it to share its secrets and help her remember the code for securing the system.

The six-digit code came to her, number by number until she remembered the entire thing and swung open the door to leave.

"Dylan?" Surprise stole her brainpower and made her freeze just inside the door.

He flashed a nice smile, not the one he reserved for public relations situations, but something glittered in the blue depths that made Skye fidget nervously.

"Can I come in?" he asked, gesturing to the living room behind her.

Skye glanced over her shoulder at her safe space, her sanctuary, and cringed. "I was actually just going out."

The smile didn't falter, though his voice lost some of its cheery edge. "It will only take a moment."

She wanted to say no, but maybe giving in would make him go away faster. "Okay."

As she stepped out of the doorframe, Dylan sauntered inside, and she closed the door behind him. When she pivoted to face him, he moved further into the living room, his gaze raking over the titles on her bookshelves, and he sneered with scorn at her reading choices. She had no doubt, the titles were beneath him.

"Can I help you, Dylan?" Skye shifted from foot to foot.

Now that she'd decided to speak with Rabble, that was all she wanted to do. She wasn't interested in a conversation with her ex-boyfriend, especially considering his involvement in her father's disgusting plot to remove Rabble from her life, again.

"You know," he said, straightening the perfectly cuffed sleeves of his button-down, "had you married me like your parents wanted, you never would've had to live in this hovel."

Skye reared back as if he had slapped her. "Excuse me? I wouldn't call it a hovel."

She loved her cottage and worked tirelessly to restore its current glory. She'd chosen the furniture based on comfort, not style, and the colors and textures of the rooms and furnishings were complimentary muted tones of soft green, blues, and grays. Her home radiated peace and comfort, exactly the type of place she desired after a long day around her amazing and chaotic job.

Dylan clicked his tongue and shook his head. "Poor, simple Skye. You just don't get it."

Her stomach cramped, this conversation felt wrong on every level. "I think you should leave."

Dylan's suave, gentlemanly illusion dropped like a curtain falling away from a broken window. The act was over, the politician nowhere to be found. Skye bet the bored, exasperated look pulling at the corners of his mouth was his primary expression, not the placating smile he displayed to everyone in public.

He stepped toward her. "Do you even realize the kind of political alliance our marriage would create? How much power your father and mine would have; how much I would have? And how that will benefit you too?"

"Political alliance? I've never cared about that. And we haven't dated in years. No one said anything about marriage except for my delusional parents."

"Skye, honey, you live with your head buried in the sand, wasting your time teaching, not paying attention to what's happening behind the scenes. I gave you space to do as you pleased, but it's time to move forward, to accept that our marriage is inevitable."

Her head spun from the words spewing from his mouth, and she grasped the doorknob behind her back. "You need to leave." Each word was clipped, not allowing any room for miscommunication.

Skye twisted the doorknob and pulled it toward her, her eye on the alarm system's panic button. But the door hadn't opened more than a few centimeters before Dylan slammed into her body, banging the door shut. Her head smacked the solid wood with a loud crack, and Skye saw stars. If only she'd agreed to let Dash install the video surveillance too.

He gripped her shoulders tightly, his fingertips digging into her arms hard enough to bruise, and he shook her. "Why must you be so stubborn?"

She cried out as her head cracked against the door again, but he cupped his hand over her mouth, so she did the first thing that came to mind: She bit down. Hard.

Dylan gave a sharp shout of pain, and Skye enjoyed a moment of satisfaction until he slapped her across the face. Her jaw throbbed, and she struggled, bucking and squirming against his hold. He jerked on the phone she held in a death grip and threw it across the room. Her keys followed, flying through the air, landing with a loud clang in the kitchen.

Fight, fight! her brain shouted.

Skye opened her mouth, another scream building in her throat. But quick as a snake, Dylan jabbed at her shoulder, plunging a tiny needle beneath her skin, the feeling like a bee sting, and her scream turned into a yelp. Her head swam, her vision went fuzzy, and Skye sank into darkness.

Chapter 21

Rabble

Rabble spent entirely too much time pacing, slowly going out of his mind. He'd practically watched Skye's heart shatter at what she overheard. Would he have someday told her about the deal he'd made with her father? He liked to think he would have, but not like this. Never like this.

The moment she processed her father's words, the light in her eyes flicker out as if someone had blown out a candle. He ached to go after her, everything in him straining to take her in his arms and beg for forgiveness. With Max and his shadow there though, Rabble couldn't do anything that would show weakness, in himself, or Skye.

As her form retreated, running as far away from him as possible, Max and Dylan both wore satisfied smirks on their faces. Rabble didn't believe in coincidences on a normal day, and that certainly hadn't changed overnight. If he had the money, Rabble would bet Max or Dylan, maybe both, orchestrated that meeting specifically for Skye to hear. The scumbags left not long after, done with taunting and trying to intimidate him.

He watched as they climbed into one of their expensive cars, waiting until they drove away before pulling out his cell phone. He called, texted, then called Skye again. Stomach twisting, heart racing, Rabble's body tensed with acidic dread. She had to know how he felt, the truth, not the twisted poison she'd overheard. He needed to show her, she was the very thing he'd been working to protect, then and now. The only person he couldn't live without. Always.

He lost his sense of purpose, of direction, and for once had no idea how to proceed. He abandoned his original destination, having no desire to go into the bridal shop and face the questions Elyza and the others would certainly have for him. With no particular destination in mind, he walked alone, his thoughts a swirling pile of useless mush. He returned to the truck as the sun began to fade. He couldn't think about anything except telling Skye the truth, needing her to understand like he needed air to breathe.

Dusk fell, and the streetlamps came on, dimly lighting his drive back to the bed and breakfast where he slumped onto the back porch swing and rocked throughout the night. He remained in the same spot as the sun rose, his clothes wrinkled and his eyes haunted.

Just after sunrise, the sky still bursting into life, the rear screen door creaked open, ancient hinges groaning with protest. The sound of heavy footsteps and the door slamming shut followed as Declan and Dash sauntered toward him. Rabble couldn't even bring himself to tense, to prepare for the dressing-down he knew was coming and he didn't bother trying to defend himself as they settled near him. Dash leaned against the porch railing, crossing one booted foot over the other, and his arms over his chest. Declan sat on the railing, legs dangling while he braced his hands by his hips.

"Go ahead," Rabble rasped, "Light into me."

Dash remained silent, watching his friend with hazel eyes that saw too much.

Declan, his brother's counterpart, let loose, "What possessed you to do something so stupid? I've made my share of dumbass mistakes, but … man what the hell were you thinking?"

Rabble stared ahead, unable to meet his brothers' eyes, shame threatening to pull him under.

"Rab," Dash said, his voice low, reassuring to Declan's simmering anger and disappointment, "You aren't infallible. We've all done things we regret. But you're going to need to give us some context here because the Rabble I know wouldn't even bother associating with those sons'-a-bitches."

His throat bobbed and he struggled for the words to say what he needed, "I, uh, well. Look, you know I don't like talking about my family, where I came from, the person I was before I joined up."

Declan nodded and Dash flexed his arms but neither spoke, giving Rabble the space to fade into memories he'd rather leave buried.

"I've told you how wonderful my mom was, I could never be ashamed of her, but the loser she married, he's a different story. Drunk, abusive, lazy, a slob, I heard it all growing up. I wasn't Rabble or even Matthew. I was the son of that good for nothing trailer trash who beat his wife and kid and drank until he blacked out every night."

Declan's frown darkened his face and Rabble wondered if he could see where this was going.

Self-loathing stirred in his chest, "Anyway. Skye's father is a real bastard too. A different kind maybe but—."

"What happened?" Dash asked, "You've said before, you and Skye spent years together, meeting at the fence without any fallout. The mayor didn't make any moves before that to stop you from being around each other. So, what was different?"

A wet track found its way down Rabble's face as he remembered the night everything changed, "My mom died."

Declan and Dash shifted in unison, their eyes taking on a type of sympathy that made Rabble's already shattered heart break apart just a bit more.

"She came to me that night, after I found out Mom was gone. I got home late, I'd been studying at the library, and Dad told me when I walked through the door. No emotion, not a single sign he gave a shit and I raced out of the house, finding my way down to the fence in the dark."

Rabble could see it happening, as if it played out in front of him.

He'd arrived at the fence, already a mess. A high-pitched ringing static in his mind. Wet splashes landed on his skin, his clothes and he realized he'd been crying. Skye hopped over the fence, her long legs eating up the distance to him and she gathered him to her as his legs gave out and they fell to the ground together. She hushed him gently, holding his head to her chest as he fell apart completely. Devastation poured from him and she absorbed it as it crashed against her. Skye held him, rocked him, comforted him in the only way she knew how.

Eventually, each breath an agony, he managed to ground out the horrifying and heartbreaking truth. Saying it aloud somehow made it permanent where it had only been a horrible nightmare before.

Memories of her soft smiles flashed through his mind, each striking another blow to his pulverized heart. Distantly, the angry voice of a man yelling, screaming for Skye, broke through the haze of his anguish, but she didn't leave. Skye stayed, holding him through the night while a part of him, the part that felt hopeful and good, died.

"Max never forgave her for disobeying, or me for leading her astray. His daughter was worth more to him unsullied by association with someone like me. If he thought I'd touched her that night, if he thought we'd—" Rabble huffed out a breath, "Skye meant more to me than anything in the entire world. But to him, it didn't matter.

"After that, I stopped going to school regularly. Dad didn't care where I was during the day, or night for that matter. No one really cared and I was better off alone. I wasn't exactly pleasant to be around. Mrs. Basket and Mr. Jack are the only ones who saw me for what I was at that point, besides Skye. A shell, a husk carrying around a rotted and dead soul."

Dash's expressionless face calmed Rabble enough to finish his tale.

"With Mrs. Basket's help, by the time graduation rolled around, I made it to school just enough to pass and I'd been trying to patch up the holes in my life. Things were kind of starting to look up. And then, Max found me. He cornered me at Mr. Jack's pharmacy after work one night, and God, he knew." Rabble dropped his head, letting it hang as he stared, unseeing at his clasped hands, "He knew exactly what to say, what to jab at to unravel every bit of self-confidence I'd started to gain."

"What did he say?" Declan asked, his face unreadable.

Rabble shrugged, "Beyond the typical, 'you're lazy trailer trash who came from nothing and will never amount to anything'? He hit me where he knew it would hurt. Skye. I had nothing to offer her, no money, no name, nothing. And she, she was on a good path, one that would take her places, allow her to make something of herself. And what was I? The son of a drunk and a dead waitress."

"Man, that's bullshit," Declan seethed.

"Maybe so, but to an eighteen-year-old kid who just spent the last three years doing everything to self-destruct that he could think of? Max's words were cruel, but true. I was a nobody. Skye deserved better than me, better than anything I could ever offer her. So, Max made me a deal. Leave his daughter alone, find somewhere else to live out my miserable existence, and he would make sure I made it wherever I needed to be. It seemed like a good idea at the time."

Taking the money had seemed like the best option; joining the military had been purely selfish, a move meant to keep him occupied so he didn't have time or energy to think about Shiloh Hills, about Skye. He wanted to give Skye the chance to grow, to become the woman he always knew she could be. She'd marry some scumbag, but at least she'd be happy. What was he other than the rabble from the wrong side of the fence, with no money or a single redeeming quality to his name? He had nothing to offer her. And she deserved it all, every good thing in this world.

Rabble struggled to think past the grief, a lead weight in his chest. He'd done this. Even after years of trying to protect her, he had caused sadness and despair in her beautiful eyes. Any pain she felt now was entirely on him.

"I have to go get Bekah," Declan said, his voice low as he jumped off of the railing and clapped Rabble on the shoulder. A gesture, not of forgiveness exactly, but of understanding and acceptance. Rabble would take it.

Dash sat next to Rabble on the swing, "Rab."

Rabble braced himself.

"You don't get to make those decisions for Skye."

Shock barreled through him, "What?"

Dash met his eyes, the frankness there that Rabble usually found comforting now made his heart pound.

"You don't get to make those decisions for Skye, any more than her father does. Love is more than blind protection. That instinct is strong, especially in men like us, but when it comes down to loving someone, sometimes the ability to let them meet challenges head on, no matter how difficult it is for us, it's part of the package deal."

A quiet fell between them, each lost in their own thoughts. Rabble turned Dash's words over in his head, examining them through the fog of the mistakes he'd made. Neither spoke until Declan returned with Bekah.

Bekah, despite her disapproving look in his direction forced a bag of chips and a bottle of water on Rabble when he refused lunch. The chips tasted like sawdust, the water like acid.

Bekah glanced at her phone for the tenth time, and she flicked a worried gaze at Declan each time. She was waiting for a response from Skye.

"She won't answer me either," Rabble said, his voice ragged.

Bekah turned toward him, worrying her lip. "No offense, but do you blame her?"

Flinching, Rabble had to give her that one, especially considering her own experiences with two-faced jackasses.

Bekah seemed poised to speak again but the subtle shake of Declan's head had her pausing and reconsidering her words.

Even though Rabble appreciated his brother looking out for him, he wouldn't blame Skye if she never spoke to him again. Maybe she packed everything and left town. He wouldn't condemn her for that either.

Bekah tried Skye's phone a few more times before Declan drove her to The Wild Bride to help Elyza with the shop. The glaring rift between Rabble and Skye couldn't stop everyone else's lives from continuing. It seemed odd that they could keep going, just another day in their existence as the world spun around him, even though Rabble felt like his world was ending.

Rabble eventually moved from his vigil on the porch swing, wandering inside to change shirts and sulk. He poured himself some coffee and returned outside where he sat on the stairs and stared out over the backyard. When the back door slammed shut again, he didn't turn around.

"Brought you dinner." Mrs. Basket said, passing him a sandwich wrapped in a paper towel.

"I messed up," he said, hanging his head.

"You did." She agreed, resting a warm hand on his shoulder. "But you'll fix it."

Then she passed him a small black felt box. He recognized it instantly and his eyes widened as he glanced between her and the box he now clutched alongside his sandwich. He set the sandwich atop one knee and carefully lifted the box lid, his fingers shaking ever so slightly. There, nestled atop a pillow of black satin, sat the simple ring he'd purchased long ago.

"Sylvie—," words failed him.

"I thought I'd save it for a rainy day."

He sucked on the inside of his cheek, refusing to let the sob out as it crawled up his throat. His sorrow must have shone in his eyes though because she patted his shoulder again, and studied the clear sky, then him, "I'd say it's a pretty rainy day, my dear."

That sob he'd tried so hard to hold back, choked out of him and she ruffled his hair with a hand the way she used to when she'd said her piece, before standing slowly and wandering back inside, closing the door silently behind her.

It took several deep breaths before Rabble could think clearly enough to close the lid to the ring box and slide it into his pocket. Then, he unwrapped the triple peanut butter and jelly sandwich and chuckled. Mrs. Basket always knew what to say when he was having a hard day. Famished, he devoured every bite.

Later, when the sun began to sink behind the bed and breakfast, Rabble overheard Elyza's muffled voice in the dining room, something about Skye not returning anyone's messages.

He frowned. That didn't make sense. Sure, she had every right to ignore him. But Skye spent most days worrying about everyone else but herself. Even if she needed time to be alone, she'd never leave her friends to panic over her, not for this long.

Fear became a living, breathing demon inside him. That voice in his head, the one that told him when he needed to be scared out of his mind, the one that kept him alive in the military, screamed at him to get to his feet.

Running inside, he threw his coffee in the kitchen sink, not stopping when he heard the telltale crack of the ceramic mug shattering against the metal tub, and sprinted into the dining room where Dash tried to calm his sister and Declan stood protectively in front of Bekah, her shoulders shrinking inward.

"I'm on it," Rabble said, pulling his keys out of his pocket. "You guys stay here with them."

Dash pulled out his cell phone. "I'll call Kellyn, make sure she's okay. Just in case."

Rabble nodded. While Declan reassured Bekah that no one had tripped the cottage's alarms, that her ex had nothing to do with whatever was going on with Skye, Rabble bolted for the front door. He jammed his truck key in the ignition and peeled off toward Skye's cottage without bothering with trying to call. She hadn't answered anyone before, and he doubted she'd start answering for him.

The alarms in his head kept blaring, getting louder the closer he got to her home. He parked on the curb; his front tire having jumped the curb entirely to sit atop the grass of the yard. Rabble took the concrete steps to her door two at a time. He swung his fist up to knock, stopping just shy of tapping his fingers against the wood. The door sat ajar from its frame, leaving a thin gap where the latch hadn't caught.

His whole being froze, and the voice in his head went from screaming to radio silence. He reached for his sidearm, only it wasn't there. A rookie mistake, he cursed to himself. He wouldn't let that stop him from breaching the house right then and there.

With two fingers, Rabble slowly urged the door open, listening past the squeaking of its hinges for any noise from within. Hearing nothing, he pushed the door open the rest of the way and stepped into the small living room, which she artfully put together. Her home looked well maintained, cared for. But in the center of the floor lay her phone, abandoned, the screen cracked as if someone had stomped on it. His breath caught in his throat.

Quickly, Rabble cleared the living room. Against his training, he rushed through the open rooms and followed a short hallway to the single bedroom kept neat in a lived-in way with wrinkles in the sheets and clothes on the floor. The bathroom appeared the same way.

The kitchen also seemed to be in order, aside from the candle left burning on the counter. The sink was clean. But in the left basin, her keys lay in a heap, making the alarm bells in his head ring double-time. Pulling out his cell phone, he dialed Dash's number, put the speaker to his ear, and prayed to whichever gods might be listening that his brother answered quickly.

"Yeah," Dash said, his simple greeting coming through on the first ring.

Rabble's voice cracked and scraped like he hadn't used it in days. "She's gone."

"We're on our way."

Chapter 22

Skye

Skye swore she could feel every nerve ending, every synapse in her brain burning and freezing simultaneously. A steady and awful pulsing behind her eyes made her wish for the oblivion she just woke from. She cracked her eyes open, her eyelids heavy and gritty as if sand dragged beneath them, and her cotton-like tongue made her long for a glass of water. She swallowed several times, wishing her mouth didn't feel so strange. Lifting her head, she scanned the room, trying to gather her bearings. Gradually, the throbbing in her skull subsided to a dull ache, and she rolled carefully to the side. Her hands and knees hit cream carpeting. Dazed, she let out a gasp. A fair amount of disgust and nausea mixed together, creating a horrible sense of déjà vu.

The pale-pink wallpaper that graced the four walls taunted her with familiarity, as if welcoming her back to a picturesque prison. The golden antique metal-framed bed waited in the corner by the window, untouched since she'd moved out. The same large, mirrored vanity perched beside the closet door. She rose onto her knees and peeked out the window, recognizing the giant leafy green bush that grew by the sterile, horrible fence. She had no idea how or why she was in her childhood bedroom.

On shaking legs, Skye stumbled across the room to the painted white door that led to the house. She grasped the doorknob and twisted. Nothing happened. She pulled, turned, and yanked on the handle, but the door didn't budge. Skye's breath came in short gasps as she struggled to think clearly.

Why was she at her parents' house? None of this made any sense. Still unsteady, she hurried back to the window and peered down. Two stories below, the ground glowered at her. She'd always been too chicken to risk sneaking out of the second story opening, but she might try today. Compared to being abducted and trapped in her parents' home, maybe a two-story drop would be nothing.

She wracked her brain, searching for any reasonable explanation that might keep her from panicking. Yes, someone had locked her in her old bedroom, but these were her parents after all. They loved her and wouldn't hurt her.

And yet the utterly terrified part of her mind didn't care if Mother Teresa held her prisoner. As a grown woman, Skye had her own life and agenda. She rolled her neck, hoping to ease some of the stress that bunched in her shoulders and didn't help her headache. She reached up to rub her neck and hissed through her teeth as her fingers found a stinging pin-sized spot between her neck and shoulder

Her eyes widened, her hand flying to her mouth. "Oh, my word. Oh shit."

Everything that happened came back in a rush. Dylan at her house. Their fight. The reason why that spot on her neck hurt.

"He drugged me," she whispered, her voice rising with hysteria. "He fucking drugged me!"

Usually she avoided cursing, but under the circumstances, it felt appropriate. The stumbling, the confusion, the pounding and persistent headache—all of it made sense. Only one puzzle piece continued to elude her. Why was she in her old bedroom?

Skye searched the room, exploring every corner and testing anything she might be able to use as a weapon. While she looked, she ran through every recent conversation she'd had with Dylan and her parents, trying to find the anomaly that would lead to this conclusion. Despite their encounters being charged with anxiety and strain, none of their words stood out as anything out of the ordinary.

They left the room like a shrine dedicated to her childhood years; the little girl they'd trained to be the perfect princess. When she left for college, she never looked back. The reason why glared at her in every inch of the room, especially the things she chose to leave behind. Nearly every gift her parents gave her sat on the vanity. Diamond bracelets. Emerald rings. Pearl necklaces. The wealth atop the vanity was staggering. Designer dresses she'd long sense outgrown still hung in the closet, the names on the tags ones she could never afford on her teacher's salary. In truth, she had no desire to own anything like those clothes again.

Maybe she was crazy to leave those here, to take the solo route paying for college, but she learned long ago that her parents did not give gifts. They traded favors to unwitting participants and then collected on the favor later, with interest.

Buying her expensive things became their apology letter, but the jewelry, the dresses, and other gifts were just a pretty bejeweled prison for a confused, sad teenage girl. Skye wished she'd seen the gifts for what they were earlier, but the bribes never worked on her. She had only ever wanted one thing, and her father had successfully ripped that away from her.

Her parents always obsessed over maintaining societal standards, spending her youth wrapped up in themselves and whatever they thought might further their social standing. With Max in the mayor's office, Gayle thrived under the attention she received as his wife. She planned parties and charitable events, anything to fulfill the imaginary expectations of the Wellington name. Skye snorted. She knew who her parents really were—power hungry opportunists, plain and simple.

Across the room, the doorknob twisted, and the door creaked. Skye spun around, putting her back to the wall. Pushing down the instinct to freeze, she bent her trembling knees and steadied herself on the balls of her feet. Every screaming part of her wanted to cower, to hide behind the bed, but she squashed it, hard.

Dylan, dapper as ever in a black pin-striped suit and tie, waltzed in as if he owned the right to the room and all of its trappings. He scanned the space with bland and hooded eyes, a smirk growing on his face as he noted her position against the far wall. He tucked his hands into his pants' pockets and for all the world appeared like the cat who ate the canary.

"Skye," he said, voice deceptively soft, "we are so glad you have decided to join us."

Beneath the gentle tone, an underlying note of condescension lurked. She'd always hated that.

She bared her teeth at him in a feral snarl, surprising herself with her ferocity. "Dylan, what the hell?"

Apparently, she should have been harsher when she broke up with him in college if he still harbored some delusion that she had any interest in him. His obsession passed from an annoyance into a different realm of concern.

He tsked. "Is that any way for a gentle lady to speak?"

Skye resisted the urge to roll her eyes, not wanting to let him out of her sight for a moment. She opted for flipping him off with both hands.

Behind him, the sharp clack of high heels on the wood floor grew louder until Gayle Wellington glided through the door.

Skye felt the color drain from her face, and her voice came out as a whisper. "Mother?"

Gayle's red-tinted lips curved upward at the corners in a sorry excuse for a smile that contrasted with her saccharine sweet voice. "Good evening, darling. Why, when you didn't wake up right away, you gave Dylan and I quite a scare."

Skye's mouth dropped open a fraction in disbelief. Surely, they weren't serious.

Gayle strode to the closet, her steps marking the seconds like a clock. She nearly floated in her grace, ever the perfect lady, and hung a hot pink garment bag from a hook on the closet door, its bottom barely dragging on the carpet.

Skye's stomach dropped. Her nausea came back in full force, and she pressed herself tighter to the wall, wishing the wallpaper would come alive and swallow her whole. Her newly discovered inner-fortitude quickly ebbed away, evaporating a little more with every new and horrible puzzle piece that clicked into place.

"No matter, sweetie." Her stepmother executed a sharp turn, the deceptively serene uptilt of her lips plastered in place. "Now that you are awake, we can move forward with the wedding."

Skye's head shook back and forth in appalled denial, her tangled hair swinging languidly about her face.

Gayle waved a hand dismissively at her and gave a small laugh, the sound like tinkling bells. "Oh darling, Dylan's been quite smitten with you since your first date. With the mayor and the senator both up for reelection, wouldn't it be just perfect for your love story to help voters make the right choices in November?"

Skye flicked her gaze toward Dylan, hoping he wasn't as delusional as her stepmother. Gayle had always been driven and manipulative, but this? This plan to force Skye, her own stepdaughter, into a marriage she didn't want? And for what—political gain, more power, higher social standing?

Dizziness coursed through her, making her stomach roll. She crossed her arms over her belly as if she could stave off the queasy, bubbling feeling as a cold sweat broke out on her forehead.

Dylan, for his part, listened to Gayle speaking with an intensity that startled Skye. She expected his eyes to glimmer with glee, but she found the solemnity in his gaze far more frightening. She contemplated pinching herself in an attempt to wake up from this nightmare. The longer Gayle stared at her expectantly, that placid smile fixed on her lips, Skye's hopefulness drained away, agitation rising to fill the emptying space.

"You cannot seriously think I'll go along with your hairbrained scheme?" Incredulous disgust rang in her voice. "Why the hell would I even stick around for this?"

Skye took a step forward, aiming for the door, but Dylan moved toward her, angling his body to block her path, his hands out to physically stop her if she continued forward.

Gayle smoothed her wrinkle-free navy sheath dress and sniffed daintily. "Come now, dear. Enough with this childish behavior. You're old enough to stop playing games."

"Games? You hear how insane you sound, right?" Skye's voice rose shrilly as she realized the sheer depth of her stepmother's delusion.

For the first time since she'd entered the room, Gayle's perfectly serene expression faltered, and her eyes flashed with ire. She folded her hands together in front of her, the bright red fingernails standing out against the dark-blue dress.

"Skye Louise," she chastised, "You're a grown woman. It's time you step up and take your place in the family. You have a job to do, just like the rest of us. Why, who knows, with your marriage to Dylan, you could be the mother of the future president."

Gayle's smile brightened, her eyes seeking Skye's, searching for the anticipated excitement at the prospect of birthing the future president of the United States.

"We aren't the damn Kennedys!" Skye yelled.

Gayle crossed the room quickly, her hand striking out before Skye could blink. The slap stung against her cheek, the sound echoing in her ears. Shocked, she stumbled back a step, her fingers coming up to cup her stinging cheek.

Her stepmother stepped back, adjusting her dress and composing herself before hissing, "Watch your language, young lady."

Skye's eyes whipped to Dylan imploring him for some semblance of sanity. He watched her, a vague disappointment tugging at the corners of his mouth.

"I am not your puppet!" Skye bit out each word, accentuating the syllables.

Dylan's displeasure turned into a full frown. His eyes going hard, "Skye."

A warning. And a threat.

Skye pulled herself up to her full height, though she was several inches shorter than both Dylan and Gayle in her heels. "You cannot keep me here. You have no rights to my body or my time. And you're both fucking crazy if you think I'll stay here for another damned minute."

Dylan strode toward her, and Skye resisted the urge to shrink back from him. His hands came up to grip her arms, pulling her tight against his body. She felt every awful inch of him against her. The muscles in his biceps, the bony angle of his hips, the hard press of his thighs against hers. She turned her head, refusing to meet his eyes, refusing to acknowledge his desire for her.

His fingers tightened cruelly, digging in with bruising force. With his breath hot against her ear, he whispered, "You forget your place, but that's okay. I'll remind you. It's time to take your place at my side, Skye. If you don't, I'd hate to see something happen to your little toy soldier."

Her toy soldier? Skye's eyes widened, fear freezing the blood in her veins as his words sank in. *Rabble.*

Near the door, Gayle cleared her throat delicately. "Well, dear, now that that's settled, I'll let the officiant know we'll be ready for the wedding before the end of the day." She clapped her hands excitedly. "There is so much to do!"

She whisked from the room, ticking off tasks she needed to finish on her manicured fingers. Dylan turned his head to watch her go. When Gayle's heeled tapping disappeared down the hall, he locked his eyes on Skye, releasing one of her arms to run his fingers through her tangled hair, then down the line of her jaw, forcing her to meet his gaze. His fingers moved to her lips, and she barely contained the desire to lash out with her teeth and tear the digit from his hand.

Dylan grinned. "See, it won't be so bad."

She tried to turn her face from him, but his fingers caught her cheeks, pushing against her viciously. Skye clasped his wrists, tugging with all her strength to move him away, to make him to let go.

Gone was the gentle concern he'd shown moments before with an audience looking on. Now, his eyes gleamed with a dark light. His lips quirked in an infuriating smirk. "I win."

She furrowed her brow and dug her fingernails into his wrists, leaving red small half-moons in his skin.

"I told you, Skye." A dark promise rang in his voice. "I play the long game."

Then he too was gone, the door snicking shut followed by the death knell of the lock sounding behind him.

Chapter 23

Rabble

Dash and Declan arrived less than fifteen minutes after Rabble called. They'd activated the emergency plan for Elyza, Bekah, and Kellyn, who were holed up at The Wild Bride. The locked doors would remain that way under threat of brotherly punishment until either Declan or Dash contacted their sister. Elyza was no fool. Knowing the world her brothers lived in, she was prepared to keep her friends and herself from any harm that might come knocking.

Rabble paced in Skye's living room, trying to analyze what he could while simultaneously losing his shit. The brothers came through the door like avenging angels, focused and determined. Rabble watched them work, reminded again why he trusted these men absolutely. After Rable told them he found the door open, they too took in the discarded and cracked cell phone, moving from one room to another, then to the house keys in the sink basin.

Rabble ran his hand through his hair in agitation, the strands already standing on end from the fingers he'd been raking through it. The sharp tug of him pulling his hair centered him, just barely.

Annoyance shot through him. Almost eight years of combat and hostile situation experience had utterly failed him. The fear that rode him nearly all-consuming, and he hated how useless and weak he felt. When his brain registered that *his* Skye was missing, not a stranger, all his training and experience dissipated like a cloud of dust, even though he needed it more than ever.

Declan investigated the rest of the cottage, finding the same things Rabble had, her relatively tidy bedroom and bathroom. Both wonderfully ordinary.

"Whatever happened," Dash strode to the living room, his hazel-green eyes clear of the panic swamping Rabble, "is localized to here."

"And it happened fast," Declan said. "With this little evidence, the police won't suspect foul play." He winced. "What I mean is—"

Rabble held up a hand to stop him. "I know what you meant. We're on our own."

Shame-faced, Declan didn't respond.

"She hasn't mentioned anyone, no parents or teachers from school who have a problem with her. Nothing. She's a fucking kindergarten teacher for fuck's sake." Growling, Rabble threw his hands in the air, hating the helpless feeling that wormed its way inside him, heading straight for his heart.

"Okay, Rab." Dash looked him in the eye, a deadly calm in his gaze. "Let's work this like a regular case."

Rage threatened to blind Rabble, and he got in Dash's face. "A normal case? This is Skye we're talking about!"

Despite the red-hot fury pulsing through Rabble, Dash didn't back down.

Declan moved to stand shoulder to shoulder with his twin, raising his voice because Dash wouldn't. "And you aren't any good to her with your head up your ass!"

As quickly as his anger surged, the fight left him, and he deflated. "You're right," Rabble said, feeling pale and shaky.

Neither brother spoke. They didn't try to console him with sugary sweet lies and promises they couldn't keep, and Rabble appreciated that more than anything as he gathered his thoughts. Each of them grasped his shoulders in silent support, keeping Rabble from falling to his knees.

"Okay, normal case." Rabble swiped at his eyes and sniffed, forcing himself to focus. "Skye doesn't have any enemies, not that I know of anyway, especially not anyone who would wish her harm. She's kind, generous, involved in the town. For fuck's sake, she's a kindergarten teacher." He reiterated with a groan, remembering the way she'd run away from him.

For the first time, Rabble told his brothers everything that transpired between himself and Max and Dylan outside of their sister's bridal shop. They'd heard some of the more damning parts from Elyza, what she'd gathered from behind the glass of The Wild Bride's front windows. Since his earlier conversation with them, Rabble now knew Dash and Declan at least saw where his teenaged mind had been when he'd messed up before. At the time, he had thought of nothing but his lack of name, family, worth, and a past so covered in rust and dirt that it didn't warrant speaking of.

Now though, now he knew without a doubt, he'd not only taken that choice away from Skye, but had undermined her at the most fundamental level, the one where she could make her own decisions, be her own person, and still love who she wanted. Even if the one she wanted, was him.

The twins kept any additional thoughts on the topic to themselves, having said their piece already. If he could do it all over again, he'd have dropped to one knee on graduation day and taken Skye with him. They could've run away and faced life's challenges together head-on, instead of wasting years on sorrow and regret.

Declan glanced at his twin, both knowing exactly which memory haunted Rabble right now. "Okay," Declan said, "so you haven't heard from her since then, and her friends last heard from Skye this morning. That leaves her family. And this Dylan guy. I say we pay a little visit to the illustrious mayor."

Rabble didn't respond. His barely controlled panic roiled beneath a mask of anger and violence. The brothers exchanged worried glances but remained silent while they hurried to their trucks. As Dash climbed into his, Declan beat Rabble to driver's door of his own pickup.

Declan held out his hand for the keys. "No way you're driving when you look like you want to plow over anything that gets in your way, and you're just wasting time if you argue with me."

Recognizing the truth in his words. Rabble tossed the keys to his friend and jumped into the passenger seat as they sped toward their destination, the courthouse.

It took Rabble all of five seconds to determine the mayor's secretary was a demon on loan from hell. At first glance, he might have mistaken her as a kindly grandmother. She was older, portly, and about a foot shorter than Rabble with curled gray hair perched atop her head. Her eyes, hard and mean, ruined the image though. Her mouth pinched and twisted with distaste at the sight of the three tall men crowding her office. She set her handbag on her desk and drew herself to her full height, her back going ramrod straight.

"Mayor Wellington isn't available right now." Her nasally voice grated on Rabble's frayed nerves.

Behind her, a shadowy figure moved about behind a translucent window. Someone occupied that space and Rabble would bet money the mayor worked late hours to avoid the uptight wife he kept at home. Rabble maintained his composure just enough not to shove the woman aside. He planned to enter the mayor's office, regardless of whether the mayor was available or not.

"Ma'am." Turning on his charm, Declan directed the entire well of his charisma at the woman, though an undercurrent of unyielding determination threaded through his words. "We really need to speak with Mayor Wellington. It's about his daughter, Skye."

"I'm sorry, but the mayor..." She sounded like a broken record.

As Rabble lost the battle rationalizing why he shouldn't charge past her and land his fist solidly in the mayor's smug face, the door behind her, the one she guarded like Cerberus at the gates of Tartarus, clicked open and revealed Max Wellington, all five foot six inches of self-righteous asshole.

The three men skirted around the flustered secretary and backed the mayor into his office. Rabble slammed the door behind them and locked it before turning to Max, an unreadable promise in his eyes.

"What's this about?" Max demanded, his face flushed red with indignation.

"Where is Skye?" Dash asked, his tone neutral.

Rabble admired how Dash maintained his composure because *composed* was the last thing Rabble felt.

Max snorted. "How should I know? She ran off after you—"

"Cut the crap," Rabble spat. "You knew she would be there. You planned that shit show so she would hear everything, all so you could drive a permanent wedge between us."

Dash and Delcan glowered, the disgust evident in their eyes, and Max backed away another step, putting his ostentatious leather executive chair between them.

"Where is Skye?" Rabble growled low in his throat.

That barely contained fury spilled through his clenched jaw. It wouldn't be long until Rabble lunged for the man. As if he could sense Rabble's hold on his control slipping, Declan moved to block him and encouraged Dash to continue. They needed answers quickly. Somewhere in the recesses of his mind, Rabble knew if he attacked Max, any chance of finding Skye would drastically decrease. He breathed deeply and reined in his rage, coiling it tightly in his chest, right next to his heart.

"I haven't seen her!" Max shouted. "Gayle said she spoke with her, that Skye was beginning to see the merit of marrying Dylan. She said Skye had big news to share with us at the house later tonight."

"Dylan?" Declan frowned, then used his most confident voice to lie in the hope of tricking Max into revealing something, anything, that would help them. "I wasn't under the impression marriage was on the table, based on what she told us about him. From my understanding, that relationship was over before it even started."

Max tugged at his shirt collar, loosening the tie that reminded Rabble of a noose. "Yes, well, Dylan never really took her seriously. He insisted she was simply playing hard to get. Women are like that. He's considered her his fiancé since college. His father and I, well, we just sort of encouraged him to continue pursuing her. I knew she'd come around eventually."

Rabble's stomach rolled again. He might truly throw up all over the man.

Dash crossed the space between them, cornering the mayor against a bookshelf behind his desk. He leaned down, face mere inches away from the mayor's sweaty face, and growled, "She is a *human being*, you sick son of a bitch."

Declan joined his brother, his usual easy-going nature nowhere to be found. Together, they created an impenetrable wall.

"Sounds to me like you have a real hard time letting your grown daughter make her own choices. Makes me wonder how far you'd go to get her back under your thumb."

"There better not be a single hair on her head out of place," Rabble said.

For a moment, his mouth fell open, and Max blanched. "She's my daughter. Why would I hurt her?"

Rabble snorted. The fact that Max couldn't see how his actions broke his daughter's heart every day for twenty-six years made Rabble realize it didn't matter what he said; Max would deflect it. He refused to take responsibility and would never be at fault for anything, ever.

Declan shook his head in disbelief, his mouth opening to tell the mayor exactly what he thought of him, but Rabble stopped him with a quick shake of his head.

Rabble's tone came out firm and flat, "We're done here."

As one, Rabble & Bros. Security team turned away from the revolting man, if he could even be considered a man, and not a ruthless snake.

They waited to speak until they stood before their trucks. Declan clapped Rabble on the shoulder. "I don't like what we heard about this Dylan. If he still thinks he has a chance with her, he's at the top of my list. Unrequited love is such a bitch. Tends to bring out the crazy in people."

A drifting cloud momentarily blotted out the moon and Rabble shook his head.

"Maybe, but Max gave himself away. Skye *loathed* that house. If she has such big news to share tonight, my bet is that's where we'll find her. And based on what we saw at the cottage, she didn't go there willingly."

Dash unlocked his truck. "Let's go get Skye."

Dash's hazel eyes met Rabble's, and the promise that shone in those depths settled Rabble's heart just a little. No matter what happened next, there were no other men he'd rather have with him than the two walking beside him.

Rabble nodded. "Let's go get my woman."

Chapter 24

Skye

Skye sat on the pink floral comforter adorning the twin bed, and stared into nothing longer than she should have. She had the surreal sensation that this was all some elaborate prank and someone would soon to let her in on the joke. Though she had no difficulty believing Dylan and her stepmother were capable of this, something so vile and repulsive that it turned her stomach. Her instincts warred with each other, freeze or flight.

Either way, she had to find a way out of the house and warn Rabble. They'd already drugged her once. She had no doubt they would do it again, and whatever shady officiant Gayle paid off for this farce of a wedding, Skye didn't trust they would care whether she gave verbal consent to be married.

Her eyes drifted to the vibrant pink garment bag hanging on the closet door. She had worked with Elyza long enough to recognize the long, protective bag for formal gowns. A bad feeling engulfed her. Driven by morbid curiosity, Skye took light steps to the closet and slowly, cautiously, pulled down the gaudy golden zipper. She sucked in a sharp breath as inch by inch she exposed horrible heaping layers of taffeta and chiffon. The monstrosity of long yards of fabric came together in sharp corners and puffy sleeves. Light-headedness overcame her as she struggled to pull air into her lungs. She wanted to scream and rage against the hideous creation, to burn the damn thing.

Skye slowly backed away from the dress as if it could grow fangs and rip into her. The window began looking more and more like a viable option, her *only* real option. She fantasized ripping the white gown into strips, tying them together, and using the makeshift rope to repel down the two-story drop. The beginning of an insane plan began to form in her mind and she shoved it to the back of her brain to mull-over.

Terror and years of obedience, to a fault, warred with her desire for freedom and her knowledge that none of this was okay. Worry gnawed at her, and her teeth tore nervously at her bottom lip. She had never been the type of person to choose fight or even flight. No, she always froze. Just like now.

"Think, Skye," she muttered to herself as she paced, keeping to the opposite side of the room and far away from that hideous dress as possible.

Two days ago, Skye wouldn't have doubted Rabble would come for her, no matter where she was in the world. But after she ran away from him, she wasn't so sure anymore. Rabble might be lost to her completely now. Not to mention she'd ignored every single one of his phone calls, text messages, and voicemails. Maybe he wouldn't even care to look for her.

Their friends had enough going on with the upcoming parade and the concern for Bekah's safety. The likelihood of anyone knowing she'd been taken against her will was slim, and that knowledge alone was enough to tear down a few more blocks of her resolve and sanity.

The door clicked open, and Skye whirled around, hurrying to put as much distance between her and the intruder as she could. Dylan strutted through the door, his self-assurance proceeding him like the peacocks at the animal sanctuary, preening and full of themselves.

He leaned against the door, making sure it closed securely behind him. Fear shivered down her spine. She had never seen this particular look on his face before. The gleam in his eye was pure satisfaction at seeing his prey cornered and helpless.

Skye pulled herself up to her full height and squared her shoulders to make herself look bigger, more like a threat. She wished she could meet his eyes, to stare him down with all of her fury, but she couldn't quite force herself to meet his gaze for longer than a few seconds. Long moments passed in silence as they sized each other up. Whatever Dylan saw made him smirk a little more. He was nearly licking his lips in excitement.

"I hope you like the dress." His gaze flicked to the garment bag that hung open, the poofy skirt threatening to spill out and pool on the floor.

Skye's face twisted. "It's awful."

As Dylan drew his eyebrows together, his lips twisted in disdain. "I chose it myself."

"Well, it's horrendous." Everything else she wanted to say wouldn't quite convey the hatred she had for him and his dress.

Dylan's smile boarded on a grimace, "I know you aren't in love with this idea right now, but you'll come around. I'll be a good husband. I'll help you accept it, to take on your role, and we'll be truly happy. Did you honestly expect me to walk away for good? You need me, Skye."

Skye's blood boiled and her ability to hold her tongue vanished, "I'm not struggling, you imbecile, and yes! I thought I'd never see you again. That's what normal people do when they break up."

She regretted her outburst almost immediately. He didn't deserve the satisfaction of her answers.

"So naïve. You can't escape the life you were born into. Seeing you for the first time at college, knowing I needed to pursue you was painful. I must say though..." He leered at her, making her feel exposed in her leggings and tie-dyed T-shirt, "I warmed up to the idea of marrying you quite quickly."

Dylan exhaled a small sigh and wrangled his expression back to bland disinterest. "You and I are both just pawns. The difference is I've accepted my position, and I don't think the life we'll build together will be that awful at all."

Like oil-slicked claws, he raked his gaze over her, and the filth of his words coating her skin made her want a shower.

"I've never cared about my father's job. He wanted to be mayor, not me. He and Gayle can scheme all they want; I want no part in this."

"Too bad, sweet-cheeks." He stalked toward her, caging her against the wall with his arms, the smell of her stepmother's pot roast and sweet tea on his breath. "The sooner you accept your role in this family, the better. Between your father and mine, they've built up a little political empire. They have plans already in motion. The next step is you putting on that white dress, and we get married. The officiant will be here within the hour. And Skye, you know what I'm most excited about?"

"You're going to tell me whether I want to know or not." Her voice trembled, and she hated herself for it.

He leaned down, his lips brushing the curve of her neck, upward, making her shiver. His hot breath rushed out against her ear. "Taking that wedding dress off."

Skye didn't think; she just reacted. One moment Dylan's mouth and words were terrorizing her. The next moment, he kneeled before her on the floor, his hands tucked tightly around his privates. Her knee smarted a bit from where she struck him.

"You bitch!" he screeched, reaching for her.

She scrambled out of the way and backed toward the window. Gingerly, Dylan rose to his feet and limped out the door, slamming it behind him. She realized two things at once: She really was going to throw up, and climbing out of the window was the only chance she had to escape.

Chapter 25

Rabble

Night had officially fallen, its multitude of stars dotting the sky as Declan and Dash drove their trucks down the road Rabble knew so well. As one, they hit their headlights, allowing the beams to go dark and they continued on, driving by instinct and the light of the moon. Rabble tried to focus on anything that might keep him sane on the drive. Through the open window, the song of the crickets and frogs hiding in the weeds reached him. Fireflies, though less than he remembered, danced across the shadowy stalks of grass, their little glowing lights like beacons, urged them onward.

Declan pulled the truck off the road, next to Dash, just before the bright white gravel driveway leading to the mayor's house. Rabble gripped the seat buckle, his fingers cramping with the effort to keep from pressing down and releasing the lock. Skye was somewhere in that house. He could feel it.

Dash jumped out of his truck and jogged over, speaking through Declan's open window.

"How do you want to play this?"

Declan's usual goofy, joking personality was replaced by a more serious version, a man on a mission, with a purpose and focused drive. This version of Declan would do whatever it took to win, to beat the odds, to emerge victorious.

Declan kept his eyes glued to the long driveway and the house beyond it. "We have a lot of unknowns here."

Rabble understood the apprehension in Declan's voice. They lacked an absolute shit-ton of necessary information, like the layout of the house and property, Skye's location, and any other active players who may be part of this fucked-up scenario. Rabble was sure of exactly one thing: Skye was here, and he wasn't leaving without her.

"Wait a second. I've got an idea." Declan grinned, then proceeded to fill them in on a classic Declan MacAlister Hail Mary.

Thirty minutes later, Rabble crouched under the thick green leaves of the lilac bush. This gift from Skye's grandmother had grown over the years since watching over them from its sentinel position by the fence. His heart ached for those long-ago days.

When Declan explained the plan to them, Rabble thought he'd crossed over from a creative thinker to something closer to an evil genius. This plan was so far from what they were used to, what they'd planned and executed for years, that Rabble thought it just might work.

From under the giant bush, he could barely see Declan walking right up to the front door. The sound of furious knocking came across the yard as Declan pounded on the door, cursing and slurring, a mostly empty whiskey bottle gripped firmly in one hand.

Dylan, the senator's son, opened the door and frowned at the interruption. "What the fuck, man?"

Declan's slurred words were barely audible to Rabble, but he could just make out his friend doing his best impersonation of a pissed-off drunkard.

Dylan stepped outside, not a hair out of place and his black suit jacket impeccable. He flailed his arms at Declan, shooing him like a stray dog.

On cue, Dash jogged up the driveway, apologetically raising his hand as he came to Declan's side and grabbed hold of his shoulder. Stumbling away, Declan swung at Dash, who ducked and Dylan took a strong fist to the jaw.

That was the signal. And what a beautiful signal it was.

In a stooped crouch, Rabble raced across the lawn and skirted around the windows until he reached the backdoor. When he opened it with a quiet click, he sent up a quick prayer of thanks for well-oiled hinges. He entered the house, muscles coiled, ready to strike, but he stopped every few steps to listen for Gayle or her staff.

During his life, he'd never been in a house that felt less like a home, and that included the hovel of his boyhood. The space, sterile and silent like a museum, made him a tad nervous. Rabble forced himself to clear each room, ensuring Skye wasn't tucked away in some random closet or chained to the stove. His mind ran rampant with off-the-wall scenarios, and he shook his head to clear the what ifs away.

After searching the entire first floor and finding no sign of Skye, Gayle, or anyone else while Dylan and Declan shouted at each other in the near distance, Rabble clenched his jaw and forced his muscles to obey him. He focused on taking the stairs one at a time though the driving pounding in his heart screamed for him to ascend the stairs faster. Despite his need to reach her, he wouldn't risk putting Skye in more danger because he couldn't think clearly.

The second floor had four closed doors around a common sitting area, the obnoxious floral pattern on the settee and sofa were enough to make him cringe. Rabble groaned. Each door offered an opportunity for someone to hide Skye, or themselves. He took a deep steadying breath and twisted the knob on the first door. Time to find out exactly what type of messed-up the Wellingtons hid in this ridiculous mausoleum of a house.

The first door opened without a sound, revealing a cream-colored bedroom, the expensive four-post bed perfectly made up, not a wrinkle in sight. The second room must have been Max's home office, the furniture all crafted from that same dark wood in the first room. The smell of cigar smoke hung faintly in the air, and Rabble quickly shut the door.

Please let this be the lucky door.

Rabble reached for the knob, but the handle didn't budge. Locked. Rabble's heart picked up. Deep in his bones, he sensed he'd found her.

Again, Rabble sent up a prayer of thanks for the skills he acquired during his days in the service—and the less savory ones he'd gathered before that. He pulled out the lock-pick set he always carried with him and attacked the doorknob. No stupid locked door would stand between him and Skye. The moment the latch snicked, Rabble was back on his feet and through the door.

His eyes took in the entire room all at once, a room designed and decorated for a young girl. Pale-pink and lacy white frills filled the space, suggesting elegance, picture-perfect expectations, and polite manners. He didn't see a trace of the Skye he'd known as a child, the one who loved dirt and flowers and reading under the lilac bush amid the spring grasses.

A long, bright-pink bag hung limply on the back of the closet door. Inside, the shelves were bare, not a stich of clothing to be found. He searched every corner, but the room was unoccupied.

Why would they lock an empty room?

Rabble's gaze caught on the twin-size bed. Tied to the metal bedpost, a thick swath of fabric made a thick knot, before disappearing out the window. Rabble ran to the ledge and peered out, shock and awe making him sputter at the sight below him.

Clinging to a rope made of sheets and torn bits of white fabric he could only assume belonged to the hideous concoction she wore, was Skye. She'd made it about halfway down, her eyes clenched tightly against the distance between her and the safety of the ground. Curse words flew from her lips in hushed whispers, and he doubted she even knew she was speaking.

"Skye," Rabble called, his voice pitched low to avoid being heard by anyone else who might be in the house. "I'm going to pull you up."

She shook her head, he tried again. "Skye, it's me. I'm going to keep you safe, okay? Just hold on and don't let go."

This time, she nodded, and her white-knuckled grip on the makeshift rope became impossibly tighter.

He braced himself against the window frame and grasped the rope. Hand over hand, he hauled her up. Even though Skye was slender, the strain of pulling her body upward wrenched at his muscles, and he breathed deeply, straining to keep his pace smooth and steady as she gradually moved closer to the second-floor opening. At the top, Rabble grasped her seeking hand and hauled her inside until they lay sprawled on the floor together, Skye slightly atop him and shaking.

Rabble pulled her tightly against his chest, his arms sliding around her in a protective embrace that she nestled into. She jerked back from him and Rabble struggled not to reach for her, to bring her back into his arms.

"No, Rabble, you can't be here," Skye's eyes widened and her voice broke with terror, "they said—they said they'd kill you."

Rabble's relief rumbled through his chest, "Honey, I won't die easy. I've got too much to live for."

Skye relaxed back into his hold and Rabble rubbed circles over her back until her shaking subsided and she sat back on her heels.

"Get this thing off of me." She flailed her arms, indicating the back of the wedding dress, her voice rising into a panic. "Get it off, please."

"Okay, okay." Rabble sat up, trying to soothe her.

He hadn't been sure what to expect when he found her, but this wasn't exactly it. She spun around, and he swore at the multitude of tiny buttons that ran down the back.

Fuck it.

Grasping both sides of the dress, muscles protesting as the fabric sundered, and he tore the dress from her shoulders, shredding it until it lay in pieces around her. Skye scrambled to her feet, shedding the rest of the dress as she went. She hopped out of it and fled to the opposite side of the room. Rabble whipped off his t-shirt, passing it to her cautiously and keeping his movements predictable. He had no idea what she'd been through during her time with Dylan, but being trapped or held against your will affected people in different ways.

Skye looked down at herself as if noticing for the first time that she stood in her bra and panties. "They took my clothes."

Fisting his t-shirt in her hand, she lifted it to her nose, inhaled deeply, and exhaled slowly before slipping the shirt on over her head. His shirt didn't cover her completely, but it hid the important bits.

"Skye, did he . . .?"

"No. He's a vile piece of shit. But no."

Rabble picked up the awful dress and hurled it out the window, watching as the gaudy material caught the wind and slowed just slightly before tumbling to the ground.

Skye sank to the floor as if her legs would no longer hold her. Going to her, he kneeled down, opening his arms to her if she wanted his touch. She burrowed into his embrace like she couldn't seem to get close enough.

"Skye?" His voice was grave, emotion choking his throat and burning his eyes.

With little hiccupping cries, her shoulders rose and fell intermittently. Then the small motions turned into full-fledged, heart-wrenching sobs, and she buried her face against his neck to muffle her cries. As she fell into him, he absorbed her weight, giving her a safe place to fall apart. He locked his arms around her in a strong, reassuring embrace.

"It's okay, sweetheart," he murmured into her hair. He found himself whispering nonsensical promises and words to console her as her body shook and shuddered.

Did they have time to sit in her room while she broke down? Probably not. Was that going to stop him from giving her every moment she needed to process this? Also, no. Rabble trusted his brothers to handle Dylan and Gayle. He also trusted them to deal with the police when they showed up. For the moment, he was exactly where he needed to be.

"You came for me?" she finally gasped out, her heart showing in every broken word.

"Always." Rabble kissed her hair and rocked her gently. "Always."

Chapter 26

Skye

What followed were the longest hours of Skye's life, including the numerous times her parents made her retake the ACT, trying to improve her already impressive score each time.

When her stepmother came in and demanded her clothes, Skye refused. But Gayle threatened to send Dylan to retrieve them, and Skye shuddered, the thought of that man's hands and eyes on her body too much to contend with. That she'd ever been with him was enough to make her sick.

She had handed over her leggings and t-shirt, her lip quivering as Gayle forced her into that wedding dress. If given the time and resources, Skye could have come up with a different escape plan. Her descent down the side of the house had started smoothly enough. The knot held, which had been her biggest concern. But when she made it halfway down, her arms and legs burned with strain. Based on the way her muscles pulled and burned, she doubted she'd be able to move much the next day. Thick red bands stood out against her palms from where she had wrapped the fabric tightly around them.

As Skye followed Rabble into the hallway, she held on tightly to his arm so he couldn't vanish with her hope. She tucked herself close to his back, stepping lightly where he stepped, her muscles quivering with the need to bolt. Skye attuned herself to every twitch Rabble made as he led her slowly down the hall, stopping to listen often and searching the area with practiced eyes.

Rationally, she understood the extra time he took mattered, but that didn't stop her nerves from thrumming violently. Impatience overrode her, and she stepped from behind Rabble, desperation fueling her movements. She closed the space between her old room and the stairs in record time, her steps light and silent on the cream carpet. Her gaze flew back to where Rabble now stood, only a few inches behind her.

"I know you want to leave, Skye, and I will get you out," he said with whispered conviction, "but you've got to stay with me. I can't lose you again."

His voice cracked, breaking through the sound of her hammering heart and settling against her panicked psyche like a temporary balm. She closed her eyes and inhaled Rabble's scent, ingrained in the threads of his shirt covering her body. Though it did little to hide her lower half, it was more than she had before and ten million times better than that wedding dress. Skye took another breath, then another, until she opened her eyes and nodded, falling back behind Rabble as they slowly descended the stairs.

Rabble stopped at the base of the stairs, his body going taut like a bow string waiting to snap. Voices sounded from nearby, likely from the den where Gayle held court with her subjects. Rabble backed Skye into the wall and crept forward. The urge to grasp Rabble's arm and keep him from continuing forward pounded through her.

"Wait," her whispered plea barely sounded aloud, yet Rabble turned his head slightly toward her, letting her know she had his attention.

"Dylan..." Skye grimaced at his name, tasting the acid of it on her tongue. "He said he'd kill you. He said—"

Rabble's answering murmur did little to calm her nerves. "He's been neutralized."

What the hell did that mean?

Voices reached them again. Skye recognized Gayle's, and her blood ran cold. She didn't know who the other voice belonged to, but if they spoke so casually with Gayle, she doubted their strength of character.

"Oh, she'll be ready any minute now." Gayle's southern Missouri dialect sounded lilting, almost musical. "And Dylan should be back shortly. He's chatting with someone at the door."

Disgust barreled through Skye. She might vomit. Or punch something. Possibly both.

The seconds ticked by unbearably slow as Gayle and the mystery man spoke of inconsequential topics—the weather, the upcoming parade, the statistics for the local sports teams. Each passing moment settled like a stone on Skye's laboring heart, and she considered the toll this entire experience had taken on her body. She could concern herself with that later though. She just needed out of this damn house.

"Shall we go see what's keeping Dylan?" Gayle's syrupy sweet tone held a sharp, irritated edge. Anyone else may not have noticed it, but Skye had heard that same tone time and time again.

Footsteps grew distant as Gayle led her guest toward the front door. Rabble refused to move for a minute, his body remaining poised for a threat while shielding Skye's body with his own. At long last, he grasped her hand lightly in his and pulled her along, through the dining room and toward the massive kitchen near the back of the house. He paused before entering, his eyes roaming over the stainless-steel appliances.

"Do you know if anyone else is in the house, Skye?" Rabble muttered, refusing to take his eyes from their roving for even a moment.

Skye worried at her bottom lip. Several years had passed since she'd lived at her parent's house, but... "The maids would have gone home already. Marsha, their cook, may still be here, but this late at night?"

Skye snuck up on tiptoe, cramming herself in front of Rabble to see through the small plastic bubble near the top of the swinging door. He grumbled, but otherwise remained silent. The appliances gleamed in the dim light over the stove microwave, illuminating the spotless surfaces and quiet kitchen.

"I think Marsha's gone home," Skye said.

"Let's go." Rabble pushed them through the door as silently as he could.

Freedom, called to her from just feet away, pulsing through Skye like a rhythmic call. She hurried after Rabble, her gaze focused solely on the dark night visible through the glass panes on the back door. Darting for it, Skye burst into the night air before Rabble could stop her. Skye took in a great gasp of air, gulping it down like a person lost in the desert and longing for water.

Her relief lasted all of thirty seconds before shrieking rent the air and she froze again, her muscles tensing with that freeze instinct that grated at her nerves. As he had inside, Rabble led her in their charge around the house, toward the awful noise that rose in pitch and vigor. Skye stumbled to a stop behind Rabble, her mouth popping open as her jaw dropped and she clutched Rabble's arm.

Skye barely noticed the still warm stones against the bottoms of her tender feet, the heat collected during the sunny day dissipating slowly with the cooler night. She didn't register Rabble, beyond knowing with certainty that he had not and would not leave her side for as long as she stood still and processed the scene before her.

Dylan lay curled on his side on the grassy lawn, moaning pitifully. Staring down at him, Skye's utter distain for that cowardly worm rose again, her disgust choking her. Another man, one she didn't recognize, sat in false calm on the front stoop, his fingers linked behind his head as if he were about to recline back and watch television. While his face appeared passive, sweat stains soaked through his button-down shirt. Nearby, her stepmother lay face down on the lawn, screeching like an angry hen. Her scrawny arms splayed out to the sides and she kept flapping her hands like she could take flight. The twins, practically growling, loomed like avenging angels over Gayle and Dylan. In the distance, the lone siren of the on-duty police officer sounded, growing closer with each second, the light of its siren breaking through the dark.

Through it all, Skye felt far away, like she viewed the entire surreal situation through a distant lens. And yet she was also painfully aware of every moment passing by, of the warm summer night breeze on her bare thighs, of the dirty violated feeling from having her choices stripped from her.

Obscenities filled the air, startling Skye, and she couldn't help but seek out the source of such profanity, her head tilting as she listened past the rushing white noise that hindered her hearing. Those words came from the last place she expected, spewing like venom from the lips of Gayle, southern hospitality personified. The sudden need to chuckle surged through Skye until it bubbled up and out of her, and she tucked her hand in front of her mouth as if to stifle the sound.

The damage had already been done though.

Gayle turned her vitriol on Skye and Rabble. "You!" she hissed.

Skye shivered at the sound of pure hatred in her stepmother's voice. She didn't understand where the woman's intense feelings came from. She and Gayle had never had a normal mother-daughter relationship, she assumed, but did she really deserve this level of loathing?

Whatever Gayle continued to shout faded into the sound of the approaching siren as the officer on duty pulled into the drive, the flashing blue and red strobe lights doing nothing to alleviate the headache pounding in Skye's temples. Instead of a deputy, Sheriff Joe Armanan stepped out of his patrol cruiser, his black cowboy hat pulled low on his head. He took in the scene with wariness, his baby-blue eyes narrowing on the key players and their respective positions in the yard.

Before the sheriff could get a word out, Max Wellington's Mercedes-Benz whipped into the drive, the suspension protesting his failure to slow down as he left the road and came onto the gravel of the driveway. His breaks squalled, the sound grating on Skye's nerves and surprising her. Max had a special place in his life for his car. That he would abuse it so didn't set right with her.

He exited his car in a hurry, leaving the door hanging open behind him.

"Maxwell!" Gayle's shrill voice pierced the air.

Max pointed a meaty finger at his wife and snapped, "Don't you say a fucking word."

Skye pulled closer to Rabble, that fight or flight feeling returning to her limbs with her father's arrival. She willed the humming in her ears to quiet so she could hear as he stormed toward the cruiser and jabbed his finger at the sheriff's chest, getting in the older man's face to the best of his ability. Considering Max stood about five inches shorter, the way he tried to intimidate the sheriff was both impressive and incredibly foolish.

"Armanan, I demand you arrest these men!" Max turned, sweeping an all-encompassing hand across the yard, catching Rabble & Bros. Security within his statement.

"What for?" Sheriff Armanan asked, his voice tired and a tad bewildered.

"Assault, for starters! Look at them, standing over my wife and Dylan like no good thugs. I'm sure we can come up with a few more charges that would stick too." With a self-confident smirk, Max turned back to the sheriff and dipped his voice, ensuring only the sheriff could hear his next words.

"No!" The scream that tore from Skye's throat scratched and scraped the entire way.

Rabble moved even closer to her, pushing her gently behind his back with a reassuring hand.

"Skye Wellington? That you girl?" Sheriff Armanan asked, tipping his hat back as he squinted into the darkness.

"Sheriff, may I speak with you?" Rabble asked, his voice steady despite the simmering violence that ran just beneath the surface.

Skye didn't know if everyone else could hear the threat or if she just knew Rabble that well.

When Sheriff Armanan motioned Rabble and Skye join him at the rear of the cruiser, Rabble stayed protectively between her and Max as they approached, lending her the warmth she lacked so thoroughly.

"Sir, my name is Matthew Raden," Rabble said. "I'm a private investigative security officer with Rabble & Bros. Security, and those two men are my partners, Declan and Dash MacAlister. Dylan Santoro removed Miss Wellington from her home under duress, and he and Gayle Wellington have been holding her here without consent."

"Miss Wellington, you got anything to add to that?" Sheriff Armanan's voice held a note of skepticism, though only a note.

Does he also know the type of secrets my parents and Dylan have?

"Everything he said is true." Skye's voice shook, and she cleared her throat to no avail. "I, I—Dylan drugged me. He said—" A sob escaped and she tried to hold it in with the rest of the tidal wave of emotions threatening to overcome her. But when Rabble's fingers found hers, she squeezed his large hand with all the strength she could muster. "He said if I didn't marry him, he'd kill Rabble. And..." She couldn't look at Gayle, her betrayal adding another layer of agony to her already bruised and battered heart. "And Gayle made me—"

"That's not true!" Gayle snarled from behind them, making Skye flinch involuntarily. "That ungrateful bitch—"

"Shut your mouth, Gayle!" Dylan and Max shouted at the same time with varying amounts of panic coloring their voices.

Sheriff Armanan sighed heavily and waved toward Declan and Dash still holding their positions, the older man's eyes taking in everything from the nervous twitching of the officiant avoiding eye contact from the stairs to Dylan squirming uncomfortably on the ground. "You boys interested in being deputies for a night?"

"You can't do that!" Max barked.

The sheriff seemed to grow in height and size right before Skye's eyes. "I can deputize whomever the hell I want, *Mayor.*"

Declan let out a whoop. "It's a dream come true!"

Dash held back a bit as he firmly told the sheriff, "Yes, sir."

As one unit, the twins hauled up the officiant and Gayle, pushing them toward the Sheriff's police cruiser.

"Mayor, it seems I don't have enough seats in the cruiser for the shit show you've managed to create. Shame, if I had another officer that sure would be a help. Now, will you drive yourself to the station for questioning, or do I need to hog-tie you to the roof?" Sheriff Armanan grinned; his gaze positively feral as he enjoyed every minute of this.

"Got a runner!" Declan hollered as he stuffed Gayle into the backseat of the cruiser.

"Shit!" Dash sprinted after Dylan, who had disappeared noisily into the brush.

Skye leaned against the trunk of the cruiser, her legs going wobbly and threatening to drop her on her ass. The rest of her body seemed to follow suit, the strength draining from her limbs like the tide ebbing from the shore, she slowly worked her way to the ground and sat against the car's rear bumper.

"Skye," Rabble crouched in front of her, his brows furrowing as she squinted, trying to pull him into focus. "Hell," he said sounding suddenly far away. "Sheriff, I'm assume we're done here?"

The Sheriff must have agreed because the next thing Skye knew, Rabble tentatively took her in his arms, his touch and eyes asking for her permission, and she melted into him, her muscles languid and limp. He helped her into the front seat of his truck, pushing aside his vest and buckling her up before going around to the other side. He hurried to the driver's seat, and she grabbed the heather-gray vest, draping it over her lap, her fingers brushing the soft material. She absently noted how much she'd undervalued Rabble's get-shit-done attitude as he threw the truck in drive, worked his way quickly around the circular drive, and back up the gravel road to the two-lane blacktop. They passed through Shiloh Hills, taking the only road south toward Grand Rock, the largest city nearby with a decent medical clinic.

He didn't falter in his determination to get her medical attention as quickly as possible. She didn't care. As long as Rabble held onto her, she could let her mind wander into a quiet space where no thoughts formed. Arm around her shoulders, Rabble guided her through the clinic's front doors and held her hand the entire time they spoke with the receptionist. Vague awareness touched at the edges of Skye's consciousness, and she had to force herself to focus and respond to questions directed at her.

The nurse led them into a triage room that smelled like antiseptic and rubbing alcohol. Skye stared distractedly at a ridiculous poster of a male and female body beside each other, both relieved of their skin and muscles while they smiled placidly. She felt ill just looking at it.

As nurses and a female doctor volleyed questions at her, Skye was grateful beyond measure that she could answer no to almost every appalling thing they asked. That she had spoken up to keep Rabble by her side for the entire ordeal gave her another measure of peace. The nurse on staff gave her a reassuring smile and offered a set of sea-foam-colored scrubs to replace Rabble's T-shirt, which, while serviceable, left her legs exposed to the cold hospital air. She hesitated to return Rabble's soft cotton T-shirt though, clinging to it like a safety blanket.

Sensing her discomfort and indecision, Rabble took the scrub shirt for himself, looking to her for a nod of approval. Skye sighed as she hugged Rabble's shirt tightly against her, the smell and feel of its cotton comfort.

"If you'd like to step out, sir," the nurse said, scowling at Rabble.

Skye's jaw clenched and she willed her boiling blood to cool. Rabble wasn't at fault for any of this. Couldn't they see he saved her?

"Skye?" Rabble asked. "I'll be right outside if you want me to step out." His gaze met hers as he waited for her decision.

How far would he go for her right now? Would he take her away if she asked? Would he stay with her and defy the nurse?

Skye forced her lips into a small smile. "I'm just going to slip on these pants. Give me five seconds."

He nodded and stepped away, drawing the curtain closed behind him. Skye dressed as quickly as possible, tugging on the pants and fumbling with the drawstring, comforted to be fully covered. True to his word, Rabble returned less than half a minute later.

At the doctor's direction, she sat atop the examination table and shifted uncomfortably on the crinkling white paper. "I think..." Her voice broke, and she cleared her throat. "I think he drugged me. I don't remember anything after opening my front door. Until I woke up."

Skye glanced nervously at Rabble standing stoically by her side, moving as needed to remain out of the doctor's way. He clenched his jaw, the anger unmistakable in his flashing storm-cloud-gray eyes. While his fury smoldered below the surface, Skye knew he would never direct that violence he kept on such a tight leash, at her.

The doctor returned to the room after a few minutes and leaned against the cabinets in the corner of the room. "At this point, I'm recommending rest. That is the number one cure for everything churning in your brain right now."

Skye didn't doubt the doctor's recommendation. Exhaustion weighed on her, and all she wanted was to close her eyes. She didn't protest when Rabble gently held her hand and helped her onto her feet, his other hand settling on her lower back protectively. Walking beside him on their way out of the clinic, Skye felt the comforting weight of his warm hand on her back, keeping her steady and warm. As they drove back to Shiloh Hills, she alternated between watching out the side window and observing Rabble's intense focus as he drove. Before Skye knew it, they were parked in front of her cottage.

Conflicting emotions spun in her head, making her dizzy. She wanted to go inside, desperately so. She wanted to burrow under her covers, in her own bed, with her own things around her, to remember that she was a grown woman with the ability and right to make her own choices.

She also wanted to avoid the place like the plague. She didn't want to see where Dylan had been, remember what he had done. That she hesitated to go inside at all made her furious. This was her home, dammit. What right did he have to take it away from her?

He didn't.

Jaw set with determination, Skye threw open the truck door and slid down from the seat, making sure to step lightly on the side runner so she didn't crumple to the ground completely. The driver's door opened and shut, and Skye waited until Rabble stood beside her before taking a step toward her home. He stayed next to her, letting her set their pace and offering silent support every step of the way. Skye was pleasantly surprised when her legs supported her and she didn't land flat on her face. She let herself in the front door, and Rabble followed.

"Elyza and the others came by after we found you and knew it wasn't Bekah's ex." Rabble smiled fondly. "They wanted you to come home to something a bit more calming."

Skye let go of the breath she'd been holding, and her shoulders felt lighter. Though it was still the dark early morning hours of the night, the scent of lasagna hung heavy in the air, the aroma of melted cheeses and tomato sauce with garlic and other yummy seasonings made her mouth water. A sticky note hung on the fridge, explaining the girls had made dinner and requesting her to call when she was ready. Elyza knew her well. Someone had plugged a new fragrance pack into the kitchen outlet. The wonderfully warm smell of cinnamon rolls paired with the savory aroma lingering from the prepared dinner, a far cry from the sweet floral scent from earlier in the day.

The sense of warmth that enveloped the house lightened something in her chest, and tears stung her eyes. Her entire life, Skye wished for friends who would have her back no matter what, friends who she could share with, the good and the bad, and they'd expect nothing in return. At one time, Rabble had been that friend, her confidant in everything.

She glanced toward her bedroom, then back to Rabble.

One of the barstools tucked under the peninsula countertop softly scraped the tile floor as Rabble pulled it out and took a seat. "I'm here."

A small thankful smile turned the corners of her mouth up. "Thank you."

She struggled not to rush through her bedtime routine, but she changed into fuzzy pajamas and brushed her teeth with extra vigor. She ran a brush through her hair until the strands were neat and shiny, not a tangle in sight, washed her face, and lathered lotion over every inch of skin she could reach. For all the world, Skye felt as normal as possible when she stepped back into the living room where Rabble sat at the kitchen bar as if he had nowhere else to be.

"Better?" he asked, the gentleness of his tone made those pesky tears threaten to spill again.

Skye nodded. "Much."

Standing, he took his time walking toward her, giving her the space to say no, to tell him to back off or freeze. She stood still, waiting for him, wanting him to come closer, to pull her into his arms. She needed the security, the tenderness of his embrace. But he didn't pull her to him. Instead, Rabble lovingly traced his thumb along her chin.

"I can't stay." His whisper was distressed as he dipped and touched his forehead to hers.

As much as she wanted him with her, she understood. In some ways, she even agreed. Too much had passed between them since they'd been together last. Pain and frustration had intermixed with love and hope.

Emotions that hadn't been as noticeable before now demanded to be acknowledged.

She nodded, though the thought of him leaving, of being alone, set her heart racing. "I know." Squeezing her eyes shut, Skye tried to shut out the frustration at the waver in her voice.

Rabble raised their joined hands to his lips, and whispered, "I can call someone if you want? Elyza would jump at the opportunity for a sleepover."

Skye huffed out a tired laugh, wariness tugging at her insistently. "Yeah, she probably would. Do...do you think she's awake?"

"She will be. I'll be here until she comes. You're safe, baby. You can rest."

The crawling panic that itched her skin and squeezed her heart lessened some, letting her breathe, albeit unsteadily, again. Her legs wobbled, the sensation of static in her nerves making her need to lie down. Skye nodded, her movements jerking as she headed to her room.

She practically fell into her bed, tugging the heavy blankets up to her ears while Rabble called and spoke with Elyza from the other room. His muffled voice lulled her as she lay still, feeling the weight of the blankets pressing her into the softness of her sheets. Five minutes later, the front door opened and shut. Elyza's quiet voice drifted through the house, and Skye let a sad smile form on her lips.

Heavy footsteps neared, and Rabble spoke up, making sure she knew who approached her door. Peeking out from under the blankets, she found Rabble a foot away, kneeling beside her bed.

"Elyza's here. She's set up on the couch." His throat bobbed. "I have to go, but I'm always nearby, Skye."

With her lip quivering, she nodded and closed her eyes, the slight pressure of a featherlight kiss grazed her brow. Then his boots grew quieter, followed by the front door opening and closing. The click of the lock sounding so final.

She burrowed back into the cocoon she'd made herself and let her tears soak into her cotton pillowcase. Concealed from the world beneath her many blankets, Skye let sleep carry her away.

Chapter 27

Rabble

R abble yanked the truck door closed with a solid thud, putting more strength behind it than necessary. If he had his way, Rabble wouldn't have left from his place at the kitchen bar in Skye's home but he knew they both needed some level of distance. He didn't know if he could make himself drive away from the curb out front of her house either. Make himself start the truck and drive away from her. He contemplated sitting there all night, his eyes firmly glued to the house and its surroundings. Would she be able to sleep soundly if she knew he sat out front? Would she expect it from him, knowing him as she did? Would it provide a sense of comfort to her?

At least he knew the answer to his ability to pull away from the front of her house, knew the answer as well as he knew his own name. He wasn't strong enough to leave her completely tonight.

Pulling out his cell phone, he tucked the speaker between his ear and shoulder. "Hey, Dash."

"Just a moment. Let me grab Dec."

Through the phone, Rabble heard Dash leaving his room and pounding on a door. Half a minute passed before Rabble heard both brothers through the speaker. His knuckles turned white as he clutched and released the steering wheel in his left hand. He straightened, replacing his shoulder with his hand to hold his phone so he could sit up and observe the hazy darkness of the night.

"What the hell happened after I went inside to find Skye?" Rabble wanted, needed, the missing information to settle into the cracks in the facts he already knew.

Dash's calm and collected demeanor soothed a little of the savage edge that still clung to Rabble's conscious. As Dash delivered fact after fact, he kept to the specifics and left out the unnecessary details. His near monotone voice provided a sort of unexpected peace, his unflappable responses differing greatly from Rabble's and Declan's more heated reactions. Admittedly, Dash's level-headed approach to their emergency encounters may very well be the primary reason any ridiculous plan of Declan's usually went off without a hitch.

Declan interjected as he felt called to, usually to add some inconsequential detail that might have made Rabble roll his eyes if the mission had involved anyone else but Skye. His Skye. From their combined reporting, Rabble gathered the details he missed during his search for her inside the monster house.

Rabble wished he felt like laughing and not growling when Declan described the colorful vocabulary of Mrs. Gayle Wellington from her jail cell.

"The woman truly has a way with curse words, like a well-educated truck driver. I mean, at times she made *me* blush." Declan snorted as he joked.

"You recovered Dylan, I assume?" Rabble asked, knowing the answer already.

Dash wouldn't have failed at bringing Dylan to justice. That worm of a man sat behind bars just as surely as Gayle and the other degenerate who had participated in Skye's abduction and every moment of terror that followed.

"Dash is not fast." Declan snorted, a little further from the speaker than he had been, likely putting space between him and his brother as he said, "He sure is persistent though."

"What about Max?" Rabble asked.

"Oh, he's beyond humiliated," Declan said. "We arrived in town at the most beautiful timing. It was closing time at the bar, so Gayle and Dylan had an audience watching as we hauled their cuffed asses into the sheriff's station. And when Mr. Mayor tried to reassure his voters, this was a misunderstanding, the sheriff threatened Max with a subpoena if he didn't get inside for questioning. Oh, man. I wish you could have seen his red face. The gossip mill is going at full force."

He should be rotting in jail with the rest of them.

Rabble scanned his eyes over the fading darkness again, snagging on the leaves fluttering in the trees and the grass swaying in the quiet breeze. Every single movement was a threat until Rabble decided otherwise.

"How's our girl?" Declan asked, his voice as serious as ever.

"Our girl?" Rabble's eyebrows rose in surprise.

He waited for the statement to make his heart jump or stutter. Instead, it felt right. The words settled in like a salve to his angry heart, and he sighed in relieved reassurance. His brothers would protect Skye with their lives, just as he would for anyone they chose. It was just a foregone conclusion.

"Don't be an ass," Dash said.

Rabble chuckled harshly, sobering as he recalled the hollow look in Skye's eyes when he'd told her he couldn't stay. Everything she'd been through brought out a violence in him he desperately tried to stave off, not wanting to startle her. He wished Dylan were nearby so he could smash the man's face in. He'd violated her space, creating memories that stained the home which should offer her nothing but comfort and peace.

"She's..." Rabble's eyes drifted to the cottage where the last of the lights had gone out. "I don't know. She's quiet and nervous. Withdrawn."

Dash grunted. "It's to be expected, nothing we haven't seen with past clients."

Rabble ground his teeth together, wanting to yell at his brother. This was Skye! She wasn't just any client. Thinking of her in the same type of situation they helped women escape brought his fury roaring back, and he sucked in a breath through gritted teeth.

Rabble promised to keep them updated if anything happened and hung up the phone, hoping both brothers would get some well-deserved sleep.

In the quiet of the early morning, Rabble let his mind drift, even as he kept a watchful eye out. He ached for the uncertainty that clouded her eyes now, the loss of innocence, and sense of security that everyone had before experiencing a violation like this. Part of him hoped she'd ask him to stay, even knowing he wasn't the right sort of person she needed, not with his temper flaring. Regardless of what made sense and what didn't, he wanted to hold her tightly, to protect her with everything he had to give.

For the first time since his confrontation with Max and Dylan in front of Elyza's shop, Rabble let out a deep breath, and the worry in his chest loosened the slightest fraction. Skye was safe. She was in her own bed tonight with Elyza nearby, and Kellyn and Bekah were both secure in their own homes.

Every time Rabble caught a shadow of movement that proved to be nothing more than the night playing tricks with him, he reminded himself there wasn't any immediate danger, not even from Bekah's ex-husband. According to his parole officer, Edward Elnor had still been in California the night the intruder interrupted girl's night. He showed up for a piss test the same day on the other side of the country. With him ruled out as the intruder, Dylan Santoro appeared more and more likely to fit the bill as the person who broke into Bekah's cottage.

Shit would hit the fan in Shiloh Hills' exclusive political circles, perhaps leaking into state politics as well, considering Dylan's influential father. But Rabble didn't care. Let Max, Gayle, and Dylan go down in flames. Hell, let Dylan's senator father go down right alongside them. As long as Skye was safe, they could all burn.

The early morning hours bled into predawn wearing by slowly. Rabble's eyes didn't leave the cottage except to methodically move up and down the silent road, taking in every motion as the moon stretched shadows over lawns and down the street. The first signs of the sun peeked at the very edge of the eastern horizon. When Skye's lights came on at three o'clock in the morning, then again at five, Rabble's his heart broke a bit more. It would be a long while before she would feel okay again. He wished more than anything Skye didn't have to face that harsh reality. At least Elyza could help when the dark became too much.

As the sun ascended into the sky, the midnight blue gave way to pinks and oranges, then a more vibrant light blue. He waited, letting the sky brighten into early morning before turning the key and starting the truck. He tapped out a good morning text message to Skye and hit send before putting the truck into drive and pulling away from the curb.

He would head back to The Sunny Morning Trellis and grab a shower, then a bite from the breakfast buffet, before checking in with Declan and Dash. He had no idea what came next, not after the events of the past couple of days. A sense of certainty stole over him though. Whatever came next, he would never abandon her again.

Chapter 28

Skye

Three days after the shit hit the fan, Skye had deleted countless text messages and voicemails, each one nosier than the last. The people of Shiloh Hills heard through the grapevine about Dylan, Gayle, and even Max and how they'd each been involved in some sinister plot to sell Skye off like a prized sow at the local auction. That the entire town knew so much about her personal business, especially something so awful, made her want to change her phone number and become a hermit. Perhaps Rabble's team could help her establish a new identity, one that wasn't plagued by scandal. With small towns though, you had to take the good with the bad, which included gossip spreading very quickly and everyone thinking it was their collective business to get involved.

The only people she answered were Kellyn and Bekah, largely because they were the only ones who genuinely cared how she was doing. The other messages were from townsfolk poking around for information.

Skye wasn't interested in feeding the town gossip mill further and left those texts mostly unread. Kellyn brought pastries and coffee from the Brick House Cafe. Wrapped in fuzzy blankets, Skye and her three friends talked about anything and everything. Sometimes, they didn't speak at all, letting the space between them warm with the presence of others who cared. Skye soaked it all in, and the knowledge of her friends' love for her settled in her chest, warming her from the inside out.

The twins came by the cottage, too, and Skye welcomed them. They seemed content to join the women, with Declan cracking jokes to help relieve lingering tension. Though when the conversation strayed into emotional territory and tears flowed, the men shifted uncomfortably on the carpet, making bubbles of giggles break out around the room. Dash especially looked like he wished he could be anywhere else but stuck in a room with four crying women.

Rabble's absence hung heavily between them. Questions flashed in the eyes of Skye's friends, but she kept those answers to herself, tucking them close to her heart where it beat with missing his nearness. Skye missed him terribly, wanting him there to hold her. But Skye recognized that brokenness in his gaze when he left her the previous night and knew more was going on behind his gray eyes than he could express in words. They were both wrecked and in need of healing. For her, that meant having the ones she loved around her. For him, that meant seeking solitude and acceptance in the quiet.

With just a few days until the Independence Day parade, Skye helped her friends and the twins finish up The Wild Bride's float. They took turns checking on Skye as they worked, making sure she remained comfortable in public and at night when their work finished. She stayed the night at Elyza's and Bekah's, doing what she could to distract herself, and each normal activity Skye completed centered her a bit more, made her steadier.

The day before the parade, Elyza found her resting under a large tree beside the warehouse. Skye rolled an apple between her palms and stared at the way the sunlight filtered between leaves.

Elyza joined her on the ground, knocking her sandaled feet against Skye's tennis shoes. "How're you doing?"

Skye smiled softly. "I'm okay. What's up?"

"I wanted to check in with you about the parade. Are you still okay with it?" Elyza kept her voice even and low, as if she didn't want her question to startle or frighten her friend.

Skye took a moment, returning to watching the speckled light play over the ground. The idea of putting on another wedding dress made her shudder but she crossed her arms with resolve. She'd told Elyza she would help, and she intended to see her promise through.

The morning of the parade dawned sunny and humid, and Skye prepared to face the world. She did her best to follow the picture Elyza sent for "dreamy wedding makeup." As always, she had everything planned, down to their staging and their beatific expressions, to showcase the dresses her boutique shop offered.

Even though Skye wasn't a makeup artist, her eyeshadow didn't look too bad. If nothing else, the concealer hid any remaining dark circles under her eyes, and the blush added some color to her pale cheeks. She curled her hair and tucked it into a low bun with some raw crystal bobby pins, adding an element of whimsy to her look.

Elyza asked them to meet at the float about an hour before the parade started, where there would be a place for them to change. The preparations reminded Skye of high school prom, when the other girls in class got ready together. Finally, her turn had arrived.

Even though the day promised to be hot, a light wind blew the heated air around, and Skye decided to walk to the warehouse where the floats waited. After days of keeping her friends nearby, she needed some alone time. She let the sound of her sneakers hitting the ground reverberate through her, and her brain enjoyed the few moments when she didn't have a single thought in her mind. The sound of her shoes crunching on the loose gravel and the way the summer breeze blew through the deep green leaves on the trees swept through her body, and wrapped around her soul in a calming song she'd enjoyed since childhood.

Skye arrived at the warehouse with plenty of time to spare, a sense of stillness in her chest. Few people milled about, organizing their floats and finalizing last details. She spotted the bridal shop's float beneath a large oak tree and sent up a silent prayer of thanks for the shade its branches provided.

Elyza, already there, tucked extra flowers in the garlands wrapped around the posts and draped from the sides of the trailer. With white, cream, and champagne colors flowing together seamlessly, various fabrics and laces created a waterfall of luxury as they wove in and out of the flowered garlands. The three bouquets they'd made sat along the tire well. The petals from the navy and ruby flowers littered the gauzy fabric covering the trailer's wooden boards. A woman stood nearby, her young twin daughters wearing long dresses with white lace bodices and thick tulle skirts, one ruby, one navy.

Those must be the flower girls.

Skye smiled. The little girls practically pranced around their mother with excitement while she tried, to no avail, to pin blonde curls atop their heads. Another woman straightened the lapels of the jacket on a young boy, a little older than the flower girls, who would stand in as a ring-bearer. Elyza had done a fantastic job in choosing participants.

With their hopping and shouting, the children were especially excited to be in the parade. They would sit on sturdy wooden boxes draped in gauzy fabric, and when the float stopped, the children would throw candy and beads to the waiting crowds.

Behind them, two couples and a lone woman, the crowning jewel of the entire float, dressed in wedding finery would wave to the crowd as if they'd just won a beauty pageant. Elyza had asked Rabble to participate, to stand in as the groom for the third bride, but he'd begged off. Skye knew what being on display in front of the town meant for him, the vulnerability and excruciating parts of his past it would bring up. She didn't blame him for finding a way out of the role, but that didn't mean she didn't miss him.

At the very back of the trailer, Elyza draped different gowns on three mannequins to showcase a dress for mothers, bridesmaids, and even prom. She would ride in the bed of the truck hauling the trailer, waving and smiling as they passed by.

Skye found Bekah and Kellyn behind the float, standing under a canopy modified with four linen walls for privacy. The cloth walls allowed a small cross-breeze to enter the space, just enough to cool the sweat that quickly beaded on her skin. Both women were in the process of slipping into the dresses they'd chosen.

Bekah's corset-backed gown fell off her shoulders, and the princess neckline accentuated her breasts and collarbone. The fabric draped around her body and Skye wondered how she wasn't melting into a puddle with all the layers on the dress. Despite the heat, Bekah looked every bit a princess, and Skye couldn't help but grin at the picture her friend presented.

Where Bekah looked like a princess, Kellyn had gone for classic with a sexy twist that made Skye's jaw drop. The silk dress flowed to the floor like liquid silver. The strapless neckline formed a heart across her chest, and a daring slit ran up one leg to her mid-thigh. A garter tattoo played peek-a-boo with the folds of the skirt. Combined with her pinned-up vibrant red curls and smokey makeup, Kellyn channeled a timeless seduction that spoke of long nights wrapped in moon-kissed sheets.

Both women were utterly breathtaking, and Skye's throat tightened with her love and appreciation for these ladies.

Elyza walked in behind her. The classy black jumpsuit she wore would keep her comfortable while also establishing her as a serious professional.

Paired with glossy black heels, Elyza's ensemble screamed business chic. Skye couldn't resist the tight hug she bestowed on her best friend.

"Hey lady," Elyza hugged her back. "I'm so, so glad to see you."

Kellyn and Bekah joined in for a group hug that went on for long seconds until Skye pulled back; they'd all been waiting for her to let go first, to be the first one to break that contact, and that meant more to her than she could ever express.

"We'll let you get dressed," Kellyn said, ushering the other women out of the tent to give Skye privacy while she changed.

Gratitude sat heavy in Skye's chest, like a brick as she turned to locate her dress.

The satiny white garment bag hung from a rolling rack in the corner of the tent. She stood across from it, as far as the tent would allow, and stared at it for a few moments. The bag itself, though different from the one that had played a role in her recent nightmare, made Skye's heart pound.

Gradually, she traversed the space and unzipped the bag, one inter-locked section at a time. Her fingers trembled a little more with each inch. When the zipper reached the bottom, the bag sagged open, reveal-ing the dress she'd chosen for herself. Skye froze; eyes wide.

Yards of cream fabric stared back at her, innocent and yet—no. No way.

Absolutely no way could she put that dress on. And no one could make her.

Her breath came in shallow gasps, the air sawing out of her in short bursts as her body shook. The idea of putting on a wedding dress, of feeling that cream fabric brushing against her skin made her stomach lurch. The room spun, dizziness creeping over her as the lack of good, deep breaths, kept her from thinking clearly. All of her coping mecha-nisms abandoned her at once, leaving her a on the edge of becoming a hyperventilating mess.

I can't do this.

Chapter 29

Rabble

Rabble glanced at his watch and frowned. He needed to get changed. He was supposed to be at the parade to watch Elyza's float make its grand debut. She'd convinced Declan and Dash into dressing up and riding on the float. Though it made him a bit uncomfortable that she'd read him so easily that day in the bridal shop when she'd asked him to help, he thanked his lucky stars Elyza backed off of him without asking the types of questions that made Rabble's skin itch.

Though he didn't feel exactly jovial, Rabble made sure to throw the twins some good-natured Ken-doll jokes, which they returned with anticipated hand gestures. They were both polite enough not to point out that Rabble's attempts at joking were half-assed at best.

Despite the fact that he was running out of time and he had places to be, he didn't want to move from the spot where he stood. He couldn't seem to make his feet move in the direction of his truck, parked just yards away.

The crude cross he'd constructed still held together, just barely. He'd whittled the sticks until they were smooth and straight and tied them together with twine that now frayed and hung loosely, allowing the horizontal stick to slant downward. Maybe he should just be happy it lasted all these years. Sitting stoically at the base of the wooden cross, the rock Skye painted with his mother's name and date of death seemed untouched by the years and weather. Rabble was thankful for that. He made a mental note to commission a true headstone, now that he owned the property.

On the way to the cabin, Rabble gathered a bouquet of wildflowers that were probably flowering weeds, he could never tell the difference. He'd grabbed whatever he thought looked nice, though he had no idea what any of them were called. Skye would know; he was certain of that.

Rabble had been up before the sun, driving around town and down the backroads on the outskirts; the sky had not even turned gray with early morning light. He doubted the chickens had been crowing when he'd hopped in his truck and decided to go for a drive. With no destination in mind, Rabble just drove, letting his mind wander along the yellow lines painted on the asphalt. He'd ended up at the property, at his mother's grave, before he realized what he was doing.

"Hey, Mama." Rabble's voice cracked. He felt like the sixteen-year-old boy he sounded like, the one who just needed his mother and hadn't been ready to be without her.

"I know it's been—a second—since I've been by. Sorry about that. I've been running from my roots for a while now. Not that it's done me any good."

He laid the bouquet on the ground at the base of the cross, next to the light-purple rock, purple because Skye knew his mother's favorite color. Of course, she did.

"I've been keeping busy." Rabble prayed his mother could hear him because it sure felt nice to talk to her again. He told her everything, from his days in the service to meeting and bonding with Dash and Declan. Finally, he told her all about Skye.

He started with those first years after they'd moved in, "You probably already knew this, but we used to meet beneath the fence nearly every day. I thought I knew everything there was to know about her."

He scoffed, "Leave it to me to think I had her all figured out. I'm so proud of the woman she became. Not that I have a right to be."

"I'm completely in love with her," he whispered, his words carried away on a warm breeze like his mother had gathered them up and whisked them away. "I've always been in love with her. And that scares the shit out of me."

He could practically hear his mother's voice scolding him, "*Language*". He bit down on the inside of his cheek, a vain effort to keep his lips from wobbling.

Rabble's thoughts turned to the way Gayle and Dylan had used Skye, had taken her choices from her, and forced her into a situation no person should ever be in. She'd just been through one of the most horrifying experiences, orchestrated by two people who said they loved her but used her anyway. The last thing Skye needed was for Rabble to show up, professing his love and assuming she would return his affection because they had a history.

"You'd still like her, Mama. She would talk flowers with you all day long, especially the native ones. She teaches kindergarten, and she loves those kids like they're her own. She's got an infectious smile and a bubbly laugh." Rabble found himself beaming at nothing in particular as he described Skye. His Skye.

His smile faded, and loneliness settled over him, smothering and suffocating him in the summer heat. He felt locked inside a glass box, able to see everything and everyone around him but unable to join them, unable to break past the barrier that kept him in the past. That kept him angry. Angry at the drunk driver who took his mother too early. Angry at his father for not giving a shit about his only son. Angry at Max and Gayle for taking away the only girl he'd ever loved, the best friend he'd ever had, and Dylan for thinking he could *possess* Skye like a trophy.

As if struck by a bolt of lightning, Rabble stumbled backward. He was angry at himself too. For being a foolish coward who didn't tell Skye how he felt. For not chasing after her harder. For not being there when she needed him. He'd taken time for himself to think and given her space, and maybe that was the wrong answer. He wanted to be there with her, be there for her, and dry every tear she cried. Better yet, he wanted to keep her tears from falling to begin with. The anger built and boiled and then ever so slowly drained from him into the ground, dissipating as the beginnings of a plan stirred in his mind.

"I've been so angry for so long," he choked out. "I don't want to be angry anymore. I want to be the man Skye needs, the kind she wants." He wiped at his eyes.

"I'm going to do something crazy," he said, no longer knowing if he was still talking to his mother or anyone in particular.

The wind kicked up and swirled around him with laughter and light. He could practically see his mother's sweet smile, then her mischievous grin, and the twinkle in her eye before she did something unexpected. Oh, his mother was here, alright. And she was just as excited about his next move as he was.

Feeling lighter than he had in some time, Rabble gave his mother's grave one more look, then headed back to his truck. His phone rang, vibrating in his pocket. When he pulled it out, Declan's name lit up the screen.

"Hey," he said, a bit confused and a lot concerned. He wasn't late yet. He'd checked the time repeatedly while speaking with his mother.

"Rab, we've got a problem. Get your ass to the parade, ASAP."

Before Declan finished speaking, Rabble ran for the truck, his heavy boots thudding in the grass and gravel. His tires spun, kicking up stones, and he sped toward the warehouse, breaking every speeding law in Shiloh Hills.

Chapter 30

Skye

The rushing in Skye's ears drowned out the noise of the parade preparations on the other-side of the tent walls surrounding her. Tremors wracked her body from head to toe, and she'd backed as far away from the garment bag as the tented space allowed. She sank to the ground, barely recognizing the grass as it pricked her skin. She gripped the short leaves, reaching toward the dirt and digging her nails into the earth. She didn't blink, couldn't move, as she stared and stared at the beautiful nightmare before her.

She'd chosen this gown; the floral lace having drawn her like a bee to a rose. Skye had felt like the goddess of spring, relishing the fit and flared design hugging her hips and accentuating her assets.

But the back of the dress... A row of delicate ivory fabric buttons descended to the floor. A long line of classic beauty. A long chain for caging her.

Despite loving the dress, Skye couldn't stand the sight of it, and the thought of touching it made her physically ill. The elegant fabric begged to be caressed, but it was a lovely prison in its own right.

Terror froze her eyes wide open. She couldn't turn away.

Sounds of others coming and going reached her as if from down a long tunnel, Elyza's voice, then a hand on her shoulder. Male voices floated outside the canopy walls, Declan and Dash if she wasn't mistaken. They were supposed to escort the ladies on the float after all. It made sense they'd be nearby. Their voices faded in and out. Declan sounded worried, and she wanted to reassure them she was okay. She would be okay. But she couldn't lie either. The words and the courage to speak eluded her. She just needed some time.

The linen wall behind her parted and admitted a gust of warm air that brushed against her neck, lifting the tiny hairs there. Heavy footsteps entered the space, a solid, reassuring presence. Familiar. Comfortable. She could feel him behind her, steady and ready to help her find control. Still, Skye didn't face him. She couldn't unlock her limbs or convince her mind to quiet enough to convey her needs.

"I can't," she whispered, the fabric walls absorbing her words.

She wasn't sure what she expected from him. Surely Rabble was disappointed in her. She certainly was.

Rabble walked in front of her, blocking her view of the dress. He was a vision in worn jeans and a button-down, sleeves rolled to his elbows. The tanned skin of his forearms stood out against the white of his shirt, jarring her and giving her something new to focus on.

Kneeling down, he gently cupped her face in his hands, brushing his thumbs across her pale cheeks reverently. He kissed her forehead, once, twice, then pulled back and studied her.

"It's okay, Skye." His voice was reassuring, affirming, everything she dreamed of.

"I don't want to be afraid." A sob she was helpless to stop escaped her chest.

Rabble caught her eye, putting every ounce of love and devotion into his words. "I know."

He stood and turned away from her, and Skye fought the urge to reach out and grab him, to keep his warmth nearby. His large hand touched the delicate fabric of the dress and pulled it out. Wincing, she closed her eyes, shrinking back from it as if the garment might bite her.

"You got this, Skye. I'll be right there with you." His hands moved tenderly over the fabric. The same way he touched her. "This doesn't define you. You're strong and capable, and you can do this. If you want to."

Skye locked eyes with Rabble, and what she saw there made her blood heat in the best way. Those storm-cloud eyes simmered with every desire he didn't say aloud, with every need that fired his blood; his devotion to her reflected there.

From her chest, a warmth spread outward, up into her arms and down her legs, unlocking her muscles and settling her a little further into her body.

Setting her jaw, Skye moved to her knees and Rabble helped her to her feet. And when she hesitantly took the dress from him, he shot her one more challenging glance before stepping out of the tent.

Skye ran her fingers lovingly along the lace applique and followed the skirt downward. It had a long train, one that would drag the ground majestically. She took a lengthy breath and let it out slowly before counting to ten and starting over. Then, before she could lose her nerve, she stripped out of her clothes and slipped into the wedding dress of her dreams.

At the first feel of the material against her skin, she slammed back into her body. This dress didn't feel like the other with its stiff, scratchy material, and the skirt didn't puff out around her, threatening to suffocate her beneath too many uncomfortable layers.

No, this dress was wholly, wonderfully different.

The crystal pins in her hair perfectly complemented the dress, as did her make-up. While nothing fancy, it got the job done, and she felt beautiful. Better yet, she even almost felt confident—an odd feeling considering touching the dress also made her want to withdraw and run away.

Skye smoothed her hands down the sides and took another steadying breath before pushing aside the tent flap and stepping into the sunlight.

I can do this. I will do this. I am strong.

While she'd been hiding, the warehouse grounds had become a hotbed of activity. People she'd known her whole life milled about, calling to each other, cracking jokes, and enjoying their lives—as if her entire world hadn't been flipped on its axis. She felt disconnected from them, further from them than she'd ever been. As they'd prepared for their town's prized Independence Day parade, she had been through hell at the hands of their town leadership. Something like envy welled inside her; it was an ugly feeling. She hated it, certain she wouldn't have experienced it just a few days ago.

Her eyes sought out Elyza, Kellyn, and Bekah, who all stood next to the float. Elyza posed everyone exactly where she wanted them, including Dash and Declan standing in for the two grooms. Declan grinned, the picture of ease and charisma in a sharp black tuxedo. Dash, on the other hand, seemed decidedly resigned to his fate, despite looking dangerously good in a slick black three-piece suit.

With the flower girls and ring-bearer in place, Elyza was ready for the brides. Dash helped Kellyn onto the trailer, his hands maintaining a respectful grasp on her waist as he lifted her gently. Dash followed her up and allowed Elyza to position them like mannequins. When she finished, Elyza handed Kellyn her bouquet with a smile. Next, Declan helped Bekah find her place, his hands decidedly lower on her hips when he gave her a boost onto the float. He grinned and winked when she gave him a playful whack with her bouquet, and he hopped up on the trailer after her. Elyza rolled her eyes but refused to let them distract her from moving them into position.

Knowing it was her turn, Skye took a fortifying breath and stepped toward her friends. Elyza saw her and rushed to gather the long train of her gown to keep it from dragged along the grass and over the gravel behind Skye.

"Oh, Skye!" Elyza put a hand to her chest and practically squealed with delight. "You are an absolute vision."

"I'll have you stand in the center, between Bekah and Kellyn since you don't have a groo—" Elyza's jaw dropped as Rabble stepped up to stand beside Skye.

"I've got her," he rumbled. And he did.

The man was gorgeous in those faded blue jeans and a white button-down shirt, his tanned forearms exposed to the summer sun, and he wore the fine heather-gray vest from his truck, dressing up the otherwise relaxed outfit. It worked for him. Better yet, it worked for Skye. And it seemed to work for Elyza too because she beckoned Rabble onto the float. After he took Skye's hand and pulled her onto the trailer beside him, he led her to stand between their friends, and Elyza handed her the final bouquet, the navy blues and ruby reds standing out brilliantly against her cream dress.

Skye could feel the heat of his palms through her delicately crafted layers, and she fidgeted, trying to get closer to him.

After checking over the wedding party one more time, Elyza climbed into the bed of the truck and tapped on the roof twice, letting Olivia know they were ready.

"Hold tight," Rabble whispered in Skye's ear, her skin pebbling as she shivered.

Skye closed her eyes and held on to him and his words for everything they were worth.

Chapter 31

Rabble

Rabble could feel Skye's coiled nervous energy pulsing around them. Maybe their proximity affected her. The warmth of her body seeped through her incredible dress, into his own clothing, and onto his skin. And he did mean *incredible*. The cream color brought out the golden tones of her skin, and those sparkling crystals on her dress and in her hair made him want to find each one and kiss them all.

Yes, it was a wedding dress, and at one point that might have bothered him, especially considering how he'd found her just days before. But now, seeing Skye choose to stand up here, facing the entire town and standing beside him, well, that alone was just about heaven.

The truck began to move, getting into position for the start of the parade and Skye jolted against him.

"Steady," he breathed against her ear, her scent intoxicating.

"I want to do this," she whispered back, the desire to persevere clear in her voice.

Rabble tried to soothe her with his gentle touch, but he wasn't sure that worked well. "He can't hurt you. Your stepmother can't hurt you. Want to know why?"

She gave a short, breathy chuckle. "They're locked away for kidnapping?"

He shook his head, a little surprised Skye was making jokes. "Well, yes, but there's another reason."

"Because you won't let them." Her tone edged toward serious, though she sounded resigned with a canned answer she thought he expected.

"Well, you're right about that too, but no." Rabble gave her a soft smile. "Because, Skye, you are too damn strong for that."

She leaned in and Rabble pulled her against him tightly, tucking her head beneath his chin. Besides, with the float moving in earnest now, he could use that as an excuse to hold her tighter, even if for only a short while.

"Tell me something good, Rabble," Skye said quietly. Her voice held such weariness, like a woman whose bright-as-the-sun personality had been hidden behind cloud cover for too long.

She was drawn as firmly as a bowstring, and he could feel her scarcely controlled anxiety crackling just beneath the surface. Skye probably didn't want him to tell her how good she felt in his arms, how his heart seemed to soar when she was near, or how amazing and beautiful she was. She already knew all of that. At least, he hoped she did.

But, again, was that really what she needed to hear?

He could give her something different to focus on. "I'm thinking of turning my parents' old land into a camp for kids from low-income and underprivileged families."

She pulled back from him, stunned. "Oh, my goodness, Rabble, that's wonderful!" Throwing her arms around him, she hugged him fiercely.

Rabble breathed out a slow sigh. He had brought up the idea to the twins the night before, unsure what they'd think, especially since they didn't establish Rabble & Bros. Security with the intent of running a children's summer camp. Typically, the two circles didn't come anywhere close to overlapping. But the half-formed idea had weighed on him since he'd taken possession of his parent's property. After tossing around the concept a few times, he wanted to look into it more, draw up some proposals and bounce them off the others.

When Skye's cornflower-blue eyes and a genuine smile lit her face, he knew he'd made the right choice. The half-moons beneath her eyes, which the makeup didn't quite hide, and the wariness that tugged at the corners of her mouth seemed to ease some.

"Tell me something else," she said.

Rabble rolled his eyes. "You're bossy."

Her smile transformed, becoming brighter and even more sincere. "I know."

Rabble looked around them. The others on the float studiously ignored them and waved to the crowd gathered along the parade route. The whole town practically shut down for Independence Day, allowing everyone to enjoy the festivities. Following the parade, the shopping booths and carnival games set up around the courthouse would become the center of the party, which would last until well after dark when fireworks would light up the sky in brilliant-colored bursts.

Noise surrounded them, from the cheering children and whistling adults to the other vehicles and tractors' exhausts. The local high school band played somewhere in front, and the cheerleaders somewhere toward the back shouted their memorized chants at the top of their lungs. All the individual sounds melded into one seamless cacophony that normally would have made him jumpy and agitated. But Rabble looking down at Skye, everything faded away until it was just them.

"Rabble?" she asked hesitantly.

He gulped. "You want to know something else good, Skye?"

She nodded, solely focused on his face, like the dissonance around them didn't exist for her either.

He gambled and went for it, saying the one thing he had wanted to say forever but wasn't confident she could stand to hear. "You're it."

Her brow furrowed in silent question.

Gazing into her eyes, he focused on the several tiny silvery-blue flecks. "You're it for me. This. You. Us. This is all I could ever want, all I've ever wanted, ever since we were young."

Rabble slid to one knee, a grace he didn't know he possessed allowing him to stay balanced even as the truck lurched forward. Skye's hand quivered in his, but she hadn't kicked him or screamed at him yet, so he took that as a positive sign.

"Rab—" Skye gasped, her other hand flying to her mouth.

"You are the only one who has ever seen me as more than a boy from the wrong side of the fence. I've made mistakes, Skye. That can't be argued with. But I swear, all I have ever wanted was to protect you. Be near you." He tried not to shift nervously when she didn't speak, but silent tears streamed down her face. He was vaguely aware of the others watching them, one of the flower girls squealing excitedly, and the crowd seemed to wait on bated breath for Skye's answer.

"So, Miss Skye Louise Wellington, would you please do me the honor of taking me for your husband and put me out of my misery?" He whispered the last part, a raw need escaping with each word.

A bubbling sob escaping her and she nodded. Cheers erupted around them. The tension in his shoulders lessened as he slipped the small ring onto her finger, an antique pear-shape diamond on a rose-gold band.

He'd had the ring since he was eighteen, all of the extra money he earned working with Mr. Jack at the corner pharmacy when he wasn't helping at the bed and breakfast, went straight toward saving for the bit of sparking rock and bright metal. When he'd left town all those years ago, he left it with a friend to dispose of, knowing it would never sit on the finger of the girl who held his heart. He couldn't express the gratitude he had that Mrs. Basket held onto it all of these years; it had sat in his pocket every moment since she'd returned it to him with a knowing smile.

Rabble surged to his feet and swept Skye into a tight embrace, the kind that came with never wanting to let go. As the cheering and whistling increased, the world started moving again, along with the float that had stopped during his proposal, not that Rabble or Skye had noticed.

The flower girls tossed candy from the trailer into the crowd. Thankfully, Elyza had the foresight to fill the girls' baskets with chocolate and not harder candy as pieces bounced off unsuspecting parade-goers. Declan and Dash clasped his shoulders, steadying and congratulating him—Declan in his usual loud manner and Dash in his calmer, more subdued way. Bekah and Kellyn pulled Skye into a screeching huddle-hug that only increased in size when Elyza jumped from the truck bed onto the trailer to celebrate with her friends.

During the rest of the parade, Skye periodically flashed her ring at the crowd, grinning like a lovestruck schoolgirl. He recognized some of them, older now than they'd been when he left town, but they shouted louder, telling him that there had always been those rooting for them all along.

Throughout the parade, Rabble stole glances at his fiancée, at the woman he knew and loved, at the woman this town knew and loved, pleased he could help her replace her earlier panic with happier memories.

Seeing her joy was all he ever wanted. And in the same way she had done for him as children, he would strive to protect her peace for the remainder of their lives.

Chapter 32

The Wedding

Skye

Handing over the reins for the wedding turned out to be one of the best decisions Skye ever made. The idea of coordinating the number of details that went into a wedding and reception, even a small one like theirs, made her head spin. Elyza, however, thrived on the chaos that came with mixing and matching colors and fabrics and flowers. She blossomed under the challenge, and Skye gladly handed over control to her friend, except for the guest list and the dress.

Skye and Rabble kept the guest list extremely limited, especially since the majority of their friends would already be standing at the front of the church alongside them. Mrs. Basket and Olivia were among the few others to receive invitations, along with Mrs. MacAlister, Elyza and the twins' mother. So long as Skye could call Rabble her husband at the end of the day, she didn't care about much of anything pertaining to the wedding.

Skye's other requirement felt more personal, so she privately enlisted Elyza's help. They met at The Wild Bride one night after closing, and Elyza made sure Skye found exactly what she wanted amid the pre-laid out selection. The thought of wearing a white wedding dress still made her heart seize with anxiety, so Elyza pulled three shimmering gowns from the endless racks for Skye to choose from. With her friend's careful attention, she left the bridal shop feeling lighter than a feather drifting on a soft wind.

Elyza made a show of revealing the venue she'd selected for the wedding and reception. A small church that had sat abandoned on the outskirts of town for years, left to fall into disrepair. Skye had always loved the church, the magnificent stained glass in delicately arched windows, the towering steeple, and ornately crafted cross at its peak. A sense of rightness went through Skye, and her heart thumped with growing excitement.

"Isn't the church a little..." Skye searched for a kinder word than *decrepit*. "Dated?"

Elyza gave her a secret smile, a twinkle in her eye. "Do you trust me?"

She balked at the question. Of course, she trusted Elyza. They were best friends, and yet... Skye sucked in a deep breath through her nose and slowly released it from her mouth, a calming technique she'd been working on. "I trust that you'll work your magic."

Elyza pulled Skye into a hug, one full of unspoken gratitude for each other. Skye found herself squeezing Elyza back fiercely, tears pricking her eyes.

"Let's get you married, girlfriend!" Elyza said with a grin.

Skye couldn't help the blush that crept up her neck, spilling warm pink onto her cheek as she giggled. "Deal."

***

Rabble

The repairs to the church turned out beautiful. Skye had always loved the place, ever since the original congregation moved toward the city center, leaving the old building to fall into disorder. Purchasing it didn't take long at all. He contacted the pastor and then his realtor. Pulling the right strings, the entire transaction took less than a week to complete, and Rabble became the proud owner of one derelict church.

They didn't have time to fix everything wrong with the structure, but fortunately the building had solid bones. Beyond a fresh coat of paint, a quick polish for the floors, and temporary fixes for the chipped stained-glass windows, everything else would have to wait. Dash salvaged four pews from a stack of furniture in the corner of the nave and dusted them for the intimate gathering.

With Dash in charge of ensuring Rabble arrived at the church on time, they pulled into the parking lot an hour ahead of schedule. The man had no patience for arriving anywhere near on time. In his estimation, if you weren't early, you were late. Usually Rabble and Declan would give him a hard time for it, but Rabble was secretly grateful for the early arrival time. He could work out some of his nerves while they waited.

Rabble took one step into the sanctuary and whistled in appreciation at Elyza's talent. She successfully concealed the unfinished parts of the church under artful wedding decorations. Cream lace and sheer wheat-colored fabric draped around the pews they'd salvaged, and vases wrapped with satin ribbon adorned as many surfaces as possible, each with simple bundles of white sweet alyssum, vibrant-yellow coneflowers, and fountain grass.

A distant voice drifted inside the church and Rabble met Joe Armanan at the door. Small-town sheriff and conveniently, a registered officiant. Was there anything the man couldn't do? As he took his place at the altar, Joe gave Rabble a small smile, though it looked more like a grimace on his craggy face.

Rabble escorted Mrs. Basket and Olivia to their seats when they arrived together. As he knelt before the older woman, tears pricked at his eyes. "Thank you," he choked out in a whisper.

She patted his cheek affectionately. "You're a good boy, Rabble Raden. And an even better man, Matthew."

***

Skye

At the back of the church, Skye hid behind a set of ornate solid wood doors. On the other side, Rabble waited for her, and that was all that mattered. The doors opened, and she ducked back into a darker corner as Declan and Dash escorted Bekah and Kellyn down the aisle. Their long periwinkle dresses flowed like water on the polished wooden floor, reminding Skye of mythological nature spirits she'd read about as a kid. While the ladies exuded grace with every swishing step, the twins looked handsome in their chambray shirts and suspenders, a tiny cluster of wheat spikes tucked against their chest as a boutonniere.

Once they took their place at the front of the church, Elyza primped Skye's hair one more time, shaking out the long curls with a loving hand.

"You ready?" she asked.

Skye's heart skittered, and her breath hitched with nervous excitement. "I am."

Elyza grinned, and her eyes sparkled. "Then let's get you down that aisle." She opened the double doors, securing them with little wooden stops, and proceeded down the aisle like a model on a runway.

Elyza stepped up to take her place as the maid of honor then, hidden in the florals of her bouquet, she clicked a small device that allowed her to control the music from her position at the front of the church. The smooth, lilting tune sounded like summer nights and gentle breezes that invited Skye to begin her journey toward the only man she ever wanted.

***

Rabble

The moment the music changed, moving into something smoother, something rich and warm, Rabble recalled long days under their fence, laughing together as the towering oak and flowering lilac watched over them.

Elyza grinned at him and Rabble's eyes caught movement at the rear doors. He froze, his body becoming impossibly still.

"Please stand," Sheriff Armanan said.

The twins' mom, Mrs. Basket, and Olivia rose to their feet, turning back to witness the vision gliding through the doors.

Rabble's eyes couldn't get any wider, could they? Surely, his chest couldn't expand anymore. His heart felt swollen with love, and he struggled to pull in breath.

Skye began her measured assent toward him, her smile beatific and gentle, though an excitement sparkled in her eyes too.

He gulped as his gaze travelled over her, taking in every minute detail. She wore her hair long, curling down her back, a few stray tendrils about her ears and cheeks. Her smocked dress shimmered with a creamy light as she walked, the slightly puffed sleeves settled off of her shoulders. His eyes lifted in surprise as he took in the hand-embroidered fall flowers and wheat that started at the neckline and hem and grew toward her heart. The details of the floras and field grasses were unparalleled, and he wondered who dared to put such colors on a wedding dress and where could he send his thank you note.

She kept her steps light and rhythmic until she stood just before him, and Rabble extended a hand, inviting her to join him at the altar of their forever. He didn't hear most of what Sheriff Armanan said, too focus on Skye's radiance, and Rabble nearly missed the call for vows.

Skye went first. "From that very first day, I knew you were mine. You have been my safe place, my calm and my crazy, and I vow to spend every day by your side from now until eternity. Because there is not a place or a time in existence in which I wish to be parted from you."

Rabble tried to swallow past the lump cutting off his voice. He cleared his throat and spoke, voice rough. "From that first day, I knew you were mine. You became my home, my peace, my silence, and my music. Not a day has passed when I haven't wanted to be by your side. And there is not a place or a time in existence where I want to be apart from you. I love you, Skye. Every breathtaking inch of your mind, body, and soul."

A quiet sob escaped her, and Rabble pressed his hand against her cheek, a small thrill going through him when she leaned into his touch.

The next words Rabble heard released a tidal wave of need and possessiveness.

"Husband and wife... kiss the bride."

Rabble cradled Skye against his body, her gaze reflecting his thoughts, a promise of long nights of love and days of staring down the world, side by side.

Chapter 33

Rabble

Clutching Skye's hand, Rabble hurried them toward his truck. Their friends stood on either side of the path holding up thin sparklers which sent tiny multi-colored arcs flying about them. Skye ducked into Rabble's side as he did his best to shield her from the bright flashes with his body. He threw his truck door open and helped her up and into the cab, carefully tucking her dress around her legs before shutting the door. Declan stood nearby; no less than three sparklers clutched in either hand which he waved about in gleeful abandon.

Rabble dodged the soaring sparks as he raced to his door and popped the latch. Preparing to launch himself into the driver's seat, he paused, watching as Dash approached. He rolled his eyes at his twin's shenanigans and held out his hand for Rabble to shake.

"See you at the reception," Rabble said, taking his friend's hand in a firm grip.

Dash gave a snort. "Yeah, okay."

Rabble couldn't stop the feral grin that came over his face. Dash was probably right. They'd make it to the reception...eventually.

Skye practically bounced in her seat, excitement radiating from her in waves. He started the truck, revving the engine a few times before tearing from the parking lot, the truck growling loudly as he headed toward the surprise he planned. He drove in the opposite direction, back through the town of Shiloh Hills and passed the Cottage District to a short, charming gravel path that led back through a thick stand of trees. The leaves had begun to change colors and shadowed the driveway in an enchanting way.

"Why are we going this way, Rabble? The B&B is back in town." Skye tilted her head, curiosity growing in her tone.

"Remember how they said the house wouldn't be ready for another month?" Rabble asked.

Skye nodded.

"Well, make that one day. The crews are coming back Monday to finish everything up."

Skye squealed and clapped her hands, joy evident in her sparkling eyes.

Another property Skye had obsessed over from an early age, the Old McGrader house had recently gone up for auction on the courthouse steps, and Skye's eyes had light up. She'd launched into a thirty-minute presentation on the integrity of the home's strong wooden beams, as well as the benefits of the adorable fruit and nut tree orchard and the large but forgotten garden. It hadn't taken long for Rabble to place his bid on the property, the only bid the county received.

One night as they lay together in bed, Rabble joked, "I've now bought you not one, but two, falling-down buildings. I'm not sure I'm so good at this being in love thing. Surely, I'm doing something wrong."

Skye had giggled sweetly and pulled the sheets to cover her body as she rolled onto her side and smiled at him. "No, you're doing perfectly! Plus, you gave Elyza the church as a gift after the fact, so technically I only have one building trying to fall down."

Smiling to himself as he recalled that memory, Rabble parked the truck in front of the new porch and jogged to Skye's side to help her down. They walked hand in hand up the three short steps, her ankle-length gown swishing about her. Rabble took the keys from his pocket, unlocking the door and shoved it open. Before she could protest, Rabble lifted Skye into his arms and carefully crossed the threshold with her cradled against him. Her laughter rang in his ears, the sweetest sound he'd ever heard.

Inside, Rabble carried Skye a little further into the home before setting her slowly back on her feet, ensuring she was steady before letting go and stepping back to watch her take everything around them in.

Skye had visited the house during the renovations, staying for short periods of time between her work and packing up her cottage, leaving Rabble to oversee the majority of the progress. The home had been transformed completely, from roof to foundation. In just three months, they added three bedrooms and two bathrooms, and they opened up the kitchen and living room to each other. Crews of carpenters, general laborers, tilers, and more worked in harmony to build, polish, and shine the beautiful old house into the perfect home for Rabble and Skye, where they could live out their lives together. Rabble could picture the two of them, raising a family and, later, rocking side by side in sturdy wooden chairs, the kind that stood up to the years and that they could pass down to their children and beyond.

By Monday, when the last of the work finished up, Rabble and Skye would finally start moving in their things, situating themselves in their new lives and home.

"Oh, Rabble," she breathed, her voice full of wonder as she looked around, a new wife in her new home.

He wished he could read her mind and see the house from her perspective. Was it everything she'd dreamed of? Had he gotten it right?

"That's not even the surprise." Taking her fingers in his, he led her forward, toward the dining area at the rear of the home.

When Rabble first saw the table sitting in the new house, he'd stopped dead in his tracks, immobile with a feeling so deep in his chest, he feared how it might effect his heart. He wiped at his eyes, trying to stem the tears that welled and spilled over.

Skye sidled up to the table, gasping. "Oh my word, Rabble, this is..."

He nodded, rubbing his fingers lovingly over the long table. "Mrs. Basket had it delivered while we weren't here."

Both of them knew the significance of the table, the meaning behind the tiny letters carved into the corner, the wood so well loved that it had become smooth with age.

"Her husband made this for her when they first married," Skye whispered reverently.

Atop the table, Rabble had a selection of fruits and cheeses and puffed pastries set out, just for them.

Skye chuckled at the small platters of finger foods. "Rabble, we have to get to the reception."

He shrugged, pulling out a chair for her. "We will get there. We've got a little time, and I wanted a moment alone with my wife."

The title slid from his lips so easily and he took a moment to bask in the glow of how it sounded as he sat next to her, waiting while she chose a selection from the trays. Once her plate held her favorite choices, he moved to add an assortment of everything to his own plate.

"I have another surprise," Rabble said, sucking on a ripe strawberry.

Did I imagine the way her eyes followed my lips?

"Another surprise? Rabble, that's two in one day. Be careful," she warned teasingly. "I might get spoiled."

He dropped a quick kiss on her cheek. "That's the point, babe."

"What's the other surprise?" she laughed.

"We heard back from the realtor *and* the lawyer today. Looks like we're good to go."

Her eyes widened. "No way! Rabble & Bros. is moving to Shiloh Hills, permanently? It's actually happening?"

Rabble nodded, loving the way her eyes gleamed. And the way she moaned when she bit into a particularly juicy berry. "Yep, the old bank is ours. Ironically, it's right across from the courthouse."

She rolled her eyes. "Yeah, ironic." Her tone suggested it was anything but.

"Want to see what they got done today?" Standing, he held out his hand to her.

Together, they walked through their home, admiring the way the new light fixtures threw the light in the foyer and the subtle sparkle and shine of the tile backsplash in the kitchen. Up the stairs, Rabble opened the door to each of the bedrooms and stood back while Skye inspected them. She twirled in a circle in the vast space, her toes burying in the soft new carpet.

The last bedroom was theirs. Rabble followed her in while she investigated the huge walk-in closet and large, immaculate master bathroom. In the bathroom, the tiled shower was big enough to hold five people, with rain showerheads on either side.

"You were listening." She smiled.

Rabble nodded and smirked. "Always."

"You know...the carpet in the bedroom is the softest on the market." Rabble's voice was little more than a rumble as he backed her against the bathroom doorframe. One hand wandered down to her hip while the other curled around the wooden board behind her, his grip tight as he barely contained himself at the feel of her body bowing into his.

Skye's eyes sparked at his challenge and she grinned. Rabble soaked in the beams of excitement and pleasure that shone on her face, basking in the intrinsic knowledge of her love that she freely gave him because she loved him for who he was. Together, they would face anything life threw at them and he would spend the rest of his life fighting to keep that beautiful smile on his wife's face.

Skye hummed, amusement and playful defiance turning her lips into a mischievous grin. "I'll be the judge of that."

Rabble chuckled devilishly. "Yes, ma'am."

Epilogue

Declan took a seat at one of the circular tables set up in the back-yard of the bed and breakfast. Several large tables littered the yard, providing enough space for the entirety of Shiloh Hills to celebrate with Rabble and Skye at their reception. They'd wanted to keep the wedding small, something Declan fully understood and approved of, but they opened the reception to everyone, and Declan dreaded the number of townsfolk who would stop by simply because they hadn't gotten over the shock of the recent drama involving his friends.

While he sat back, Elyza directed caterers, the DJ, and anyone else who showed up with a purpose. His sister could be a force to be reckoned with when she wanted to be. She loved fiercely and would do just about anything for someone she considered family or friend. A small table off to the side held the three-tiered wedding cake, and another held tray after tray of delicious appetizers.

Kellyn and Bekah stuck close to Elyza's side, running short errands as needed, even as Kellyn mingled with the guests as they arrived. Owning the cafe meant she spent much of her day among the public, and he didn't know how she tolerated it. As for Bekah, her smile made Declan's own lips turn upward. Her light-brown hair was swept into an elegant updo that left straggling strands of long curling hair to kiss at her neck. His eyes lingered where those teasing strands whispered across olive-toned skin. The bridesmaid dress fit her petite frame, snuggly at her bust, then flowed down into an empire waist. Elyza would be proud of him for remembering that style after all of these years.

Dash had disappeared almost as soon as they arrived, and Declan would bet his twin actively hid upstairs in his still rented room, avoiding people for as long as possible. Maybe some of the townsfolk blamed him and Dash for their roles in the mayor's shameful retreat and the arrest of his wife and that senator's spoiled son. But he and Dash did their job, relishing in the knowledge that another person with ill-intent no longer walked the same streets as them. That desire had driven them to join the military, and it carried through into their civilian lives as well.

As Declan sat back and sipped a glass of sweet tea, the backyard filled up, more townsfolk flooding in to mingle and sway to the soft music the DJ played from the corner of the back porch. Younger members of the crowd tried out the faux dance floor and smiled at the tap, tap, tap sound their little feet made against the fake wood.

The appetizers filled people's plates, even though Rabble and Skye had yet to arrive at their own reception, a fact that made Declan smirk.

He could guess where they'd gone, and Declan didn't blame them for making a pitstop to be together.

When he and Dash helped Elyza bring out several dinner trays, Declan's stomach growled, and his throat constricted a little more with each new face until Rabble and Skye finally arrived, their hair slightly disheveled and Skye's face a brilliant shade of red. Declan couldn't wait to tease her about that—good naturedly, of course. As Rabble's wife, she just gained two new brothers and a sister whether she knew it or not.

He made his way through the crowd to congratulate his friends, his eyes landed on Bekah standing slightly away from the rest of the women gathering around Skye. Without thought, he changed course for Bekah and halted abruptly when the color drained from her face. Pushing himself forward, he hurried to her side, and when his hand landed on her back, she turned into him. Gently, he guided her away from the heartbeat of the party.

Beneath the glow of the dusk-to-dawn light, he pitched his voice deliberately low, aiming to soothe her. "What's wrong, Bekah?" He grasped her arms tenderly, hoping to help ground her.

With her hands shaking, she nearly dropped her cell phone as she passed it to him. Declan shrugged from his suit jacket, draping it around her shoulders as he pulled her close. Her petite frame fit against his larger one as she tucked into him. Despite the relative warmth of the early evening air, Bekah's skin felt clammy against him, and he rubbed her back to soothe and warm her.

Steeling himself, Declan looked over her shoulder and tilted her cell phone screen toward him. She'd been reading an online news article, dated yesterday, in the state of California. At first, he wasn't sure why she had wanted him to see a photo of a house's charred and burned-out shell.

Then he read the headline, *Home of Alleged Criminal Accountant, Edward Elnor, Burned Down Overnight.*

Using his thumb, he scrolled down, and the article revealed some of Edward's more notable charges, including human and drug trafficking, as well as laundering money—details Bekah had either kept from them or simply had not known. After receiving a call from a neighbor, Kostner Fire Department had found the structure fully engulfed in flames when they arrived, and they would be conducting an arson investigation.

Declan's thumb froze as his gaze snagged on the next line. "Mr. Elnor shared the home with his wife, Catherine Elnor, but neighbors indicated they have not seen Mrs. Elnor in several months. However, Kostner Fire located the remains of one individual inside the home, assumed to be Mrs. Elnor at this time."

Each word caused Declan to tuck Bekah further into his side. He exited out of the article, which took him back to a text message. An unknown number had sent her that article, along with a separate picture of a bloodied pocket knife on a sheet of paper and charred wooden table. The scarlet blood contrasted with the white paper and its hastily scrawled note, *You can't hide from me.*

Well, shit.

Coming Soon

Return to Shiloh Hills in Book 2, *The Secrets We Share*, coming soon! With Summer fading into Autumn, Bekah and Declan explore the undeniable chemistry that sparks between them. But, danger lurks in the lengthening shadows, even in seemingly safe small towns.

Thank you for reading The Fence Between Us! I hope you loved the town and the characters as much as I do. If you did, make sure to leave a review and spread the word. There is no better gift to an independent author than a review and a recommendation.

Interested in staying updated on news from Shiloh Hills and S.E. Fisher? Join the newsletter and follow along on social media!

https://sefisherauthor.com

Facebook & Instagram: @sefisherauthor

Acknowledgements

I cannot believe this day has finally arrived! Years of dreaming and doubting have come to an end and I can't wait to start the next story. This journey has taught me so much and I couldn't have completed this first step without the stalwart support of so many people.

My husband has to get the primary acknowledgement because he is the other half of my soul and his unwavering belief in me is the only thing that kept me going, kept me typing away some days. Whether he spent his time listening to me plot aloud, or provided IT Support when I inevitably broke something on my computer, or the extra time he spent in parenting and household duties that allowed me time to write, he provides the foundation of my heart.

My children, for your silly smiles and innocent views of the world that kept me laughing throughout this process. I am thankful beyond measure that I'm your mama and I pray everyday that I get to keep watching you grow. I hope in all of this, the creativity, the hard work, and dedication, that you see it and use it to help you pursue your own goals and dreams one day. I'd love to support you as you've supported me.

My family, especially my parents, have perhaps, endured my ramblings and writings the longest and never once made me doubt my abilities or worth as a writer. From late night and pre-dawn conversations with my dad to random phone calls throughout the day to plot over the phone with my mom, thank you for accepting my awkward nature and mind that leaps from one thought to the next to the next. You've always done a remarkable job of following my random train of thought.

My friends, Sierra, Lydia, Alisha, Bailey, and Sarah, thank you for your listening ears, your wonderful minds, your beautiful personalities, and your unyielding patience as I sent you copy after copy of the same draft of logos, paragraphs, character descriptions. Even when only a small facet of the topic had changed, you didn't tell me where I could get off. Having one friend like you is rare. Having an entire group of you, statistically improbable and yet, I find myself with an entire gaggle of amazing and supportive women.

A special thanks to Ms. Sharlynn Cochran, my high school English teacher for encouraging me to follow dreams that others scoffed at, not only in my writing, but also in my life.

And a big shout out to everyone who helped bring The Fence Between Us into fruition.

To Sandy Betros, Klancey Bush, Samy Fleetwood, and Sarah Hoog, for taking the time to help proofread the final copy of *The Fence Between Us* and the ARC readers who came before the official release date.

To KiWi Cover Design of The Author Buddy, for creating such a beautiful cover.

To Revision Division providing a manuscript evaluation and helping *The Fence Between Us* gain 15,000 words.

And a final shout out to Erin P.T. Canning, my line editor, book coach, and mentor through this process. Independent publishing is not for the faint of heart and Erin helped me navigate the intricate ins and outs of the process with extreme patience. Without Erin, this book may have taken another several years to see the light of day.

Shiloh Hills Book Club

Questions to Ponder After The Fence Between Us

Book friends make the best friends! Here are some questions you can discuss after reading *The Fence Between Us* with your book besties!

1. Was the relationship between Skye and Rabble believable? Why or why not?

2. Do you think Skye forgave Rabble too easily? Did Rabble deserve a second chance?

3. Do you think Rabble did the right thing in leaving Shiloh Hills? Why or why not?

4. What do you think happens to the main characters after the novel ends?

5. Do you think Skye and Rabble can be content in Shiloh Hills now? Why or why not?

6. Was the relationship between Rabble, Declan, and Dash believable? Does having that found family element create additional interest or detract from it?

7. Did you have a favorite side character? Why?

8. If this book were made into a movie, who would play the main characters?

9. Were there any passages that stood out to you?

10. If you could change one character's actions, which one and what would you change?

About the Author

S.E. Fisher is an idealistic romantic who believes in soulmates and happily-ever-after. She believes in real life knights-in-shining-armor and strong heroines who lean into each other's strengths to create a formidable team.

A lover of fairytales and mysterious places, S.E. spent much of her childhood writing whenever she could, on whatever she could, regaling friends and family with tales of strong and stubborn individuals and mythological worlds. Today, S.E. still enjoys finding new ways for her heroes to overcome obstacles.

Introverted by nature, when she isn't writing, S.E. can be found reading romance and fantasy or partaking in one of her many varied crafting hobbies. S.E treasures spending time out in nature and devotes every spare moment to gathering with her family.

A born and bred Missourian, S.E. Fisher resides in central Missouri with her husband and three children, along with a variety of fuzzy and feathered creatures.